FOREVER DECEITFUL

A FOREVER FAITHFUL SERIES

BOOK TWO

DANIELLE KATHLEEN

Created with Vellum

For my siblings,
who have gone to every book show with unwavering love and support.

Plus, what other author gives away cookies that have their book cover as a giveaway?

I love you!

A FRIENDLY FACE

My fingertips strained towards the fence to seek a connection while my body tensed at the sound of a twig snapping behind me. My hope faded as I realized my time alone was dwindling.

When I heard a man's voice pierce through the air, interrupting my thoughts and causing my heart to race.

"Don't!" he warned. "You'll get electrocuted. This fence is turned off for repair but will be reactivated in forty-five seconds."

My skin erupted in goosebumps at the sound of his voice, which triggered a sense of familiarity within me. Its gentle yet husky resonance had been my only companion during captivity.

Tears welled in my eyes as I heard his lifeline voice, reigniting a glimmer of hope. Afraid the familiar voice was in my head, I held my breath. I turned around and saw him standing about thirty feet away.

"Zak?" I choked out, my voice shaky and hoarse.

He stiffened at the sound of his name, eyes widening with surprise as he recognized me.

"Liz?" he exclaimed in disbelief, confusion etched across his face until recognition set in.

My heart raced as I caught a glimpse of Zak for the very first time. The very sight of him took my breath away, leaving me with dry lips and an overwhelming surge of emotion.

Through tear-filled eyes, I saw his image waver before me, the man who had been my pillar of support during our time together in the oppressive darkness. But upon arriving at this place, they separated us. I had worried about his well-being and inquired after him with a heavy weight of anxiety and sadness.

While Amara, Yasmin, and Esther were there to offer their support, it was Zak I longed to see and hear from.

As the hum of electric currents filled the air, signaling an impending charge, I heard him call out my name. My fingers clawed into the soft earth as I tried to pull myself out of the knee-deep pit I had dug. My skirts caught on something below and onto the bottom of the fence, making it impossible for me to push myself up and out. The air grew warmer as the impending charge came from the fence, filling me with fear and uncertainty as I struggled to free myself from the trap I had.

Zak instinctively jumped down and grabbed me under my arms to pull me to safety. The roar of the surge grew louder as he pulled, our movements frantic as we tried to escape. Panic surged through our grunts, and he stumbled and tripped over something, bringing me down.

My face pressed against his abdomen. I couldn't hear anything over the loud hum. I covered my ears with my hands. I was amazed watching the display of the electric pulse charging in shades of purple and blue. The air was thick with the smell of earth, mixed with the stench of fear and sweat lingered in the air.

As the spark ignited, the air filled with our labored breathing. With the rustling of our clothes, my heart thudded in my chest as we stood on our feet.

Zak's strong hands reached my shoulders, reassuring me we had escaped catastrophe. It dawned on me that I still held onto my ears, trying to block out the echoes of nature's symphony mixing with the unnerving sound of electricity. In that fragile moment, we were caught between the threat of electrocution and the peaceful rhythm of our surroundings.

As the pulsating energy faded away, a harsh reality set in. We were on the brink of death, where the gentle hum of electricity had turned into a deadly force. It was only by chance that both Zak and I were still alive.

Zak got to his feet, his chest rising and falling, catching his breath. The shock was wearing off, and we shared a knowing look. Smiles spread across our faces as we embraced, seeking comfort and reassurance.

Considering this was our first face-to-face meeting, it struck me how accurate my previous assumptions about Zak's appearance were. Our faces had been covered during our kidnapping, and we were shoved into the back of a van - a cramped and soundproof space. In that darkness, our only connection was through the sound of our voices.

Zak's features were illuminated in the dim light as the soft golden hue from the sun began its final stage setting in the West. His unruly, thick hair glinted in the light with a slight curl at the ends. The stubble on his jaw was thick and coarse, giving him a rugged appearance.

A jolt of memory made me recall a moment together. Our kidnappers had moved us from the van to the back of a train car. The walls were padded, and the darkness was all-consuming. We had no concept of time and no one to tell us why we were here. But at least we had each other's words for support and comfort as we stumbled in the pitch-black space. I could feel wooden boxes stacked against the iron bars that split the cargo area in half.

We tried to climb those bars for hours, desperate for any chance of escape. But I struggled, not as strong as Zak. On my final attempt, I lost my balance and fell over him. I remembered his aftershave's sharp, arctic smell as we lay there, catching our breaths.

It had been days since we were taken, and that clean, fresh scent was a reminder of the outside world. His comfort reminded me of my husband, Brant, and how I was desperate to return to my husband's embrace.

But when we arrived at this unknown destination, they separated us; he was with the men, and I was with the women. Zak was like a security blanket to me, and what I wanted more than anything was to hear his voice and smell that crisp aroma that brought me comfort. I was afraid I would never recognize Zak, but I would know his voice.

In the fading sunlight, I couldn't help but notice the progression of his facial hair, noticing a slight reddish hue mixed in with the thick black scruff. I couldn't resist studying him, taking note of the width of his jaw, which was the widest part of his squared face. His dark blue eyes focused on my bruised face as he looked down from his straight nose and slightly parted lips.

Our attention was cut short and diverted when my furry feline companion landed beside me with a soft thud. It rubbed against my legs and let out a contented meow. I had forgotten about my injuries for a moment and smiled at the creature before reaching out to pet it. But Zak snatched my hands, examining the damage I had inflicted upon myself.

Bruised, battered, and bloody, I wanted to pull my hands away from his grasp. He held them firmly for a moment before loosening his grip.

"Let me help you," he said in a deep voice that interrupted my thoughts and caused me to pause.

With a sigh through his nose, he was gentle as he inspected my hands and carefully removed any dirt or debris caught in the cuts and scrapes. There were some twinges of pain as he worked, but they dulled as I concentrated on the dusk, and time had enveloped us with its soft glow.

My furry friend settled at the hem of my skirt, grooming itself without a care in the world.

"How did you find me?" I asked, trying not to wince at the throbbing pain of my hands.

Zak's hands were busy picking small remnants of leaves, wiping off the thick dirt on my skin. He reached into his bag, bit off the cork from a bottle, and poured water over my hands.

"It's just water." He grinned. "I happened to be heading out this way to check on the fence when I saw you on the surveillance screen. My heart dropped when I saw you digging with your bare hands. I hurried down here."

So there are cameras in this direction. Liz, why didn't you think of this? You should have planned better!

Feeling foolish for following a cat through the woods in my exhausted state, I tried to justify it as a sign from the universe. But my desperation to escape clouded my judgment. I can't afford to make a mistake like this again.

"I'm surprised no one else came with you."

Zak reached back into his bag and pulled out some strips of cloth to wrap around my wounded hands.

"We need to get these cuts checked out."

I pulled my hands away from his grasp before the medical strip could touch my clean skin. "You just don't get it," I muttered, shaking my head. "I can't trust them."

One of his hands reached back out to take mine, his raised eyebrows showing his disapproval of my hesitation.

With a heavy sigh, I was reluctant to give in and let my shoulders relax as our hands met, and he began bandaging.

"Neither do I," he whispered, his voice gentler than before. "I've been looking for you."

"Really?" The words warmed my heart.

"I made a promise to you, Liz," he said as he knotted the bandages. "I've been scouting and studying the perimeter."

As he moved on to wrap my left hand, sealing in all of my emotions, a smile spread across my face. After countless tearful nights spent in darkness together, he promised to help me escape and return me to my husband and boys.

The last time we were together, Zak was brave enough for the both of us and fought off two men who tried to capture us. We were blinded by bright lights after being kept in darkness for who knew how long. I made a desperate attempt to escape by jumping off the cargo train while still weak from the drugs they gave us. I landed on my torso without being able to run and ended up being captured and drugged again by Reynard, who called me by another name: Rebecca.

WHY WE STRUGGLE

Zak tied the last knot, securing my medical bandages on each hand. His touch is gentle and careful, as if handling a small child. My loyal feline companion scurried away as I moved, disappointed that my skirts were unavailable to lounge on. I was gazing up to meet Zak's eyes like I was staring at Brant. Their height is close; Brant might have had a few inches on Zak.

However, Zak's broad shoulders and muscular torso hinted at his solid physical fitness. A mental reminder cautioned me not to stare for too long or blush.

"It's nice to finally see the person behind the voice," Zak said with a kind smile.

A loud crackle from the electric fence startled both of us. The air was charged with electricity, casting a warm glow over the landscape beyond the wall, showcasing its vibrant greens and browns.

Zak suggested we hurry back to the tower while there was still daylight, his hand a gentle reminder at times, guiding me by my elbow.

But I focused on the hole I had started digging under the

fence, desperate to escape. The thought of freedom fueled my determination despite my unsuccessful attempt.

As I stepped away from Zak's grasp and looked toward the fence, I couldn't help but notice the colorful stream now devoid of its usual blue and purple hues due to disrepair.

"I need to escape," The atmosphere echoed my plea.

Zak reached out for me, but I instinctively backed away. He reminded me that cameras were in this area and I wouldn't survive trying to crawl under. I would be electrocuted.

The thought of returning to the castle grounds, enduring another day of misery, and listening to the followers' dreadful stories felt like an unbearable weight pressing down on me. With each passing moment, I only added to that burden, leaving my feet rooted.

I turned my gaze in the direction Zak wanted to go, but I knew I didn't have the strength to follow him. The low hum of the electric fence drowned out any other sounds, creating a haunting atmosphere that seemed to beckon me toward the wall.

I focused on the magnificent landscape beyond the barrier. A sad thought lingered in my mind: I could walk straight into this deadly fence and end my suffering. My feet lift one step at a time, pulling me closer. The attraction of the mountains, with their thick forest and promise of relief, was more alluring than returning to our village.

As each second passed, the tension in the air grew denser, and the humming of the fence took on a foreboding beat. The weight of my decision bore down on me, and the outcome made every step toward the wall a journey filled with inner turmoil.

"Liz?" Zak's deep voice held a hint of concern. "What are you thinking?"

I ignored his genuine worry. In my mind, following my

fierce feline companion had brought me here for a reason. Zak's presence only reassured me that he was safe and healthy after our time apart. But even seeing him now couldn't dissuade me from what I knew was coming--a dark and uncertain moment ahead.

My fingers reached out, unsure how long I could hold on, yet desperate with the hope I wouldn't feel anything because death could come sooner. Fear crept in, slowing my movements and causing my heart to beat faster. The weight in my chest and the steady rhythm of my breathing accompanied each step.

"I can't go back." I declared.

The landscape before me was a breathtaking combination of faded pinks and oranges in the sky, thin white clouds casting a golden glow on the trees and mountains in the distance. I took a deep breath, savoring this last beautiful memory before everything went black. My arms stretched as if reaching for something beyond my grasp. The thought of facing his Grace's wrath, enduring Hunter and Mother's terror, and dealing with the inevitable consequences made me almost eager to leap. I didn't know how long to hold on, but I was determined to give it my all before succumbing to fate.

Zak's voice, which should have been commanding and urgent, was a whisper in the background as I approached the wall. With each step closer, the humming grew louder, drowning out all other sounds.

"Liz? Stop!" Zak's faint voice pleaded.

My mind was clouded, and I was unable to reason. Before I knew what was happening, he grabbed me by the arm and yanked me away as my fingers felt the warmth of the fence.

"You don't want to do that." Before I had time to gather my thoughts, he had enveloped me in another tight embrace, his chin resting on my head. "I need you here with me, Liz."

His words were a whisper in my ear. "Please don't make me be the one who has to remove your lifeless body."

The continuous hum reverberated in our ears, a menacing reminder of our danger. The moment's tension was palpable, making each second feel like an eternity. I couldn't deny it; he was right. I needed to stop and think before acting on my emotions. With my face pressed against his chest, I apologized for my rash behavior.

"Your voice saying my name was a relief to know you were here and ok," he shared, his words breaking my defenses. I was triggered by the familiar scent that reminded me of memories from the back of a van and on a cargo train —a sweet musk with added hints of pine and sweat.

We pulled away from each other with gentle care. His hands cupped my face, and his lips curved into a smile. His blue eyes radiate warmth.

"You are strong. I made you a promise, and I intend to keep it." His hands moved to my shoulders, grounding me with their weight. "Don't give in to the darkness."

His tone was comforting and familiar, keeping me calm amid the chaos. The sun setting over the mountains cast a chill over my skin as it did every night. I shivered as the wind drifted by, unable to rub my arms due to my injured hands. The cold seeped through my muscles and bones, causing them to ache.

Zak placed his hand on my upper back and guided me toward the village. "We don't know who's watching, but we should go back," he warned.

I thought about the cameras and realized we didn't have much choice. We had no idea who could be watching us. But beneath his calm exterior, an underlying tension hung in the air, reminding us that our journey was far from over, and the challenges of escaping our captivity still loomed ahead.

I looked at the fence, its appeal fading under the darkening mountain sky. The once welcoming scenery now felt unsettling on the other side.

As the sound of the humming fence faded into the background, Zak's voice filled my ears with comforting warmth.

"You're not alone anymore," he reassured me.

Our path ahead was obstructed by thick tree stumps, causing us to lean forward and navigate through the steep hills I had just defended. At times, it seemed like I was going to lose my footing.

In my exhausted state, my body ached, and cramps from dehydration made themselves known. I reached my breaking point by settling onto a tree stump and allowing myself to catch my breath.

"You know, I had a slight vision of what you would look like," I said as we rested.

"Did I disappoint you?" He joked.

"A little. I thought you would be taller," I replied with a smile.

"Funny, I thought you would be blonde." He chuckled, propping his foot up on the stump.

"Me? Why blonde?"

"You sounded like a blonde," he teased.

With my arms crossed, I felt a little insulted. "I sounded like a typical blonde," I was taken aback.

He shrugged, "Well, you know…being from California. Aren't most women there blonde?"

He had a point. I didn't want to argue, so I closed my mouth and thought about the women I knew. Most of them fit the description, whether natural or not.

"Okay, fair enough," I conceded with a smile.

He sat down next to me, resting his elbows on his thighs.

My fingers wanted to pick at the thin twigs growing from the stump. I needed to clear the air. "Thank you for pulling me back."

"There's no need to bring that up again," he shifted.

We still had one more uphill stretch before reaching the greenhouse. My stomach twisted as we approached the main grounds, the immediate familiar scent of dirt and manure scents.

“I’m glad you saved me," I muttered.

"We'll find a way out of here," he reassured me, standing up and giving me space. "But it will take time."

I appreciated his promise, but he didn't understand what I had been through, and patience wasn't something I had much of anymore.

HESITATION

As Zak and I trudged through the dense forest, the night sky loomed above us. Our steps grew heavier with fatigue, but we pressed on, trying to ignore the distant laughter and chatter of the villagers. They seemed so carefree and content, but their sense of community felt like a cult I was determined to avoid.

I felt Zak's hand reach my upper back, a comforting gesture that spoke volumes without him needing to say anything. We both stood in silence for what felt like an eternity, acknowledging the weight of our situation.

On the other side of the greenhouse, I could hear the villagers' voices discussing their new lives and sharing their backstories from their previous lives. I was uninterested and chose to drown out their words. Getting to know them meant I would end up trying to find a connection to them. The less I knew, the better off I was. Returning to the village meant accepting this new reality, at least for now.

I had to trust in Zak and his plan for our escape. The thought of pretending to fit in and adopting a persona that didn't feel natural was daunting. I had never been good at hiding my emotions or pretending to be someone I wasn't.

I shut my eyes and let the noises around me wrap me in a cocoon of senses - the cheerful chatter, the crackling fire, the clinking glasses, and the rustle of nocturnal creatures settling in for the night. Squirrels scampered up trees while a single owl hooted overhead, and the swaying treetops mirrored the gentle mountain breeze.

My nightmares often crept into my perception of reality. Walking towards the village conjured a mirage behind me. I turned to see my house, a one-story stucco building with a small patch of grass and bushes lining the path to the front door. I couldn't help but see myself being taken from it, just like when I was kidnapped - separated from Brant and my boys. Vivid images replayed in my mind as I watched myself being dragged away against my will while the door creaked behind me. Brant and the boys looked sad while they waved goodbye. This only served to deepen the growing distance in my heart.

Shaken by this vision, I saw the same scene before me - the back of the greenhouse looming over everything else. The thought of returning to the village and facing its inhabitants once again filled me with dread, but I knew I had to put on a facade to protect myself.

"I'm ready," I whispered to myself.

Zak nodded in understanding, and we returned to the village. What surprised me was that no one seemed to take notice of us. I half expected the Watchmen to be on high alert, ready to apprehend or send me to that ominous locker. But instead, we were met with casual greetings, nods, and salutes, which helped alleviate some of my anxiety.

"Do you want something to eat?" Zak asked.

"Liz!"

Startled by the worry in Amara's voice, I whirled

around. She rushed towards me, clutching her skirts as she slowed to take in my disheveled appearance. Her eyes scanned me from head to toe, noticing the bandages on my hands.

"Where have you been?" Amara's gaze lingered on my wrappings. "Are you injured?"

"No, I'm fine. I just fell and..." I turned to Zak. "This is Zak. He helped me with the bandages."

Amara's eyes widened. "Oh wow, this is the Zak?"

Zak extended his hand to Amara. "I am the Zak."

"It's nice to meet you finally," Amara said, relief evident in her tone. "And I'm glad to see that you're okay. Liz has been worried about you since she woke up with us women."

For some reason, my cheeks flushed at Amara's words. Knowing he knew my concerns and secrets, I hoped Zak wouldn't get the wrong impression. With each passing moment, the tangle of emotions seemed to grow tighter.

"Anyone would be," I was quick to reply.

Unable to resist, Amara took my hand and examined the bandages. "Nice wrapping job, but I think we should clean it properly, no offense."

"None taken," I responded with a small smile. "We were limited on resources."

In my peripheral vision, I could see a prominent figure approaching. Turning, I saw Reynard walking towards us with his usual stern expression. He stopped beside Zak on the other side, causing Amara to stiffen and suck up a sharp breath.

Offering him a faint smile, Amara greeted Reynard, who cleared his throat and nodded as if he had lost focus.

"Is something wrong, Reynard?" Zak asked with concern in his eyes.

He turned his attention towards me. A nagging feeling in my mind told me someone would be approaching me soon.

Zak had mentioned we were being watched, and I suspected that Aldrich or his Grace had been alerted.

"I'm supposed to accompany Liz to his Grace's study. He and Mother are expecting her," Reynard stated matter-of-factly.

After Zak insisted, he accompanied us as we moved through the halls. I, on the other hand, felt relief. Both stood on either side of me, shielding me from the constant fear of being pursued by Hunter or pulled away without warning. My stomach growled as we passed the dining hall with an empty table, taking notice of Mother and His Grace absent from their dining table. After navigating through several long hallways, we reached the study room.

Reynard knocks and announces my presence. The fireplace seems to be the only source of light in the room. His Grace is seated at a small table in front of the giant fireplace, playing a game of cards with Mother. He slaps the cards face-down when he sees me. He is without his crown, dressed in a loose cream-colored long-sleeve shirt that reveals a hint of his chest through the deep V-neck. As protocol dictated, I performed a curtsey upon seeing him.

Mother's intense stare conveyed disapproval, starkly contrasting her usual comforting demeanor. When I entered, His Grace invited me to sit on the couch with them. Mother moved to the center couch while holding a goblet of wine.

Declining His Grace's offer of wine, I asked for water instead. I needed to be careful due to my empty stomach. The last time I got drunk from Aldrich's vodka shots, I was inebriated because of my empty stomach and then was assaulted by Hunter. I needed to be alert and aware of my surroundings.

His Grace pours another cup of water and sits back down, relaxed.

"Liz looks like she's been wrestling in the wilderness," His Grace said as he gestured for me to join them. "Please..."

Taking a seat a few cushions away from Mother, I took the cup of water to quench my thirst. Despite my less-than-perfect manners, relief washed over me as I eagerly drank the cool water. Before I finished, His Grace got up and refilled my cup, pouring some for himself and placing the pitcher back on the table.

He returned to his seat and appeared more at ease than I expected. His left ankle rested on his right knee, and his arms stretched over the back of the couch. A smug expression played across his face as if he was proud of something.

"Now tell me," he said with intrigue, "how far did you get?"

THE SECRETS WE KEEP

"I'm sorry?" My dehydrated lips parted from the goblet as I responded to His Grace. I decided it was best to play the innocent role, allowing him to reveal more than I was willing to share.

He gave a small smile and shook his head. "Alright, let's play along." Setting down the goblet, he leaned towards me, resting his elbows on his knees. "What were you up to?"

As he tried to strike up a conversation, I couldn't help but feel suspicious of his intentions. He tried to appear friendly and approachable, but his approach felt forced and insincere. While part of me wanted to trust him, my years of experience working with families had taught me to always be on guard for hidden agendas.

"I found a cat. I went after it," I leaned back against the stiff couch cushion.

"Your hands?" His gaze fell to my bandages. "Did you catch the cat, and it fought back?" Something about his question struck me as odd.

Hadn't he seen all the footage of me trying to escape through the fence? Why would he bring that up now? Raising my hands, I revealed the dirt and tiny smudges of blood seeping through the fabric - a reminder of how close I had come to being caught or electrocuted.

“I slipped while chasing after that pesky cat.” I sipped on the refreshing water. It was the best-damn-tasting water I have ever had.

Relaxing on his couch, His Grace shifted his hands back on his thighs. One of his eyebrows arched as he watched me, taking in my story.

"Why would you even bother chasing after a cat?" Mother interjected with a snarky tone.

I couldn't help but give her a disapproving look. No matter how hard I tried to keep a serious face, I was always guilty of wearing my emotions.

"Maybe because it's the only sweet and innocent thing I've found since being here," I retorted. She tensed up, ready for a comeback, but his Grace raised a hand to silence her.

"It's Aldrich's cat, Shadow. He found her as a kitten when we first started building here," His Grace explained, standing from the couch and walking towards the dying fire. He used a poker to toss in some logs and rearranged them to encourage them to catch flame.

Mother and I remained silent, staring into the fire as His Grace tended it. I could feel Mother's eyes on me, but I didn't have the energy or desire to acknowledge her.

"Is there anything else you need from me, your Grace?" My tone even as I set down my goblet and stood up.

“Mother wants to speak with you. I'm relieved you're safe, but please stop chasing after creatures.” His Grace bid farewell with his heavy footsteps, leaving the room. As soon as the door closed, Mother sprung up from her seat and glared at me with clenched fists.

"How dare you," she snapped, pointing her finger at me.

Her sudden change in tone took me aback. "Me?" I asked, confused.

Mother's heels clicked on the stone floor as she approached me with a wave of intense anger. My blood boiled inside my body, making me feel as hot as dancing in flames.

"I have done everything to ensure your comfort here, yet you try to escape after all I've done for you," she seethed.

We were almost nose to nose now, and I could feel her breath of red wine on my face.

"I don't owe you anything," I snipped. "You took me by mistake, and now, according to His Grace, I am not going home."

Some time ago, she approached me with a proposition that seemed only to benefit her. We both suffer from a medical condition called bicornuate-uterus, which prevents us from carrying a pregnancy to full term. This was a constant sore subject and struggle for me because I wanted a child of my own, and Brant was pleased with the boys, two boys he and his widowed wife shared. I am a stepmother to those precious boys but share no DNA with them. We always argued because of the cost and low chances of success. Brant hated taking financial risks.

Being trapped in this place, with Aldrich having access to all my personal information, I confessed that I couldn't have children. In the back of my mind, I hoped they would see me as damaged and let me go home. It was a long shot, and my cheerful optimism got me nowhere.

Mother shared the original plan. Doctor Ferrarius was an expert in the field and planned on performing the corrective procedure. When I was taken by mistake instead of this Rebecca woman, Mother saw it as a sign that if the surgery didn't work, I was the backup plan. She offered that if her surgery didn't take and she was still in the same position, the surgery could be performed on me. I would have to give her my first-born child, and then she would find a way to sneak me out, and I could go back home to Brant and try having another baby.

This plan seemed insane, but I would have to settle on being here for over a year when I wanted to return home as fast as I could. How did Mother think that arranging surgery on my uterus would make things better? And why should I be grateful? As I sat there with my hands pressed together in prayer, I took deep breaths to calm myself and gather the strength to speak again. I refused to show any sign of weakness in front of her.

"I have not agreed to anything," my tone firm, pressing my hands together to hide their shaking. "Your plan comes with a hefty price that I am not willing to pay - giving up my first-born if your procedure doesn't work is too much."

Mother stood rigid, her hands clenched at her sides. She pursed her lips as if holding back the words she wanted to say.

"His Grace viewed what I wanted him to see. I assure you, Aldrich showed him only what I deemed necessary."

"Should I be grateful?" I asked, unable to relax my folded arms at my waist. My bandages were hot and sweaty on the inside; the adrenaline pulsing through my veins could have been blood seeping through, but I felt no pain.

Mother shook her head and walked over to stand by the fireplace, her tone now calmer. "No, you shouldn't have to be grateful. You never asked for any of this. It would still be my problem even if Rebecca were here instead of you." She rested a hand on the mantel. "I see you as fate intervening in my struggle. A sign to help me with my problems, and that is terrible because you are a human being with feelings and once had a life outside these walls."

"I still have a life outside these walls," I corrected her.

Mother nodded. "My apologies." She was now composed and soft-spoken. "It was unfair of me to make such an offer, putting so much pressure on you and risking your life for it."

A memory flashed through my mind—earlier today when I had wanted to run and throw myself into the electric fence, ending everything. Zak had stopped me. I wouldn't be standing here now if he hadn't been there.

Mother's voice continued, cutting through the tense silence. "I know there have been rumors about Hunter. Please confide in me. I know there is more to your story."

The memory of Hunter's hot breath on my neck and his hands on my body made bile rise in my throat once again.

Mother's eyes started to water at my lack of response. "I want to protect you, but how can I if you don't open up to me?"

My voice was dry as I spoke, "After everything that has happened, I don't know who I can trust anymore."

"Except for Zak," Mother added.

I pressed my lips together, knowing she was right. Zak was the only one I could trust. But I remained silent, not wanting to reveal anything beyond what she had seen on the footage.

She cleared her throat and offered, "The offer still stands. Take all the time you need. Hopefully, one day, I can earn back your trust."

Her calm demeanor diffused some of the adrenaline coursing through my veins. But I still didn't know how to navigate this strange request and delay the possibility. Mother gestured towards the door, indicating that I could leave.

"Just remember, you can always come to me and share anything."

I nodded and lifted my skirts as I left the room, my mind still racing with conflicting emotions.

BRANT

"We'll try to get home as soon as possible, son. I love you," Brant said before ending the call to his son, Steven. Both boys struggled to understand why he and his brother were stuck at Aunt Shannon's house for another night. In the cramped and dilapidated hotel room, Julian, his brother-in-law, paced back and forth on the phone in the background. This place was nothing compared to the luxury of the Edgewater Hotel, but Brant had maxed out all of his credit cards. He was still waiting for a refund for all the reservations and plans he and Liz couldn't enjoy.

"I promise we're doing everything we can, sweetie," Julian reassured his wife, Shannon, over the phone.

For the past twenty-four hours, Julian had gathered updates from city officials and footage from other police departments that may have been relevant to their case. Having an FBI agent like Julian on their side was a huge advantage and blessing. They received footage from the surrounding areas faster as Detective Knight had to pull warrants. Each new lead led to another dead end.

Brant understood that Detective Knight, assigned to their case by the Seattle Police Department, came with limited resources compared to the Government. She had no political ties like Julian. She was waiting on statements and video surveillance, and no one seemed to want to cooperate, which made Brant more suspicious. To Julian, this was nothing new.

"People can be lazy these days. Everyone is afraid to get fired or get their company in legal trouble," Julian told Brant one evening as they dined at a Denny's Restaurant.

When Julian hung up the phone, he let out a long sigh. His dress shirt looked rumpled and wrinkled despite being only two days old, suggesting that he hadn't slept much since Liz went missing. His head hung low, indicating that whatever news he was about to share would not be good.

"Shannon wants the boys to know," Julian relayed.

Brant was frustrated. He had already told Shannon that he would be the one to tell the boys about their mother's disappearance. In his mind, Liz was still out there, and they needed more time to find her.

Julian ran a hand through his messy hair, attempting to keep his composure. He had dealt with similar situations before in his specialized field of work. Kidnappings were draining and filled with moments of hope and despair.

"I understand where you're coming from," Julian said, remaining calm and raising his hands in a sign of peace. "But Shannon is equally worried. Liz is her sister, too."

Brant sighed and sat on the uncomfortable bed, which creaked under his weight. He realized that he had been inconsiderate towards Shannon's feelings. She was battling cancer and couldn't join him in the search for Liz.

Their conversations revolved only around Liz: how could they find her? Who could they ask for help? What else could they do? When they exhausted all their ideas, silence fell between them.

A few days ago, Julian had shared that finding Liz alive was a small percentage Brant couldn't ignore. It was less than twenty percent. Now, her case was running cold, and at this point, the police weren't as persistent because they expected a body to turn up at this stage in the case. But Brant refused to believe it. He still felt like she was alive despite all evidence pointing otherwise. Whenever he wanted to feel close to her, he would touch his wedding band and twist it around his finger. But now, even that brought no comfort.

Deep down, he refused to believe she was dead. Even when Detective Knight thought they had found her body and they went to the morgue, even she and Julian were fooled into thinking Liz's corpse was lying before them. But Brant knew better. The woman in front of them was not his wife. He had seen this woman the same day Liz disappeared during their visit to the Chihuly Gardens. Not only does she bear an eerie resemblance to Liz, but she also wears the same jacket and pants. This woman had been murdered at the Gardens, just fifty yards away from some stage, and based on her autopsy report, she had been killed a day after Liz went missing.

Julian received another call and excused himself from the room. When this occurred, it meant it was about work, and Brant wasn't cleared to overhear any information.

In the corner of the room, Brant noticed Liz's suitcase. The unattractive green box with a worn brown stripe stood upright, ready to be taken with him at any moment.

Brant got up from the bed, hearing the creaks of the rusty springs as he relieved them from his weight. He walked over to the suitcase, picked it up, and placed it on the bed.

As he unzipped the suitcase, Brant was struck by the disorderly manner in which her clothes were thrown inside.

This wasn't like them; they were neat and organized. But she wasn't there to gather her things, so it was up to him now. He threw her items into the suitcase and zipped it up, his hands shaking from making the sudden movement.

His fingertips brushed her clothes delicately as if they were as fragile as her once-was presence. Feeling the fabric was like touching a part of her essence. He feared losing his connection to her if he stopped feeling the clothes.

Examining the colors and styles of her clothing, memories flooded back to him. He remembered how she used to complain about those jeans he loved so much because of his comment on how amazing they made her look. The dark blue floral blouse revealed more cleavage than she would like to show, but she had worn it just for him. It was their little secret.

Gathering a handful of clothes, Brant brought them to his nose and took a deep breath, trying to capture the sweet tulip scent lingering on the fabric. With each inhale, his shoulders trembled, and his whole body quivered. He buried his face in her clothes at the overwhelming absence of her presence.

PAINFUL REMINDERS

In the following days, I moved through life as a mere ghost of myself, living in a world void of excitement. My daily routine consisted of attending sewing classes and creating unimpressive designs on throw pillows. My skills were considered inadequate enough to cut fabric for others. In this foggy state, nobody seemed to care about my well-being, and I reciprocated by not caring about their opinions.

Avoiding social interactions, I retreated into my world. The twins assumed my injuries were from the story I had shared with Mother and His Grace about chasing after a cat. Amara was the only one who tended to my wounds.

Every day, I searched the dining hall and other areas for Zak. I worried that he may have faced consequences for helping me. Whenever I thought about approaching Reynard for information, the ever-watchful Hunter would deter me with his piercing gaze, casually leaning against pillars or walls in the hallways or lurking in corners. Amara reassured me through her connection with Reynard that Zak was safe.

He and the other men had been warned not to speak to any women who were not their wives yet.

"Even Reynard shouldn't speak to me as much," she whispered.

Mother was sharp enough to notice that I needed space. Her hesitant looks in my direction were forced smiles. As she kept her distance, I couldn't tell if she wanted me to approach her. It was as though she wanted me to reach out and depend on her. I made small pleasantries but stayed away, showing her I didn't need her.

CORINA ASKED me one afternoon for help with laundry duties. I was tasked to fold shirts and deliver them to the seasoned, faithful homes. A spicy scent of ginger and citrus filled my nostrils, making me feel invigorated and alive. But underneath that was an underlying sourness, like spoiled fruit, that mixed in with the steam and hung heavy in the air. The hot steam made everyone perspire as they walked in. What this change in scenery did for me was it gave me the solace I craved. I didn't want to engage in small talk or pretend everything was okay. All I wanted was to be left alone. They gave me that, toward the back, with piles of laundry in baskets to be folded and sorted. This was perfect.

I kept coming back. As my small conversation pieces and quick responses hinted to everyone else, I wasn't in the mood to chat or get to know them. I was left alone folding and delivering baskets, and I found this task perfect. While folding shirts for the blacksmith and his wife one day, I noticed Aldrich's basket at the table's end. It had been a while since I last saw him, that night when I drank too much in his living quarters in the tower. I haven't seen him around at all.

I folded the last shirt and placed it on the blacksmith's basket before grabbing Aldrich's and leaving. I announced to anyone interested that I was making a delivery, but no one bothered to respond. With the women gossiping as they cleaned on the other side of the room, they were unlikely to notice my absence.

My usual assertive knock now sounded weak, a physical representation of my current state. My hands were bandaged, thanks to Amara's nightly care. Her lavender oil helped the deep cuts heal, but my hands still felt tender and limited my movements.

Aldrich opened the door to his staircase, looking exhausted with dark circles under his eyes from a restless night. He wasn't surprised to see me and motioned for me to enter as he opened the door wider.

"I've been waiting for you," he said.

I followed him upstairs into his modern-style, white apartment with one bedroom. Setting down the laundry basket on his coffee table, I stood with my hands on my hips, struggling to put my thoughts into coherent words. During my last visit, I took a survey as part of His Grace and Aldrich's algorithm to help me assimilate better into this community. But that night, I ended with Hunter assaulting me.

The memories flooded back as I stood in this room, where I had typed out personal information about myself, my life, and my family. All of it was used to determine who I should be paired with, a decision left up to a calculation to ensure everyone's happiness. Getting my thoughts in order proved difficult.

As Aldrich closed the door, silence settled between us. Just before the latch clicked into place, a meow interrupted, and my furry companion, Shadow, appeared at the windowsill.

"Shadow says hello," stated Aldrich.

A smile tugged at my lips as I walked over to pet the

animal. The feline rubbed against my hand, taking in the lavender scent before purring contentedly under my touch.

"Is Shadow a boy or girl?" I asked.

"Girl," replied Aldrich.

I scratched Shadow's spine, enjoying her affection and grateful for her presence. She reminded me of the day Zak and I were reunited, comforting my heart. But as Aldrich began removing items from his basket, I was reminded why I was there.

"Tell me something," I said, folding my arms and facing him. "Why didn't you report my assault when I left your ridiculous test?"

His reaction was immediate, freezing up at my words. But I kept moving toward him slowly, determined to hear his explanation for not protecting me that night.

"Liz, just wait a minute," he pleaded, uncomfortable and nervous as he backed up against the wall with nowhere else to go. "I didn't see what happened."

But even as he spoke, I continued moving closer, clenching my fists at my sides to intimidate him. He was more afraid of me now.

“You have eyes and ears everywhere in this place.” My heart races as I face Aldrich.

He stretches his arms out to defend himself against my angry fists. “You vanished from the frame. I couldn’t see you anymore.”

My feet stay rooted to the ground, only six inches from him. For some reason, this gives me pause. Is it because of the desperation in his voice that makes me want to believe him, or is it the teacher in me that wants to hear his side of the story?

Aldrich points towards his monitors, insisting he can prove the truth to me. "Look, I'll show you."

He leads me to a wall of monitors and pulls footage from

the night I left his place. I watch myself stumbling down the hill, not looking as graceful as I would have liked under the influence of a few shots of vodka.

Seeing myself from a different point of view reminds me of reality TV shows back home. The frames switch every three to four seconds with a new point of view. As I watch, my pace slows as I search around and wander to the right. I hadn't even realized I was doing that. Then, the frame freezes, and within a split second, I disappear.

"See?" Aldrich points out the time stamp on the footage, showing how it continues to roll backward. "It took me a moment to realize what was happening, but then I found you about six minutes and two seconds later."

The footage revealed a heartbreaking scene outside the castle walls near the women's showers. I could see myself on the ground, huddled in distress as tears streamed down my face, a victim of Hunter's attack. It all made sense now; his sudden departure hinted at his awareness of the cameras' time frame. He must have managed to manipulate the footage, ensuring that it didn't capture the painful memory of him assaulting me, pushing me against the wall, and making his intentions clear.

"That's enough," I muttered, distancing myself from the disturbing images.

Aldrich paused the footage of me on the ground, his lips wanting to find the right words, his eyes shifting from me to the ground. When he found the courage, he spoke up with cautious sensitivity.

"Liz, later that night, I saw Reynard bringing you out of the women's showers soaking wet." Sensing my discomfort, Aldrich kept his distance out of respect. "I asked Reynard about it that night, and he said you fell. I didn't know what happened until..." He trailed off, realizing he couldn't bring himself to tell me. He gestured for us to sit on his white couches by the coffee table.

My feet were tired, and my lower back ached, so I welcomed the chance to rest. I approached the conversation with caution.

He sat across from me with gentle care. His voice carried genuine concern as he asked, "Can I ask what happened?"

"What difference would it make? What can you do?" My tone was bitter and doubtful.

"I swear," Aldrich placed his hand over his heart. "If something terrible happened, His Grace would never tolerate such dishonor."

I could feel the sweat beads on my forehead as I squirmed in my seat, trying to escape the memories clawing at my mind. My throat tightens, and a lump forms, making speaking almost impossible. Aldrich's kind eyes bore into mine, filled with unspoken understanding and compassion for the pain I'm struggling to keep hidden. It takes strength to push out the words, knowing that saying them aloud will unleash a torrent of agony and anguish.

"He almost...but time ran out for him, and he knew it." The memories flooded back, causing my chest to feel heavy.

"Did anyone hear you? No one said anything?" Aldrich's disbelief showed his surprise that no one else in our village had mentioned or reported anything.

"I'm not sure...maybe someone did, but no one has said anything to me."

He brought his fingers to his lips as he reflected on the events of that night and what he had witnessed on the footage. "I couldn't shake off the unease I felt that night. I went to the server station the next day to review the footage, but Zak was already there. I asked him to help me figure out what had occurred."

My stomach twisted as Aldrich spoke. The thought of

someone watching those moments embarrassed and ashamed me. "Zak saw me--"

"He didn't know it was you," Aldrich interrupted. "I told him I lost sight of someone and asked if he could see what happened on the footage," he stressed.

My heart dropped as I realized what he was saying. "He saw Reynard carry me out?"

Aldrich's expression turned solemn as he nodded. "Liz," his voice was above a whisper. "I want to make this right."

There was something about Aldrich that I couldn't quite understand. Maybe it was because I felt vulnerable or wanted someone else on my side. But there was also something genuine about him that made me believe he wanted to help.

"Hunter." It took all of my strength to say his name out loud. As soon as I did, Aldrich's eyes widened and then turned to anger in the next second.

"That son-of-a-bitch!" The pure hatred in his tone was evident as he gritted his teeth. He slammed his fist onto the couch cushion, then brought his fingers to his lips, deep in thought.

"I feel like Hunter is watching me. It's unnerving." A chill ran down my spine, and I couldn't help but shiver.

"Now that you and Zak have reunited, I'm sure he has your back." Aldrich sunk further into the couch cushions, his chin resting on his thumb and index finger as he pondered our conversation.

I shrugged my shoulders. "I haven't seen Zak since we returned from the forest."

Aldrich considered this for a moment. "Perhaps Zak is laying low. It's no secret that His Grace doesn't want single men and women interacting until the courtship announcement."

As he announced the word courtship, my eyebrows lifted,

and my dry skin scrunched in disbelief. This new culture was becoming more absurd by the day.

"Could you explain this courtship tradition to me?" Although I didn't like the idea, understanding the details might help me navigate this foreign place.

"Don't forget, you are not a Faithful yet. Men and women are prohibited from socializing until courtship, followed by marriage. Men have been strictly warned to stay away from women. Some have even faced lashing as punishment in the past."

I could feel my mouth almost drop open, and my eyes bulge out of their sockets.

"Lashing? That's barbaric."

"It sends a strong message." He waved his hand dismissively as if it were equivalent to putting a child in timeout.

I reminded myself that this wasn't my fight. My presence here wasn't meant to challenge their beliefs or way of life. But my mistaken identity had already left a bad impression on the Faithful followers. They view me as a rebellious outsider who refuses to understand their ways.

I observed Aldrich, noting a newfound ease in his demeanor. The exchange of pleasantries seemed like an attempt at reconciliation. If he genuinely wanted to help me and make up for Hunter's violence towards me, I needed to see tangible actions before trusting him.

NEW TASK

A reminder of our first Faithful Service was posted downstairs on the women's tower by the front door. In elegant, handwritten calligraphy, it bore a message from His Grace:

Dear Future Faithfuls,

I invite you all to join us for our weekly Faithful Service on Sunday. This is a time for gathering, listening to my words through the service, and truly understanding what it means to be a Forever Faithful follower. After breakfast, your presence is required at the hilltop church, where we will welcome you. Women who have not yet converted into the Faithful must sit on the left side. Please ensure your clothes are clean and your hair is presentable, combed, and worn down.

I am looking forward to tomorrow's service,

His Grace

THE TWINS FOLLOWED me to the dining hall, and when they saw the same notice posted outside the door, we all pursed our lips to hold back laughter. The three of us walked together to breakfast. Yasmin mentioned needing help filling jars with supplies at the medical building.

The twins were a source of comfort for me. They were almost identical in every way, though Yasmin had a fiery personality while Esther was more reserved. I was jealous of their waist-long black hair, which was always braided or styled in a unique fashion. My mid-length fair brown hair didn't glimmer in the sun like their hair did.

The twins haven't been prying into my personal life; they barely acknowledge anything. They are too preoccupied with their daydreams and the men in this place. Their wandering eyes are fixated on the Watchmen. Yasmin is confident and often smiles or waves back if she catches their attention. On the other hand, Esther is shy and seems to think she isn't as pretty as her sister—ironic considering they are identical.

In the past week, I couldn't help but notice that the twins were being flirtatious, and the women around me displayed signs of seduction. They whispered about men and their desires in the hallways, during meals, and even while we worked. I saw their eyes linger on the men carrying heavy loads or working hard in the fields. They licked their lips and waved flirtatiously as the men passed by. But as soon as Mother or seasoned Faithful approached, they straightened up and pretended nothing was wrong. It was a constant game of temptation and control, with each woman fighting her desires behind closed doors.

I was trying to move forward. Among a select few of us, I was given different tasks each day, perhaps meant to bring out hidden talents or interests that would benefit our village. We were known as "the lost ones." My teaching credentials meant nothing here until women started having children; then, a school would be built.

The actions and hormonal discussions made me long for the feel of the weight of my wedding band and engagement ring. But they were gone, taken from me upon my arrival. I missed the white gold band molded around the small quarter-cut diamonds that aligned across my finger. My beautiful engagement ring was the prettiest piece of jewelry I had ever owned. A soft cushion half-cut diamond sat elegantly on top of the prongs. Yet, as I traced the space on my ring finger, the indent seemed to have still the curve that once held my rings in place—a constant reminder of who I used to be: a married woman.

Yasmin's questioning gaze brought me back to reality. I assured her I would help in the medical building and didn't care what needed to be done. I was eager for any new task to distract me.

Angela would have no problem assigning me to work at the medical building. It would also mean less stress for her as she wouldn't have to correct my lack of sewing abilities. I always knew that when she tried to be patient with me, she would curse under her tongue with her Bronx accent.

"Maybe my jar-filling skills will finally come in handy." I joked.

MY TASK was deceptively simple yet an odd satisfaction.

Yasmin's instructions were clear: pour the coriander pepper balls into the smooth marble pestle bowl and grind them into a fragrant powder with the matching mortar.

The aroma of freshly crushed spices filled my nostrils as I watched with care, turning the handle, the coarse balls slowly breaking into fine dust. With each turn, I learned to control my breaths, avoiding inhaling too much and risking the sharp particles getting stuck in my throat. It was a delicate process that required patience and precision. But as I continued to crush the pepper balls, I lost myself in the rhythmic motion of grinding and releasing their unique scent into the air.

As I worked, the air filled with a fusion of scents—the tangy kick of citrus oils, the earthy aroma of dried herbs, and the subtle sweetness of floral essences enveloped me before fading as the day went on. Hints of lavender and cinnamon lingered in the air, giving off a warm feel and reminding me of autumn. I also learned about the calming effects of patchouli oil as Yasmin had me take a whiff from the jar.

Amara and Yasmin brewed their remedies in the back area of the medical building. There were plentiful rows and wooden shelves lined with jars and vials of all sizes. Their concoctions contained the purest scents of nature, imbued with symbolic healing powers.

From barred windows, countless jars and bundles of dried herbs filtered in sunlight, casting a mesmerizing glow on the aromatic treasures adorning the space.

My curiosity got the better of me. "So what exactly does coriander do?"

As she balanced the remnants on the scale, I funneled the crushed coriander into a four-ounce jar marked with its designated label. I tapped to ensure only the fine powder entered the small clear jar. Yasmin brought back clean and labeled jars for me to fill, inspecting my work with evident satisfaction. Despite being new to the process, I had already filled two jars.

"This is used for headaches and also treats fevers," Yasmin explained.

I was intrigued by this information. "That's fascinating. Are there more coriander bags? It looks like this is empty."

Yasmin's expression turned to surprise as she examined the empty bag of coriander, making her bite her bottom lip in thought.

"I think I'll need to go up to the storage area near the front of the castle. You're really fast. You're hired!"

"I don't work for free!" I joked with a playful smirk.

Yasmin laughed and left. As I finished securing the cork in the jar containing my meticulously crafted batch of coriander powder, I took the jars. I delivered them to the medical supply closet near Doctor Ferrarius' office on the other side of the hall.

Doctor Ferrarius greeted me as I entered, expressing his gratitude for my help.

"Remarkable!" He exclaimed in his slight German accent. "You have no idea how much this helps us."

The urgency in one of the Faithful nurses' voices caught my attention as she hurried down the hallway toward Doctor Ferrarius. "Doctor, Susan's water broke," she said, panicked.

"Excuse me, Liz," the doctor responded before rushing off to assist with delivering a baby into our village.

Our village?

I scolded myself for feeling a sense of camaraderie with the pregnant woman in labor. The sounds of her breathing and moaning filled the room, but my feet walked with caution closer to her. I couldn't resist the curiosity surrounding the first childbirth in our village, even though I stayed back at a safe distance. The other nurses and Doctor Ferrarius escorted her into her room. Despite her flushed face and wild hair, she exuded strength and determination as the sun shone through a stained glass window, giving her blonde locks an almost fiery appearance.

It reminded me of a cartoon character I once saw who had been electrocuted by an umbrella on a rainy day. I couldn't help but feel drawn to sneak down and witness this miraculous moment, to hear the cries of a newborn and be filled with innocent joy. But then reality hit me as I placed my hand on my lower abdomen, a constant reminder that I couldn't bear children. Mother could arrange for me to have corrective surgery if I wanted it, but that idea came at a price.

Word was spreading like wildfire. I glanced out the window and saw the other villagers tiptoe or walk cautiously as they approached the building. Though newcomers weren't permitted to mingle with the Faithful, that didn't stop them from gathering around, anticipating the newborn's cries.

Only one individual, a tall and slender man, sprinted toward the building. He seemed anxious but also exhilarated as he darted past the curtains. Through his excited whispers, I could hear him boasting about Susan's strength and how this was their miracle.

Yasmin appeared around the corner and spotted me. She gave me a curious look and then glanced behind her. Both of us were listening to Susan's Lamaze breathing in the background. Yasmin's shoulders slumped when she saw my hand resting on my stomach. I regained my composure and cleared my throat.

"What else can I do?" I asked, hoping to be helpful.

She handed me a stack of clean rags with instructions to head down four curtains to the right. "This patient needs his wounds cleaned. Nothing bad, a small amount of blood." Her eyes fixed on the delivery area. She was just as eager to be down there and see the miracle delivered.

I nodded before rushing past her to get the job done.

As I made my way down the hallway counting, I could hear a hoarse voice calling out from behind one of the closed curtains. My curiosity sparked, and I approached to investigate. When I pulled back the curtain, I found Zak lying in bed, lost in his dreams, seeming to be in pain. His bare chest revealed a muscular physique adorned with fresh scratches that were still oozing blood. My cheeks turned pink at the unexpected sight.

With my eyes, I counted to verify that this was the fourth curtain down, impressed by Yasmin's cleverness in having her tend me to Zak's wounds. She knew I had not seen him and worried. Walking into the room, I noticed a cart containing ointments and a water bowl. Without hesitation, I grabbed a rag and began tending to his wounds.

I dipped the rag in the water bowl before dabbing at his bloody chest. Suddenly, he grabbed my hand, startling me. His eyes opened in confusion but softened when he recognized me.

"Liz? What are you doing here?" he asked as he loosened his grip on my wrist.

I continued tending to his injuries as we talked. "I'm volunteering," I replied.

The scent of lavender and menthol oil wafted over from a nearby cloth, reminiscent of Amara's healing touch on my own hands.

Zak winced and grunted as the cloth wiped at his deeper cuts. I glanced away, trying to maintain professionalism while also being aware that I was blushing at the sight of his toned upper body.

Pull yourself together!

"Liz?" Zak's voice snapped me out of my internal struggle. I met his confused gaze before refocusing on his left side, which was now free from blood and soaking wet from the water on his bed sheet.

"What happened? Did Shadow scratch you?" I joked, but his confusion prompted me to clear my throat. "Sorry, Aldrich's cat—that's what I meant—my furry friend I chased into the woods."

Zak raised an eyebrow. "That's Aldrich's cat? And he named it Shadow?"

"Don't tell him I told you."

"I won't, but he's getting some teasing from me." Zak winced. "I was installing a new camera when a branch gave way, and I came tumbling down."

EMOTIONS

"Can you promise no more tree climbing without proper safety gear?" I held my hand to Zak, indicating a binding agreement, and waited for him to shake it.

Zak hesitated, reluctant to commit after boasting about his successful week of climbing. But I kept my hand steady, and he gave in, rolling his eyes as he gripped my hand. Upon feeling my firm grip, the twinkle in his eye was the best part. We shook on it, and I gave a slight tug that made him wince. He tried to hide the pain, but his clenched jaw gave him away.

"When I seal a deal with a handshake, it's sacred," I declared.

Wincing as he sat up in bed, Zak grabbed his bloodied shirt that hung over the railing on the other side.

"A handshake is an unbreakable promise to me," he explained, his voice cracking as he stretched his muscles. "I don't make deals with people I don't trust."

An immediate smile spread across my face. "Good to know."

Yasmin pushed back the curtain, carrying several jars. She glared at Zak, questioning our interaction as he was about to put his shirt on.

"What exactly are you doing?" Yasmin interrogated Zak.

"I'm leaving?" Zak sat back down in slow motion, like one of my kindergarten kids who got caught trying to leave time out. "Your nurse already dabbed that oil on me. I should be fine."

Yasmin squinted, analyzing the situation. She handed me the bottles and instructed me where to put them on the shelves.

"Well, she's not really a trained nurse. Nice try. You have open wounds, and if they get infected…"

I discreetly slipped out of the room, leaving Yasmin to continue grilling Zak. As her voice faded into the background, I couldn't help but feel giddy inside.

THE AROMA of garlic and rosemary infused the dining hall, making my mouth water as I took a bite of the juicy chicken thighs. The mashed potatoes, seasoned with real chives, added a crispiness to the meal. After weeks of bland food, this was the most delectable thing I had tasted. Yasmin couldn't resist teasing me.

We were celebrating tonight. Susan was still in labor, and His Grace wanted a delicious meal prepared for the occasion. On the other hand, I was looking forward to the women giving birth if we would receive delicious meals like this.

"Are those sounds about the food, or are you daydreaming about someone?" she quipped, grinning at me.

Esther and Amara joined in, adding to the playful interrogation. As they pried for more information, I tried to hide my emotions by focusing on chewing my food.

"Who is it?" Esther's eyes gleamed with curiosity.

Clearing my throat, I hesitated before answering. "It's not..." I struggled to find the right words as all attention turned to me.

"What do you mean? Tell us!" Yasmin took a bite of her steamed carrot. "How hard was it for you to tend to Zak's wounds, touching those abs." She winked at me, sharing how she had orchestrated the situation. "And can we blame you? Zak is an exceptional man." Yasmin teased, oblivious to the line she was crossing.

Esther's eyes widened, and she blushed. "Shirtless?" She asked, her voice full of excitement. "Liz, did you touch his abs?"

I felt a surge of irritation and lost my appetite for the meal. I didn't even finish half of it before grabbing my tray and standing up abruptly.

"Liz, please don't," Amara pleaded.

I turned away in front of everyone in the dining hall, not caring about potential judgment. "So that you know, he's just a friend. I would never act inappropriately, especially as a married woman!" The clattering of silverware against the wooden plate echoed in the room. "I'm stuck here, yearning for my husband every day, and the one time I smile at someone who has been kind to me, you automatically assume it's flirting."

The other tables fell silent, and Yasmin and Esther sat ashamed, their bodies hunched over like children who knew they were in trouble.

I stormed over to drop off my tray and utensils before storming out.

"Liz!" Amara called after me when I was halfway down the hall. "Please wait!"

But I didn't slow down for her or anyone else. All I wanted was to be far away from the twins who had been insensitive about my feelings for my husband - the man I cried over every night while they slept like babies on the other side of our shared room.

Amara gasped for air as she touched my shoulder, complaining about cramps and struggling to keep up with me.

"Can we take a break for a minute?"

I was reluctant to slow down, but as Amara chased after me, I did stop at the edge of the garden corridor, the women's tower looming in the distance. All I wanted was to retreat to my bed, bury myself under the covers, and trace the names I had carved into the wooden frame.

"I'm not in the mood for you playing devil's advocate tonight. What she said was completely offensive." I could feel my anger bubbling up inside me, tightening my chest and shaking my voice as I fought back the urge to lash out at Amara, who had done nothing wrong and was only trying to help.

"Come here," her soothing tone caught my attention, leading me to a stone bench on the grass. "Don't do this to yourself."

"Do what?" I snapped.

"We all know your story. We all know how you feel." Amara's soft hand held my tight, clenched fist. "It was in poor taste but wasn't meant to hurt you."

My fist clenched so tight that I felt my nails dig into my palms. She noticed I wasn't in the mood for this conversation as my chest rose with each breath, my face soured, and my dry skin scrunched.

"She's a woman, you're a woman, and Zak is an attractive man." Amara tried to help me understand. "It's natural for her to tease and assume you two have some connection."

The cool breeze brushed past us, and I felt myself starting to calm down. I wanted to shiver from the sudden drop in tension, so I exhaled, letting my anger dissipate and be carried away by the wind. My hands relaxed, and I dropped my anger as she took one of my hands in hers for comfort.

"I don't see Zak like that," I said, folding in my arms. I felt shame and guilt because I knew I blushed when I saw him without his shirt. "Small places like this love their gossip, and I don't want to be the center of it."

Amara nodded, her eyes sympathetic to my cause. "No one doubts your love for your husband." She squeezed my arms a little. "We all know how hard this transition has been for you."

"It's a constant internal battle," I confessed. I looked up at the starry sky above the mountains, fighting back the tears. I didn't want to break down in front of Amara again. She knew my story. She saw my struggles.

"Tomorrow is Sunday, our first service," Amara offered, standing up and extending her hand to help me up, too. "Let's go upstairs, talk to the twins, and get some rest. One day at a time."

I took her hand and was grateful for her support.

FIRELIGHT

When I clicked on the door latch, the twins' gazes snapped towards me, but they turned away. Their posture reminded me of guilty children awaiting a scolding from their parents despite being grown women in their mid-twenties. Like scared children, they stood up from Esther's bottom bunk and folded their hands at their stomachs, shoulders hunched and eyes focused on the ground. They were expecting to face consequences. I hurried over to them and wrapped my arms around their shoulders in a tight hug.

"I shouldn't have snapped at you," I said.

"I'm sorry," Yasmin replied, returning the embrace.

"I just miss my family," I admitted. "I took what you said wrong because I miss my husband."

Yasmin placed her hands on my shoulders and looked into my eyes.

"I was in the wrong. I'm ashamed of how I behaved."

"Me too," Esther chimed in.

At that moment, I realized I needed to relax. They meant no harm and intended to have playful banter. I had taken everything too seriously and jumped to judge when they meant to have fun. What we needed was a chance to talk and relax. I brought Yasmin over to sit next to me on my bunk.

"You know what I really miss?" I said, wrapping an arm around Yasmin's shoulders. "Coffee." The scent of lilacs wafted off her hair, and a smile spread across my face as I thought back to the small patch of lilac bushes in my garden. The scent was my favorite, making me miss the lilac oil that Brant got for me every year for my birthday.

"I miss Coffee so much," Esther exclaimed. Her longing for the delicious beverage made her whine, causing all of us to laugh. I reassured Yasmin because I knew we would get through this together. She wrapped her arm around my shoulder in response.

"I appreciate you not hating me," Yasmin's shoulders relaxed as she exhaled.

"Hate is a strong word in my book. I'd rather give someone a hundred excuses than hate them." I stated matter-of-factly.

With that affirmation, as I said the words, I recoil when thinking of Hunter. He was someone I despised with every fiber of my being. I couldn't tell which word was worse because I had never gone through something like this. I thought I despised math or Alex Hill when he broke my heart in high school when he cheated on me with some girl from Chatsworth. For the first time in my life, I could state that I had an actual enemy. It was a deep-rooted disgust and resentment that I couldn't find it in myself to move on from.

Esther motioned to the corner of our shared bedroom, where our new Sunday dresses were wrapped in delicate, light brown paper and tied with a blue ribbon. I reached out for the dress but hesitated before opening it. The thought of seeing my new dress filled me with dread instead of excitement. Wearing fancy gowns to attract potential suitors was not something I looked forward to. All I wanted was a peaceful night's rest.

"You not going to open it?" Esther said as she held her package in her hands.

I shook my head. Her eyes dropped down. I sensed the remark because she wanted us to open it together. It was a custom in their culture that when the same gift was given, they opened it simultaneously.

"How about tomorrow morning," Amara stated as she climbed up to her bed.

After the four of us dressed for bed, we said goodnight. The moonlight shining through the small oval window illuminated my carved names. My fingers traced over Brant's name, hoping he could somehow feel a connection. I wanted him to sense me in his surroundings, hear my voice in the breeze, or dream of me knowing I was thinking of him. At some point, I had fallen asleep, only to be awoken by Amara's whispers and the nudge on my shoulder.

"Let's go downstairs," she whispered.

I noticed the twins sleeping with synchronized breaths, curled up on their left sides. Curiosity sparked inside me as I followed Amara out of the room, torn between wanting to sleep and wanting to know what was on her mind. We tiptoed down the stairs without making a sound.

The fireplace's flickering flames danced along the last remnants of a giant log, their warm orange and yellow light barely reaching the corners of the dark room. Amara gestured for me to follow as we descended the stairs towards the comforting heat. It was eerie to be the only two in the room, surrounded by the sound of crackling embers and the faint smell of burning wood. I tugged on Amara's sleeve.

"Is everything okay?"

Amara motioned for us to sit in the armchairs closest to the fire, her hands fidgeting and her expression uncertain.

My eyes scanned the room, ensuring no one else was present to eavesdrop on our conversation. The tapestry hanging on the walls, depicting peaceful scenes of nature, seemed darker in some areas, adding to the eerie atmosphere.

"What is it, Amara?" I asked, feeling a sense of unease wash over me.

She let out a deep breath through her nose as she prepared to share whatever was on her mind. Her fingers intertwined as she spoke.

“Something else happened the day you ventured into the woods,” Amara was hesitant.

Her tone caused a knot to form in my stomach. "Okay," I responded, bracing myself for what she was about to say.

"It's about Nellie," Amara said, referring to her travel companion, who had been placed in the locker since their arrival. "I haven't thought much about her. I'm just relieved I don't have to deal with her. But Mother came to me and asked if I would visit her."

My skeptical brain kicked in. "What was her reason?"

"She wanted to know how I felt about seeing Nellie again. She's been asking about me," Amara explained, shifting in her chair. The warmth from the fireplace was fading, and she rubbed her arms for comfort.

"I don't want to see her," Amara admitted, sensing the guilt weighing on her. "I can't handle listening to her after everything she put me through. Our journey left me almost as crazy as she is."

Amara and I often talked about our journey to this place, but I had it easier with Zak as a travel companion than Amara's experiences. She crossed her legs, staring into the flames. Her teeth rested at the tip of her index finger, her coping mechanism as she spoke to me as if trying to rid herself of a heavy burden.

"I haven't told you that Nellie knows things about this

place, and everything she has shared so far has turned out to be true."

This information was weighing on her. She had been optimistic and supportive since we arrived here, but seeing her like this worried her.

"I just thought it was all an act, you know?" Amara admitted. "I assumed the stress of being kidnapped and our journey here had made her lose touch with reality."

"I can't say I blame her," I replied, understanding the severity. I pulled my armchair closer to hers and placed a comforting hand on her knee. My touch seemed to reassure her that she was safe with me in the present moment.

"She used to try and hide in one corner of the van," Amara continued. "But when we transferred to the train, it was like she never slept, always on edge. She would mumble nonsense to herself or scream out in bursts."

Listening to her share her rough time traveling here made it hard to imagine myself in her shoes. I couldn't imagine listening to someone else scream randomly, speak nonsense, or outwardly act out when all you want is silence.

I was thankful for my situation and counted my luck in knowing that Zak was my travel companion, not Nellie. If I was locked up with someone going crazy and losing touch with reality, I could see how that could break someone.

"She kept hinting that she knew what was going on, but she only gave me small pieces of information," Amara recalled.

"Like what?"

"She said a man named his Grace was a time traveler. We would have a new mother and lose everything we knew but become devoted followers."

The gravity of her words erupted goosebumps under my thick cotton gown.

Amara put her hand on mine. "She told me she was hand-selected, and her brother would protect her."

My face went pale. Amara locked eyes with me, sadness filling her gaze. I leaned back, holding my fingers to my lips.

"Who do you think her brother is?"

Amara shrugged. "Your guess is as good as mine. She speaks in riddles. Sometimes, when I'm alone doing something mundane, I try deciphering her words in the back of my mind."

"That must be exhausting," I empathized. "Why didn't you tell me this before?"

Amara's composure was slipping away as she tried to explain the situation. "You have to understand, she sounded insane." Her voice rose in pitch. "Dealing with her was like dealing with a different level of madness." There was a flash of anger in her eyes as if she was reliving a moment.

"I've had to block out most nights to cope." She took a deep breath. "Sometimes, I would sit or lie down with my hands over my ears, hoping she would pass out from exhaustion. But now Mother tells me she's been asking for me as if my visiting her will fix or maybe settle her down. I don't know." The weight and stress over her situation were evident all over Amara's face.

"You know what you have to do." Brant appeared behind Amara, arms crossed against his chest as he leaned against the wall. Seeing him didn't scare or excite me - I knew he was a manifestation of my subconscious. His presence brought comfort because I trusted his guidance.

He was in his dark blue jeans and green-collared Titleist polo, which he wore on our casual Fridays. My heart skipped a beat, imagining him standing there and still trying to find a way to connect with me and help me. Earlier, when I wished for my connection to be strong with him, this may be my gift from the universe. Having these moments where I can see and have him as my subconscious, I can remind myself that our love is still alive.

"You need a distraction. Maybe you can save Nellie from the locker?" Brant suggested.

He was right. Or, I should point out to my psyche that I am right. But I needed to be careful with my words. I had to remind myself getting someone else involved wasn't about me keeping myself busy. I needed to see this woman for myself, to understand the level of madness Amara stated.

I couldn't shake the idea of how Nellie could be in this state after being in the locker for so long. I had no medical training or expertise, but she needed a friend, someone to trust or guide her in making the right choices. The desire to make a difference in someone's life made the adrenaline rush in my veins. Was this really what drove me? Or was it something deeper, something darker that I didn't want to face?

Squeezing Amara's hand, I wanted her to look into my eyes. Her shoulders slumped, and she struggled to decide what to do. She confided in me because she trusted me and needed my help.

"How about we do this together," I offered. "I can go with you and see for ourselves."

SUNDAY

The soft morning light illuminated my bedroom, and I stood in front of my dresser in only my undergarments. On top of the dresser sat a package that had caught my attention.

The twins, full of excitement, couldn't wait to open their wrapped packages and reveal their new floor-length dresses made of cotton. Delicate ruffles adorned the neckline, adding a touch of allure. Yasmin couldn't wait any longer as she slipped into her dress, twirling around with youthful joy. Esther followed suit, draping a long linen bodice over her cotton dress and cinching it at the waist. The golden yellow color of the bodice complemented Yasmin's complexion, giving the whole outfit a medieval charm.

Amara noticed my hesitation in joining in on the transformation as I changed behind them.

"Refusing to participate will only draw more attention to yourself," she shared, urging me to do as they did.

With a sigh, I grabbed the package and revealed an emerald green bodice to accompany my cotton gown. Amara whistled in approval as I slid my arms through the smooth and clean fabric and complimented how well the rich color looked against my skin. Her gentle violet bodice highlighted her features and her wide brown eyes.

"Let me assist you." Amara's graceful steps in my direction made me smile as she came over to help tie the front of my bodice. "This looks lovely on you."

Her kind words resonated with me. The twins held arms and lifted their skirts, skipping in circles with contagious joy. Amara gave a gentle tug as she secured the final knot of my bodice, catching my attention.

"You can do this," she reassured me.

I nodded in appreciation. The atmosphere was filled with excitement as we headed to breakfast and the long-awaited ascent up the hill to attend church service.

THE CRISP morning air made the uphill journey pleasant while the sun's warmth shone down on our backs. When we reached the top, I was met with a breathtaking view - a sprawling lawn surrounded by a pine forest with a stone church at its center. The towering perpendicular spire almost rivaled the grandeur of the mountain looming behind it, casting a shadow over the entire structure.

Our guide, Alex, a blacksmith and devoted member of the Faithful, and his wife, Elen, shared details about the church's construction, including specific details of its use of ham stone. He spoke about the challenges of mastering this craft. Terms like doulting and lias were mentioned, though their significance eluded me. I walked alongside him at his rapid pace, listening while also stealing glances at some men led by members of the Watchmen on the opposite slope.

I scanned the group of men, hoping to glimpse Zak among them. They were uniformly dressed in sturdy black pants, leather vests, and boots, topped off with long-sleeved cotton shirts. They blended as a cohesive unit against the backdrop of the hill.

As we approached the front tower, I craned my neck to take in its grandeur, feeling small in comparison. The building was adorned with intricate details - carved parapets, decorative bell windows, and niches housing statues of wildlife from the surrounding forest instead of human figures. Expecting to see menacing gargoyles perched on the edges, I was surprised to see crows in place.

Our procession narrowed as the Faithfuls formed two lines on either side, welcoming us. In my mind, I gathered my skirts and counted six steps before reaching the imposing front doors. Mother stood at the entrance, ready to greet us. A sense of peace and awe washed over me as I passed through the heavy wooden doors. The elongated hallway had arched ceilings and rib-vaulted structures that seemed to transport me back in time despite the newness of the church.

Sunlight filtered through stained windows on each side, casting vibrant colors onto the flagstone floor like a kaleidoscope. The windows depicted scenes from nature—a majestic stag in a meadow, a bear catching Salomon in a river—surrounded by various other wildlife animals on large stained panels.

Alex and Elen led us to the entrance, where a beautiful fountain welcomed us. They instructed us to dip our fingers into the cool water, place them over our hearts, and then take seats on the left side. Amara and I exchanged a look of confusion before following their guidance. The cold water sent shivers through our fingertips as we complied with the ritual. Alex explained that the centerpiece, a hand-carved stone fountain, was chosen by his Grace. Its flowing streams created a soothing atmosphere as it descended from tier to tier. Intricate sculptures of wildlife adorned each level, with fish appearing to swim downstream within the tiers.

As we entered the space, I couldn't help but feel a sense of warmth and hospitality. Amara and I walked in without saying a word, entranced by every detail we encountered. The air was faintly scented of wax and aged wood. Rows of pews lined the room, cushioned with soft red velvet. As everyone took their seats, I noticed a section reserved for the Faithfuls at the front. Amara and I chose to sit towards the back.

After the men on the right side had taken their seats, a profound silence fell over the room as we settled into our seats, only interrupted by occasional coughs or throat clearing. The anticipation was tangible as we waited for the next part of the ceremony to begin.

The blaring of trumpets blasting through the speakers startled most of us, causing an involuntary jump. His Grace made his way down the aisle, his intense gaze fixed on Mother. We all rose and performed curtsies or bows as he passed by. The Watchmen stood guard in the back, but a glance revealed no sign of Hunter. Relief washed over me, mingled with a hint of fear. I scanned the room, wondering where he could be lurking.

His Grace ascended the stage, where Mother sat on a purple cushioned throne on the left, and I assumed His Grace's red throne was on the right. The noticeable distance between them struck me as strange. Behind the podium, His Grace instructed us to take our seats. Like obedient children, we fell into silence.

"Before we begin, I want to update you all that Susan gave birth late last night to a baby girl named Aster." His Grace beamed with joy.

Everyone erupted in applause, and I, too, joined in, relief that everything would be okay with the new mother and baby.

"This moment means everything to me," His Grace

echoed through the speakers. "I have devoted my life to our Faithful ways, and now I will show all newcomers that following the Faithful path is a new beginning for the mind, body, and soul."

His pacing across the stage allowed him to make eye contact with each of us as he spoke. "This is not like any church you may be used to. Remember that part of your life is behind you now. The ways of the outside world are not welcome within these walls. Why?" He paused, waiting for answers from the crowd, but even his devout followers remained silent.

"Out there," he gestured towards the outside world. "I once believed in its potential, its system of hope." He suppressed a small laugh. "Even after achieving success and wealth beyond my wildest dreams through my business, I was still unhappy."

The people around me seemed to be nodding their heads in agreement with his words, and a part of me felt like I was being subjected to his ways, which felt like a moment of submission.

"I've climbed the corporate ladder and built an empire using this," he said, pointing to his head with his index finger. "But it was never enough for everyone else in my world. They always wanted more. I remember sitting in my office one day in disbelief that all my accomplishments still weren't good enough."

He paused, leaning on the podium to gather his thoughts before continuing. "That's how people made you feel in your past lives, didn't they? You were a number, a credit score. Your accomplishments were measured to pin one person against another. The people in this room can relate because no one in your life said 'you' were good enough."

The crowd's buzz surrounded me as I watched him effortlessly charm and manipulate everyone around him. It was hard not to be impressed by his brilliance and cunning tactics. But at the same time, I couldn't help but question the means he used to gain power over those who had started with nothing. Sitting back with my hands in my lap, I couldn't shake off the unease and discomfort lingering in the air.

He continued, "As you sit here in this audience, you may be wondering why this happened to you," His Grace descended the steps one by one. "But I ask, why not you?" He approached the front row, gesturing towards the Faithfuls seated before him. "You all took my test when I offered it in other cities because you wanted a different life. You were unhappy with the one given to you. So let me offer you a fresh start. You were pressing reset when you clicked that 'complete' button."

His boots echoed in the room. His hands were outstretched towards the villagers before him.

"Let us welcome you into our family. Here, you are not just a number; you are family."

I whispered to Amara, "Do you believe any of this?"

Amara leaned over, "As implied by the salvation of sinners and blessings bestowed upon us."

"What?" I thought I had lost her for a split second, and she spoke a different language.

"That's what the word 'grace' means." Her eyebrows lifted as though warning me what we were up against.

FIREPIT

The Faithfuls were the first to leave, with a sparkle in their eyes and heads held high as they exited the church. Those of us at the back exchanged nods of acknowledgment, and a feeling of hope lingered among the departed.

I observed other women nearby beginning to embrace this same sentiment, wiping away tears and engaging in hushed conversations about the change and the potential for a second chance. Despite this hopeful atmosphere surrounding me, I couldn't help but feel like an outsider. I hadn't endured the same struggles as these women; my past wasn't as rough. I embodied everything they might desire, making it difficult to connect with them.

Amara was an exception, and perhaps the twins, but even they seemed more focused on each other than forming connections with others. As we exited the church, Mother blocked one side of the aisle while guiding us onto the field, where refreshments and food awaited us. At that moment, my eyes met Zak's, and I realized that all the men in our row had been fixated on us women. Some gazes felt flattering, while others were objectifying, reducing us to mere pieces of meat.

"Eeww," Amara joked, breaking the tension between the glances.

I caught Zak's smile in response and wrapped my arm around hers as we walked out together. The sky above was a brilliant blue, stretching endlessly over the field and offering a view of hills and a picturesque mountain range with lush green hilltops. The serene beauty of the scene carried the fresh scent of dewy grass while the warm sun spilled its rays through clouds that seemed to have been smudged by someone's hand.

"It's almost too beautiful here," Amara mused, her eyes fixed on the captivating landscape.

As I took in the breathtaking view alongside her, I understood the sentiment behind her words. Choosing such a peaceful and scenic location would make winning His Grace over followers easier. Living in a desolate desert would not have been as appealing.

We leaned against the wall of the building on our left, watching as others made their way down the steps to join the Faithful on the grounds below. Scattered tables offered refreshments like juice, water, or tea. Another giant table had meats, fruits, bread, and cheeses, while a large fire pit was a focal point for gathering and conversation.

As the men exited the church, it was time for socialization. His Grace joined them outside, standing on the steps. Thanks to a still-active microphone, his voice carried through the ground's surround sound. This was our chance to get to know each other and engage in courtship after every service.

"Please take this opportunity to mingle and enjoy refreshments and snacks," With a loud clap, His Grace signaled the start of this designated interaction time. The resounding echo of his hands coming together drew everyone's attention. "The rules are simple: Sundays after service are reserved for courtship. These rules remain even when you leave this field. Remember not to engage in behavior that would disgrace our Faithful ways while my cameras watch."

"Now, let us all bask in this beautiful day." Mother slipped her arm through His Grace's, and they descended the stairs together.

A gentle medieval melody played through the surrounding speakers, setting a serene atmosphere as everyone mingled. His Grace and Mother, standing tall and proud with noses in the air, like the elegant couple they were, making their way through the crowd, accompanied by soft music.

"It feels like we're attending a sad Renaissance fair mixed with a weird family reunion," Amara commented as she grabbed a cup of cold tea from one of the wooden stands.

Trying to suppress a laugh, I bit my lip, struggling to hold back the humor and disbelief written on our faces.

"Are they serious about this?" I whispered to her.

"I'm just waiting for the crowd to break into a choreographed dance," she snickered.

We couldn't contain our amusement, but our playful banter was interrupted by Hunter's voice calling out my name, instantly souring my mood.

"Now is not a good time," Amara tried to intervene, but he disregarded her efforts.

He stepped closer, and when Amara put out her arm to stop him from coming any closer, I could feel the tension radiating off him. His disdain for her was evident.

"I have every right to approach whoever I want, whenever I want," he declared, his eyes never leaving mine.

I turned around to face him, meeting his chilling expression head-on. His dark brown hair, slicked back, gave him an air of confidence mixed with arrogance. The Watchmen, dressed in royal blue vests and puffy cream-colored shirts, only amplified his authority.

Feeling Amara's arm extended towards me, I placed my hand on hers, reassuring her that it was okay.

As she lowered her arm, she didn't hesitate to approach him.

"You do that again. Next time, I'll scream," she threatened, keeping her voice low. "I'm sure your commander is waiting for the right opportunity to put you away." Her eyes narrowed on him.

Hunter remained silent, his jaw clenched as his eyes darted between Amara and me. Her words did not affect him, and he dismissed her altogether. Taking a step closer to me, my instinct was to take a step back. I didn't want him anywhere near me. Gesturing with my hands, I clarified that I didn't want him close to me.

I snapped, "What do you want?"

Hunter's sly grin and piercing blue eyes swept over my figure. "You look stunning."

My bodice tightened around my waist, squeezing me like a plush doll. I placed a hand over my stomach, my fingers wanting to rip open the bodice so I could breathe. My heart pounded in my chest at his presence. The flash of heat was like someone flipped on the sun, and its rays scorched down on me. At the same time, my skin broke out in goosebumps when his sour stench drifted into my nostrils. The taste salivated my mouth, choking down the bile and threatening to rise.

"Did you hear me?" Hunter took a step closer.

Stepping back, the side of the church and its cold stone wall stopped me from any more movement.

"I think you made your point," Amara interjected, staying close to me.

But Hunter ignored her, his gaze fixed on me. "Elizabeth, you are the most beautiful woman here."

His whispered words chilled my skin, and the goosebumps formed hard pebbles that made my hair itch under the thick layer of my cotton sleeves. My stomach churned as his gaze met mine with his malicious intent.

Just then, Zak appeared to our right and handed me a cup of tea. Seeing his friendly face was a welcome relief. I exhaled and took the tea, linking my arm with his.

Hunter snapped his eyes at Zak as if I were his prize and Zak was stealing me away. The pupils in Hunter's light blue eyes cast a cold and beady glare. There was no exchange of words necessary. I managed to lead Zak in another direction and walk away.

I stared straight ahead, avoiding looking back. If I did, he could assume that I was playing a game with him or making this move to make him jealous. Like a child, he would stop if I didn't pay him attention. Today, there were too many witnesses for Hunter to make a scene.

Zak led me toward the fire pit. "Even through this thick shirt, your skin feels like ice," he remarked.

Amara was on my other side and glanced back at Hunter with disdain.

"He's such a creep," the bitterness of her tone didn't go unnoticed.

"Don't worry, you're safe now," Zak reassured me with a gentle smile.

Feeling the warmth of the fire, I held onto two cups of tea and needed to discard one as we walked through the crowd. With skilled hands and patience, I poured one cup into the other with the most room to spare. This helped quench my thirst as my dealings with Hunter dried my mouth.

"Don't worry, I've been keeping an eye on her. Hunter won't get another chance." Amara added.

Zak glanced at me, awaiting an explanation of what Amara meant.

"Not here," I managed to say.

TEA TIME

Mother's voice rang out through the speakers, announcing it was time for tea in her garden. Zak asked me to promise him I would share what Amara's comment meant. I hesitated, wanting to find a quiet place. I wanted to finish the conversation before joining the other women, but there was not enough time. My gaze saw the sea of people, and the single women picked up their skirts and walked away from the suitors who occupied their time. Mother positioned herself in the center of the group, keeping a watchful eye on all of us.

"I promise I'll share," I assured Zak before walking away.

I felt a twinge of sadness and disappointment in his gaze, knowing he wanted to hear all the details. Amara whispered an apology as she linked her arm with mine to guide me in the direction where Mother was waiting.

"Was it me, or does he not know?" Amara asked.

"You did nothing wrong," I reassured her.

We lifted our skirts to avoid getting stained by the grass as we walked across the field and down the hill. I wondered how much I should tell Zak about what had happened. The last thing I wanted was for him to feel obligated to get involved. The consequences could be dangerous, and I didn't want him to take that risk.

MOTHER HAD transformed her garden into a picturesque trellis setting for afternoon tea. As we walked down the path lined with white roses and blooming yellow jessamines, their sweet scents filled our noses.

The tables were draped in white linen and adorned with silver tea sets, while trays of cookies and an array of cakes sat on silver cake stands arranged for our enjoyment.

"Please, ladies, choose your seats," Mother beckoned us into her crafted garden, bordered by a stunning Italian stone and timber pergola. In the center stood a grand fountain of limestone and white marble, surrounded by fish swimming upstream.

Amara and I chose an empty table, but Angela and her friends approached us before I could speak.

"Mind if we join ya?" Angela's Bronx accent was unmistakable.

"Of course," I gestured for them to sit.

As they took their seats, six more chairs were filled. The twins who passed by looked disappointed, and I mouthed an apology for not having enough room at our table.

"Ladies," Mother's voice echoed through her surround sound system, even in the open air of the garden. She never strained her delicate voice. "As you know, it is important for young women to learn proper manners and etiquette after Sunday courting sessions. His Grace and I want all of you to carry on these traditions."

Angela rolled her eyes behind Mother's back. She made a crude gesture with one hand while the women at our table bit their tongues to keep from laughing.

"By the time we finish this tea, snowflakes will ye shoulders," Angela whispered, feeding off the energy of making everyone smile.

MOTHER SAT alone, tucked away in a peaceful corner of the garden. Above her was an archway covered in vibrant Virginia creeper leaves as Wisteria flowers intertwined with its vines, wrapping around the walls and stretching across the beams to envelop a peaceful serenity. Aligned with the walls were bright, Dazzling Daffodils radiant in the deep contrast with the lush grass. The table she sat at was adorned with white linen that stuck out like a sore thumb compared to the floral arrangement around her. My knowledge of horticulture was above average, thanks to my mom's love for gardening when I was growing up. She would collect magazines with cut-out pictures from gluing on her poster board, which would resemble, to her own eyes, the perfect dream garden. It was her sanctuary from my sister and me on difficult days.

As I look back, the pieces begin to fall into place. My mom's struggle with postpartum depression after losing her baby boy at thirty weeks pregnant was evident in her constant need for an escape. And that escape came in the form of gardening. It consumed her body and soul as she poured all her pain and longing into creating the perfect garden for our backyard.

But there were obstacles in her way. Our backyard was small, thirty feet deep, and covered in concrete with a trampoline and chalk designs. The grass strip on the backside was hard as a rock, making it difficult for anything to grow. But my mom was determined. She attempted to create planter boxes and bring a sense of serenity to the space, but it never quite compared to the gardens she had seen in magazines.

Despite this, my mom made it her mission to teach my sister and me about the beauty of flowers and how nature provided us with these beautiful plants to enjoy. I still remember her careful hands showing us how to plant and nurture seeds as they grew. And even though our backyard may not have been ideal, my mom always found ways to make it memorable.

One of those ways was setting up tea parties for the three of us on the small patch of grass. Worn-out plastic lawn chairs were pulled out and arranged around the table. The anticipation of my sister and I waited to stroll from the house in our Easter dresses, hats, and purses. The plastic heels scratched and clicked on the concrete. On that day, our backyard transformed into a magical wonderland filled with laughter, love, and the beauty of nature.

The grand round table was adorned with pristine white linen embroidered with intricate floral patterns. A mismatched tea set, collected over the years, was placed on the table along with an assortment of store-bought cakes and cookies.

I still remember my sister's squeal of delight, giddy with excitement, as we prepared for our afternoon playtime in this elegant setting. But as I grew older, I could sense the strain on our mom's face. She reveled in the picturesque scene before her, like something out of a movie set, but it also seemed to be a heavy burden she carried.

My sister and I were expected to abide by strict etiquette and manners, knowing our proper places as young girls should. Any misstep would result in being banished from the playtime we cherished. Our mom's dream was to host the perfect tea party, and everything had to be staged perfectly for her vision to come to life.

I still recall how even the smallest crumb on the table or a spilled drop of tea would send our mother into a frenzy, her happy thoughts shattered by these imperfections. But here I am, sitting at a lavish tea party dressed in a custom-made gown, surrounded by the stunning gardens. My mom spent hours flipping through magazines and cutouts all over the floor, wishing she could tend to them. If she were here, she would envy the moment I am experiencing in her beloved setting.

Mother's eyes lit up when she saw me approaching, and she set down her teacup on its saucer. She greeted me and gestured for me to sit down. With good manners, I bowed my head before taking my place at the table.

"How are your hands?" Her eyes flicked down to my faint scars.

"They're healing," I replied.

"What brings you here?" Mother's gaze shifted. "Is something on your mind?"

I leaned back in my chair, mirroring her relaxed posture. Her eyes watched my behavior.

"Nellie."

Mother's surprise was evident at the mention of that name. "What do you know about her?"

She poured herself another cup of tea and then a cup for me. The steam from the pot billowed into our cups without spilling a drop. Her eyes stayed fixed on me. As she added a cube of sugar to our cups and stirred with her small silver spoon, the sound grated against the porcelain, like nails on a chalkboard. She watched me, tapping the spoon on the saucer before setting it down.

The cup's warmth in my hands was comforting as I sipped chamomile tea—the subtle hint of apple added to its soothing effect. Mother sat across from me, her piercing gaze questioning why I visited again.

"Amara told me about how you asked if she could visit

Nellie," my tone even, as if this conversation was as casual as I could make it.

"And your point?" Mother's voice was sharp. Her keen eyes stayed fixed on me. "What role do you play in this situation?" she asked with a curious tone.

"Nellie is not well," I added. "I don't see any harm in offering support. Lord knows I need something to do."

Mother's fingers tapped anxiously on the armrests of her carved chair before she abruptly stood, her hands clasped at her stomach. She appeared lost in thought, her brow furrowed and her eyes distant. As she made her way toward the archway, every movement seemed to mimic a classical painting I had admired in a museum.

Her lavender dress cascaded down in soft ruffles, rustling against the grass. Her back was perfectly straight, exuding an air of regality and grace that transported me back to a fourteenth-century era. She paused in front of the archway with deliberate steps as if considering her next move with great care.

I couldn't help but think of my mom back home in Los Angeles, wishing she could relish my serenity. She would be at peace here. I believe my mom would welcome being trapped in this place. She could tend to the gardens day and night. I don't think she would miss anyone if she were in my place.

"Fine," Mother agreed, her words snapping me out of my daydream. "Reynard will go with you and Amara to the locker, but we must set some ground rules first." Her gaze narrowed on me. "You are not to touch anything or anyone. I don't need His Grace to get a report that something went wrong, am I understood?"

With this, I was on my way to a task of some importance in this place. I needed to know Nellie and find out who her brother was.

IMAGINATION

I had not expected Mother to suggest visiting Nellie right now. My mind was preoccupied with thoughts of a dark and dank medieval cellar, and I wasn't in the mood to ruin my dress.

Mother assigned Wallace, one of the Watchmen, to accompany me and inform Reynard of her plans and rules.

It had been a while since I had seen Wallace. As we walked side by side, our shadows stretched out on the grass before us. He towered over me like a giant while I felt like a small child.

"It's been a long time," I said, talking with him.

He grinned in response. "I've been on night shifts for the past few weeks. Have you missed me already?"

Was he flirting with me?

Surprised by his comment, I glanced at him and saw the mischievous twinkle in his green eyes.

"Let's not get ahead of ourselves," I replied, keeping my gaze ahead as we reached the top of a small hill.

Wallace chuckled, unable to hide his delight. I couldn't

help but laugh along with him, and when I looked back at him, he winked and gave me a wide smile.

Oh dear, what have I gotten myself into?

As I descended the stone walkway toward the dining hall's gardens, I spotted Amara leaning against one of the pillars, her chestnut hair twirling between her fingertips. Reynard was standing close to her, enraptured in conversation with only each other.

Amara took a sly stance, flirting with him and biting her bottom lip as he leaned closer, resting his arm on the pillar. They were absorbed in each other's company, their gazes never breaking even as Wallace and I approached.

Wallace slowed and whispered, "Should we give them more time? Hate to interrupt whatever's going on."

But as I glanced up, I saw a camera in the corridor's corner. It reminded me that everything we did was being watched. Per the rules, single men and women were prohibited from being close or socializing.

Feeling uncomfortable, I picked up my pace to get ahead of Wallace. Even when I reached them, they were so engrossed in each other that it took them a moment to realize I was there.

Amara's eyes darted to me, and she straightened up, trying to act innocent like a child caught doing something forbidden.

"Liz, I didn't see you coming." Her wide eyes and quick words made her more evident as her cheeks flushed.

"Change of plans." I ignored their closeness, moving on to break the tension.

When Wallace approached, he and Reynard shared a glance, then exchanged a nod as they understood without saying a word, as if they had just communicated telepathically. Wallace motioned towards the right, and Reynard nodded in agreement.

“You are going to escort Amara and Liz to see Nellie,” Wallace announced.

Amara's eyes widened, and she fidgeted with her hands, shaking her head.

“I won't go.”

“I'll be right there with you.” I followed with.

Amara mouthed the words, “Why me?"

“Are you sure about this?” Reynard's expression seemed to question Wallace's decision.

“You can ask Mother yourself.” I gestured towards the garden where we had come from.

“She's...” Amara hesitated, her hands dropping to her hips as she squeezed her sides. “Nellie is going to blame me for being in the locker.”

“Why would she blame you?” Wallace asked with a confused look on his face.

Amara took a deep breath and let it out through her lips, trying to calm her nerves. "I'm the one who reported she tried to escape in the middle of the night," she explained.

Wallace turned to Reynard. "Did you know about this?"

Reynard nodded, reminding Wallace that he and Hunter were the ones who had taken Nellie in.

The giggling behind us made us turn our gazes as women flirtatiously waved at Reynard and Wallace as they strolled by.

"I have to go back to Mother's garden." Wallace's face was filled with annoyance. "It's how they look at me as if undressing me with their eyes." He complained.

Reynard grunted in response to the comment, his expression hardening as if he had flipped a switch. In an instant, he had transformed into Watchmen mode, his demeanor becoming severe and focused.

"We must hurry before nightfall," he instructed, striding ahead with purposeful steps.

As Amara and I followed behind, Wallace stayed by my side, his gaze fixed on me. I could sense him waiting for a reaction, but I bit down on my lip to suppress a laugh at his annoyance. He said he didn't like it when women looked at him in that manner, and I wanted to remind him of the constant alertness we all had to maintain since the beginning of time, but I decided to save that comment for another time.

When I glanced at him out of the corner of my eye, that spark in his eye made him giddy. Then I felt guilty, but Brant suddenly appeared beside Wallace wearing the same Watchmen attire.

Brant's hard eyes bore into me. He looked Wallace up and down, matching our pace, before shifting his gaze back to me.

"Seriously? This oaf is making you blush?" His tone had a hint of jealousy. But then again, when it came to guys being nice to me, Brant always assumed they had ulterior motives.

"Don't be absurd, Brant. I'm not blushing," I retorted. "He's just being polite." The long strides trying to keep up made my skirts heavy. I gripped them to pull them up, knowing how it helped quicken my pace.

"Right." The sarcasm in his tone stretching out the word made me want to roll my eyes.

I knew Brant would react this way because he did the same thing when we were dating. If any guy was nice to me, he automatically thought they were trying to get into my skirts.

My cheeks turned red at his words. My blood pressure was rising because I was now annoyed at his behavior. I debated with myself in silence, feeling guilty for wanting to argue with Brant.

Brant chuckled. "You're both stuck in a village with limited options. I'm sure that's all he thinks about, how to make you blush. Trust me -"

"Trust what?" I interrupted, speaking out loud.

Reynard, Amara, and Wallace all stopped and looked at me. My outburst startled them, but Brant was nowhere in sight.

Amara raised her eyebrows. "Are you okay?"

I cleared my throat and straightened up, trying to regain my composure after my sudden embarrassment brought me back into reality.

Wallace is one step from turning right and heading back to the garden. He stopped, concerned about my outburst.

"Liz, if you're not feeling well, I can walk you back to your room."

I felt Brant's presence behind me as the familiar scent of Drakkar cologne—basil, lavender, and lemon mixed with juniper and cedar—filled my senses. The sudden surprise of the familiar scent made me want to close my eyes and inhale. I knew Brant's presence wasn't real; it was just a figment of my imagination, but I missed him, and my heart ached each time.

"Oh, he definitely wants to take you back to your room. This guy will use any excuse to be alone with you." Brant's jealousy poured through the words in my left ear.

As I turned to look at where Brant would have been, his scent disappeared in the wind. The painful reminder that he wasn't there.

"Liz, are you sure you're okay?" Amara asked with caution as she came closer.

I let out a sharp exhale and nodded. "Let's just continue."

THE LOCKER

My legs strained to keep up with Reynard's long strides while Amara matched his pace. But it was clear that even she was getting winded.

As we descended the hill towards the front of the castle, a breathtaking landscape unfolded before us. The grassy slope extended down to the purple mountains in the distance, and on the left, a creek flowed under a drawbridge connected to the castle.

"Hey, Liz!" Amara's voice broke through my reverie.

I hurried to her side, crossing the drawbridge as salmon swam below us in the crystal-clear water. As I approached, I noticed a sign carved into the castle wall reading "Locker." My stomach turned at the thought of what awaited us inside.

Amara's hand reached for mine, giving it a reassuring squeeze. Reynard pulled out an electric stick and scanned the padlock, which turned green and emitted a loud grinding noise as it unlocked.

The electronic door opened for us, releasing a pungent odor of mold and body odor that made us instinctively pinch our noses in disgust.

The hallway was a gloomy, lightless place that seemed to suck away any trace of sunlight. Before Reynard entered, he turned to us with his focus on Amara.

"Stay in the center of the aisle, and don't touch the bars," he said in a firm tone.

We nodded like obedient children.

"Stay close to me," Reynard ordered, holding his electric stick as we followed him into the darkness. His pace was slower this time.

As we ventured further into the castle's dungeon, dim LED candles flickered on every few feet, with its sensors alarmed by our movement. Chandeliers hung from the ceiling, providing some light but not enough to reveal the occupants of the cells lining each side. I could tell the candles weren't real, just as no wax or fire-burning odor existed. The candles looked like all the rest, but these were dimmable by their faint glow.

My hand tightened around Amara's as we walked together. A chill draft made my teeth chatter, and the dripping water echoed in the eerie silence. The musty smell of mold filled my nose and threatened to make my stomach turn.

How long would I be able to endure this putrid stench?

I heard sniffles and coughs coming from within the cells, but no one called out or stepped into the faint light. Each cell was challenging to make out in size, with only the outline of bars visible from floor to ceiling.

After what felt like an eternity of navigating through the dark, musty, long hallway, we reached the end. The chandeliers were now few and far between, making it difficult for our eyes to adjust.

Reynard stood near the last cell on the right. His arm was outstretched as a silent warning to stay close.

As I peered over to what I thought was the end of the

long hallway, I noticed four small cutouts along the wall, letting in slivers of light and revealing glimpses of what lay beyond. My curiosity piqued, and I strained my eyes to make out the scene before me.

The space between us and the wall felt as though there was more to it and stretched on, the four cutouts of faint blue squares of light of some sort or natural sunlight, but either way, it gave off an eerie glow against the shadows of the prison.

Amara grabbed my arm, her nerves evident in her grip. In front of us, the faint light from a hanging chandelier a few feet behind made it challenging to see all the details. As our eyes adjusted, we could make out corroded iron bars, and before our eyes, we saw long fingers methodically wrap around the bars from inside the cell and squeeze.

Reynard announced our presence. His deep voice echoed off the walls, with soft whimpers and cries from nearby cells. Reynard grabbed a lantern hanging just out of reach and illuminated Nellie's face behind the bars.

"Nellie, you have a visitor."

All of us jumped back when Nellie made her appearance by slamming into the bars, and her pale face pressed against them. Both arms reaching out, a desperate play on our reaction. I clutched my chest as my heart pounded. Amara's instinct was to grab Reynard's bicep out of fear. She covered her mouth to stifle a potential scream.

Nellie's piercing gaze, intensified by her big, round baby blue eyes and deep, weathered circles beneath them, was reminiscent of a character from a horror film. Her demeanor and intense look reminded me of the movie where the children found the witch in the woods, her long stringy hair matted with dirt, and the rustling of leaves and twigs appeared permanent like moss on a tree. The long, gaunt face and the crazed look in the witch's eyes. The stare of looking beyond and into the soul of someone, but with ill intentions.

That's what Nellie's stare reminded me of. It held an eerie stillness like her eyes were devoid of life. She wasn't looking at me but somehow through me. As the others stood frozen in fear, Nellie released her grip on the bars and faded into the darkness beyond. It was like a scene from a nightmare come to life.

"Reynard, I only wanted to speak with Nellie. Who is this woman?" A seductive voice slithered out from the shadows.

"Let's be civil. Mother wanted you to meet Liz," Reynard urged, his jaw clenched as he tried to maintain composure.

"The Liz who isn't supposed to be here?" She responded with a curious slip of her tongue.

The pit in my stomach grew as I felt the blood rush down my face. I went to take a step forward, and then I felt Reynard's thick fingers resting on my shoulder, pulling me back.

I went to shake him off, but his fingers dug deeper. "How does she know? She's been in here the whole time." My nerves got the better of me as I blurted out.

Nellie seized the opportunity, slithering out of the darkness and gripping the bars again. Sensually gliding her hands up and down them, it was an unsettling performance reminiscent of watching a stripper behind bars. She skillfully manipulated the metal to appear seductive. When she wasn't getting the reaction she hoped for, her patience was thin.

"What do you want?" She leaned back and stood straight, her big eyes hidden behind dirty, tangled blonde hair. With an exaggerated flip of her head, she continued, "You never ask about me. I thought we were friends." Her high-pitched and manipulative tone was like that of a whiny child, and it caused me to grip my dress and bite my tongue in disdain.

"You wanted to see me," Amara answered, ignoring Nellie's rhetorical question.

Nellie's top teeth bit down her bottom lip, dragging up and over her lips as she stared at Reynard. He cleared his throat, unamused by the sentimental action, and bore the face of annoyance.

This sprung a tinge of jealousy to Amara. "Nellie, what do you want?" She took a step forward, wearing her annoyance.

Nellie ignored Amara and bent over to flip her skirts as her skin pressed against the bars. "Come on, Reynard!" Despite her tall and skinny appearance, the intensity in her eyes revealed a disturbing presence.

Amara took a deep breath and stepped forward, with Reynard behind us and his electric wand ready. A tense silence hung in the air as Nellie flipped her head from side to side.

No words were exchanged. The whimpering and soft cries from others in the cells made the air colder. Amara turned to leave in frustration. But before we could react, Nellie was quick to reach out and grab onto Amara's dress and viciously pulled her back, wrapping her arms around Amara's throat in a chokehold.

The cell's iron bars jolted out a loud *BANG!* Amara's body slammed against the iron bars as dust from the ceiling sprinkled down on them. My eyes glanced up for a second to see the corroded holes from Nellie's rattling of her cage. She worked on the iron bars as the solid rock was worn down.

This caused the other cell mates around us to moan and beg for her to stop. The wild and crazed look in Nellie's eyes, like she won the biggest prize, revealed yellow-stained teeth. Reynard went to react and reach out, and Nellie tightened her grip on Amara's throat.

Reynard's grip on the lantern dropped as his electric stick

powered on, adding intense energy. Reynard's big hand gently pushed me to one side, taking a defensive stance.

"Nellie, you know what happens when you do that," he reminded her, his chest rising and falling intensely.

Amara struggled against Nellie's grip, weakening and trying to give her throat relief. "Nellie, please," she gasped. "I'm here for you."

But Nellie's jealousy consumed her. With a scream that sent chills in my body, she declared Amara as just another whore of a friend who used her. The other prisoners in nearby cells began pleading with intangible comments, everyone all at once. It was hard to decipher what they were saying.

"Now that you have someone else, you no longer need me," Nellie spat venomously into Amara's ear.

Reynard's eyes never broke away, and he calculated his next move. "Nellie, you know His Grace will not be pleased with this. You've been doing so well," his tone was cautious and calm.

I stepped back, sensing that my presence might only worsen her agitation. She wasn't thrilled with my friendship with Amara. If I retreated into the shadows, Reynard could negotiate her release of Amara.

"She's my friend!" Nellie yelled, tightening her forearm around Amara's neck.

In a flash, Amara lunged forward, causing Nellie to slam against the bars and lose her grip, earning herself a painful welt on her forehead and a bloody nostril.

I expected Nellie to explode in anger, yet she wore a wicked grin that spread across her face. Wiping away the blood from her upper lip, she revealed menacing stains on her yellowed teeth, creating a disturbing image when she smiled.

"I knew you had some fight in you," Nellie declared, spitting blood in one corner of her cell.

Reynard helped Amara to her feet and made sure she was okay. He maintained a tight grip on his electric stick, and even in the dim light, I could see his knuckles whitening from the pressure.

"You broke the rules, Nellie," Reynard growled with deep-rooted anger. His nostrils flared as he assumed a dominating stance.

Nellie tilted her head, biting her bottom lip and dragging it with her top teeth.

With a taunting smirk, Nellie declared, "You can touch me. I know you want to." She slid her hand up her skirt, pulling it up to reveal her long, pale legs. She continued to touch herself brazenly in front of Reynard, beckoning him with her seductive gaze. "I know how much you've been craving this," she teased, letting her leg dangle between the bars to expose even more of herself. Disgusted, Reynard turned his head away from us.

"Can we be done here?" He snapped his head in our direction.

"Please," Amara chimed in.

Reynard gestured for us to continue. We walked about thirty feet down the corridor while Nellie cried out and shook the bars behind us.

"Come back! I promise I'll behave! Liz, you need to know why!" Her desperate pleas were disregarded as we pressed forward. The cries of other prisoners echoed around us as we huddled together in the center of the corridor, avoiding any potential contact with the surrounding cells.

"Reynard!" Nellie's voice rang out behind us, sending chills down my spine. "You promised him!" she screamed.

Just a few feet away from the exit, Reynard's heavy footsteps slowed in front of us. With a heavy sigh, he stopped.

“Just stay here for a bit.” His tone was gentle, and he directed his attention to Amara as if he would do anything not to upset her.

Amara grabbed his forearm. “What are you doing?”

He placed his other hand on top of hers. “Let me calm her down. She’ll cause chaos for everyone else here if we leave now.”

My eyes couldn't help but notice the tenderness in his gesture and how he appeared to rub the top of her right hand. It was clear that they had more in common than friendship. His direction leaned toward going back.

Amara's body tensed up, not wanting him to go. She pulled him back.

“I don't feel safe here.” She said.

Reynard responded by approaching the door and using his electric stick to open it.

"I won't be far behind." His eyes smiled, reassuring Amara.

I tugged on Amara's sleeve. I couldn't handle another second in this place and needed fresh air. We took off and rushed outside to the bridge.

My hands gripped the railing on the bridge to steady myself, taking in long, deep drags of the crisp air, in through the nose and out of my mouth. It helped both of us settle our nerves. When our eyes met, it was an understanding that this woman would be a lot to handle.

AMARA SAT on the examination table, her head tilted to the side as Doctor Ferrarius examined her neck. I could see a hint of red marks under her jaw, evidence of the chokehold Nellie had done to her. Reynard entered through the curtain, and his face fell when he saw Amara's condition. Doctor Ferrarius asked him to wait in the hallway; he followed right after, asking his side of the story.

Amara gripped the table's edge, her knuckles turning white from the pressure. She was trying to be strong, but it was clear she was agitated and in pain.

"I warned you about her," Amara's voice was soft yet annoyed.

I hung my head, frustrated with myself for not recognizing the severity of Nellie's mental state. Amara released her grip, folded in her arms, and looked at me with deep thought.

"I'm sorry," I whispered.

Amara exhaled and shook her head. "You have no idea what you've unleashed. Just do me a favor and keep me out of the drama. If you think you can help Nellie, go ahead. But don't involve me."

"I don't understand--"

"It's who you are," Amara replied. "I could tell when I shared the other night, and there was that flicker in your eyes," she paused. "You have the quality of how your motherly/teacher instinct wants to jump in and save her." Her shoulders relaxed, and she reached out a hand to me. "Just understand what you are getting yourself into." She pulled me close, her head settling on my shoulder.

I took in what she said, understanding and appreciating her warnings. To make light of the situation, I knew what to say to make her smile.

"You plan on sharing what happened with you and Reynard?" I teased.

As she perked up, her immediate grin was evident. In a secretive voice, she said, "It's just been little moments, but he has been keeping a close eye on me, and I have been doing the same." She blushed.

"You two have been obvious," I remarked. "But when did it start?"

"It's been glances here and there, then the day you and

Zak emerged from the forest," she admitted. "After that, we found subtle ways to be near each other."

I felt genuine joy for Amara. I remembered what she shared about her complicated past and lack of family support, and I understood the value of finding companionship.

"Aren't you worried about His Grace choosing someone else for you?"

She shook her head, keeping her lips sealed. I nudged her with my elbow, eager for more details.

The idea that Reynard might have his sights set on Amara made me smile and happy for her. But lurking in the back of my mind was a sense of unease. Hunter had mentioned the privilege of choice given to Watchmen. And then there was Wallace, who had also shown interest in me. I couldn't help but wonder who would be next in line to make their choice.

NELLIE

The echo of Nellie's shrill voice, repeating the words 'you need to know why,' reverberated in my mind. I couldn't shake off the feeling of unease and restlessness as I lay in bed, surrounded by my roommates' soft snores and deep breathing. After tossing and turning for hours, I gave in to the urge to escape. Wrapping myself in my warm blanket, I crept out of the room and into the crisp night air.

My feet sank into the damp grass as I approached the stream along the castle's left side. The gentle murmur of water calmed me, just like it had countless times before when I played it through my speaker back home. It had taken some time for Brant to get used to it, but he couldn't sleep without it either.

As I reached the castle's edge, bathed in moonlight, a sense of peace washed over me. I closed my eyes and took deep breaths, letting go of all my worries and fears for a moment. In this tranquil setting, nature's symphony was all I needed to lull me into a deep, peaceful sleep.

I was at the locker entrance once again. I hesitated,

unsure of what to do without an electric stick to open the door and no knowledge of what lay beyond. A feeling inside me told me to wait, so I stood frozen for thirty seconds before deciding.

The electronic stone door opened as if by my own will. But reality set in as I realized someone was coming out, possibly even escaping. Without hesitation, I raced back across the drawbridge and hid behind some hedges, observing Aldrich stepping out, looking exhausted. He had a frown on his face, and his hands were stuffed into his pockets as he walked towards his home to the mill tower.

Once he was past me, I leaped up and made a mad dash across the drawbridge, leaving my blanket in the bushes and squeezing through the narrow opening before the door closed and almost caught my fingers. I couldn't help but question my actions in the dark, damp hallway. What was I thinking? I hadn't thought this through at all. As I took caution, descended the stairs, and went down the long corridor, I could hear snoring and deep breathing.

The soft glow of LED candles illuminated my path as I continued forward, careful being light on my feet so as not to disturb any sleeping bodies.

"I knew you would be back." The sliver of Nellie's tongue broke through the silence.

"What are you doing here?" Brant's voice echoed in my mind. His presence trailed alongside me.

He was at my side, and I pictured him shirtless in his black pajamas bottoms. He refused to wear a shirt. He joked that he felt suffocated at night wearing clothes but settled on wearing bottoms because of the boys.

"Liz, this isn't a good idea," Brant said, crossing his arms.

As I took a step forward, his memory faded away. I positioned myself near the sensor, keeping the light on to see Nellie's face.

She moved closer to the bars, revealing a knot on her forehead, a black eye, and a bruise on her nose from earlier. Despite the injuries, I kept my composure. After all, she had called me a whore. There would be no love lost between us. Remaining calm and collected was second nature to me - an essential teaching skill, particularly with challenging students.

Nellie tilted her head as if inviting me to speak first. When I remained silent, she smiled and gave up on trying to make small talk.

"I'm sure sweet Amara told you about our journey," she said in a playful tone.

In this conversation, I needed Nellie to feel in control. One wrong phrase could trigger a violent outburst. When she dragged her feet toward the corner of her cell, her fingers tapped the bars, creating a melodic sound in the cold, hollow iron she was working on, trying to make me lose my patience. She was trying to discover what made me tick.

"They want me to be crazy...you know that, right?" Nellie's voice was desperate and pleading. "Every village needs a scapegoat."

My heart went out to her. The time spent in this cell made it clear that this place was only worsening her manic episodes instead of helping her.

Earlier, Nellie shouted at me as she knew more about why I was kidnapped. She got what she wanted, piqued my interest, and I wanted answers. The cold air seeped into my skin, intensifying the ache in my bones.

Her matted, dirty blonde hair was unkempt and unwashed for who knew how long. Her playful demeanor changed like the wind; now, she sat curled up in the corner with fearful, vulnerable eyes and pouty lips, like a small child trapped in a scary situation.

I crouched to her level, my knees touching the damp,

moldy ground. I wanted to show her that I meant no harm. Her eyes fixed on me, and she leaned into the corner of the cell bars.

"He comes here to see me, you know," she said, her words laced with bitterness. "He takes advantage of me."

My body tensed at the thought of someone exploiting her vulnerable state. "Who?" I asked, trying to hide my anger.

A flicker of memory brushed against my mind as I watched Aldrich exit the door. He appeared tired, his shoulders slumped, and his movements slow. Dull circles hung under his eyes, hinting at a lack of rest. It was hard to imagine him as a person who could play such a disturbing character. But then again, those who seem innocent often hide something sinister within.

Despite the rushing questions and judgments in my mind, I managed to maintain a calm facade. I had come here for Nellie's sake and because I needed closure. But in the meantime, I couldn't help but remind myself to keep a watchful eye on Aldrich, unsure of what secrets he may be hiding beneath his worn exterior.

"I allow it," she replied, a twisted play on her words. "He needs me because he can't have you."

Anger boiled within me as I clenched my jaw and gripped my nightgown with white knuckles. I urged her to reveal who had been using her. A single tear rolled down her cheek.

"You don't belong with us," she continued, her voice dripping with resentment. "You can't understand us, yet he wants you."

I felt empathy for Nellie. She was playing me and wouldn't give me a straight answer. She controls the situation, only allowing what she wants me to hear. Her desperate desire for attention through harmful means saddened me.

"They make excuses to keep me locked up here," she said,

reaching out from behind the bars before retracting her arm. "Every village needs a villain."

"It doesn't have to be you," I whispered, wanting her to see that she didn't need to settle and accept being a villain. I wanted her to want more for herself.

She chuckled at my comment before pausing and standing up. She tapped her fingers on her temples as if deep in thought.

"I want out from behind these bars. You want out from beyond the walls," her eyes narrowed at me as she grinned. "Why don't we have a common ground and learn how to help one another." Her thin fingers wrapped around the bars. "As long as you stay out of my way, I'll be the focus. They'll be too busy with me and will forget all about you. Isn't that what you want?"

Am I so desperate to think this could work?

I rose to my feet, watching Nellie and scrutinizing her body language. Her expression shifted from playful to desperate, signaling she had to count on me as much as I needed to rely on her. The stakes were getting higher, and I didn't know if this was another desperate move to get me out of here or if it would cost me everything.

In the same second, I thought I should entertain her. What could be the harm in listening? She could have good ideas. I didn't have to go along with anything that she would say. This reminded me to keep some sanity that I had left in me.

"How do I do this?" I pondered aloud, considering the potential risks.

Nellie's lips grinned, "Go find my brother. He'll assist you. He's been trying to save me for years." Her tone was suggestive yet tinged with annoyance.

"Alright," I was reluctant. "Who is your brother?"

"It wasn't long ago he was here. Then you managed to

creep in. I know you saw him." Her playful suggestion was sly.

"Aldrich?" I asked.

Despite the dirt and grime covering her, I could see similarities between her and Aldrich. The facial structure of their jawline, long straight noses, and deep set of big blue eyes brought it all together. However, hers were more prominent and rounder.

"Aldrich, is your brother?" I inquired, but Nellie blinked at me.

She was playing a game, giving just enough to intrigue me and keep me returning for more. It was a tactic often used by narcissists seeking attention, whether positive or negative. I proceeded with caution, hoping to earn some of her trust through our coy interaction.

"Nellie, I want to help. Can you share with me who takes advantage of you? Does your brother know?"

My question had an instant effect on her mood. She gripped the bars of her cell and shook them, causing a commotion that woke the other inmates as the dust from her ceiling rained down on her. Her laughter was directed at me, knowing it would hurt my ears and disturb the others.

"You know, it's how he squeezes my face, then pushes it to one side. His hot breath is on my neck, and he whispers, promising me I would want more." Nellie slides down the bars and then pops back up. "It's what he does; he hunts his prey."

Nellie's words hit me like a ton of bricks and left me breathless. The description she gave echoed my own traumatic experience with Hunter, the man who assaulted me, pushing my face to one side, his hot breath on my neck telling me once I had him, I would want more. Instinctively, I stepped back, my hands gripping my clothes, clinging onto them as if they were the only comfort that enveloped me.

Her cackle echoed through the dimly lit cell, sending me shivers. It sounded like a menacing monster unleashing its deepest, darkest secrets and finding joy in sharing them with me. Her laughter was deafening, drowning out the desperate cries and pleas of the other inmates. The sound reverberated off the cold stone walls, filling the air with fear and unease. I couldn't help but wonder what twisted thoughts were behind that maniacal laugh.

"Where are you going?" Nellie's tone was playful as it echoed down the corridor.

I retreated down the corridor. I tried to block out the chaotic sounds around me and focus on getting to the door. The memories of Hunter assaulting me flooded my mind, his scent lingering in the air as he covered my face. My neck muscles could still feel the intense pain of his strength. I shuddered as my cold hands touched my neck, a mental reminder of the skin he touched. I covered my ears to run down the hall, escaping this nightmare.

The sound of a stone door grinding open gave me a glimmer of hope. I watched as it slowly revealed Aldrich in my view, disappointment etched across his face.

He shook his head and remarked, "Looking for trouble?" His eyes scanned me up and down.

My socks were damp, and my nightgown was dirty from where I knelt on the floor. My hands and body are shaking from the cold. I didn't notice before, but he had my blanket in his hands. He came over and wrapped my shoulders.

"Better?" His kind eyes suggested.

I nodded. The wool blanket was an instant savior. I went to speak, but he held his index finger to his lips and suggested I follow him.

ALDRICH GUIDED me into the dining hall. The warmth

beneath my feet thawed my freezing toes when my wool socks touched the stone. I sat across from him. I could see the worry in his eyes as he rested his hands on the back of his neck, trying to find the right words.

"Rough night?" he asked.

I shrugged, trying to shake off the chill that crept into my bones. The rough wool blanket I had wrapped around myself brought some relief. Its comforting weight provided a sense of security. It was like a shield against the outside world, a barrier between me and reality. But as much as I wished for it, I knew I couldn't disappear into the soft folds like a magic trick. It was just a temporary comfort, not a solution to my problems.

He put his elbows on the table. "Why were you in the locker?" he asked, "be truthful with me. Why visit her?"

"You mean, why would I visit your sister," I spat out.

Aldrich maintained a neutral expression and tapped his fingers on the table, unsure if he wanted this information to be revealed. "She told you."

"In a roundabout way," I confirmed. "Why would you bring her to a place where she could be punished like this?"

"Don't judge me," Aldrich's defensive tone was sudden. "You have no idea what we've been through. You couldn't possibly understand how much money I've spent on treatment."

"She's sick, this isn't the place for her." I snapped back. "She obviously doesn't mean that much if you're willing to toss her aside and keep her hidden."

My words cut through him. I saw intense anger in his eyes. He got up from the bench like I was the problem, the disease that plagued his life.

"She is everything to me," he seethed. "My parents sacrificed everything to save her." He stepped back, realizing he had shared information meant to stay a secret.

I raised my hands, a sign of truce. I didn't need Aldrich as an enemy. I needed him to be my ally.

"I'm sorry," my tone softened. "I don't know everything, but she deserves better than the locker. I'm sure that's why you both came to this place."

Before my eyes, Aldrich's mood deflated. He sat back across from me, his nails digging at the crusted particle of food on the table.

"When she tried to escape last time, and Amara told on her, she hadn't been taking her medication. Believe it or not, she's gotten better," he shared.

"I want to help her transition into our society. I know she isn't well, but I don't see her as a lost cause," I responded without hesitation, knowing that impulsivity could sometimes lead to positive outcomes.

THE STRIKE

"Are you out of your mind?" Amara's mouth hung open, arms crossed, and her eyes wide with shock.

We were gathering fresh berries for Maestro Roberto in the greenhouse this morning. Angela was on the other side, picking raspberries, when she poked her head around with a puzzled expression.

"Why would you sneak out like that?" Amara placed her basket on the cart behind us and tried to comprehend my story. "I understand that you feel guilty, but she..." Amara couldn't bring herself to finish her sentence. She dismissed the conversation, grabbed her basket, and left Angela and me alone in the greenhouse.

"You're going to pitch the idea that you can rehabilitate Nellie from the locker to the village?" Angel's Bronx accent became more prominent, indicating her concern.

I continued plucking blueberries off the bushes, making sure not to squeeze them too hard. Maestro Roberto would consider those spoiled and toss them aside, cursing in Italian at anyone who mishandled food.

“We can’t ignore her, Angela. We have a responsibility to help anyone with a mental disorder,” I argued.

Angela threw up her hands in defense. “I’m no psychologist, but sometimes, we need to accept when there’s no hope for improvement and stop making excuses for erratic behavior.”

I didn't want to get into a debate about this. Exhausted from lack of sleep, I kept to my task and plucked more berries, keeping to myself.

"Fine, you win," Angela sighed. "I'll be back later."

As I stood amongst the sounds of nature in this breathtaking greenhouse, I couldn't help but feel captivated and revitalized. The various scents of fruits and vegetables filled the air, yet there was no overpowering odor; instead, it was a delightful combination of sweetness and earthiness. The grounds emitted a crisp, fresh fragrance with specks of dark brown soil floating around like burnt wood or the subtle aroma of a bonfire. The temperature-controlled facility was separated into different sections, some providing a humid environment for plants to thrive while others maintained hotter or drier conditions.

I wiped the sweat from my face. I could feel the heat rising outside, adding to the oppressive humidity. With my basket halfway full, the recommended amount, I decided it was time to find Amara. As I turned around, I was startled to see Hunter standing in the distance, fixated on me with his intense gaze. The thought of his slow, mocking smile and how he relished in my discomfort made my grip on the basket handle tighten.

Hunter's eyes never left me, enjoying his power over my nerves. His cold blue eyes roamed over my body as if I were an object waiting for him to claim. Every second he stared, it felt like a bold attempt to undress me with his eyes.

"You look beautiful today," he remarked, sending shivers down my spine in its sinister echo.

His words sliced through the peaceful atmosphere with their chilling effect, prompting me to take a step backward for every step he took towards me. We were locked in a dangerous game of cat and mouse, his smile revealing a cruel satisfaction. His familiarity with these grounds gave him an advantage, making it impossible for me to tear my eyes away.

In one quick motion, he lunged forward and grabbed me with one arm, spilling the berries and basket onto the ground.

"No!" I screamed, struggling against his hold. "Let me go!"

Instead of letting me go, he found amusement in my resistance, and his sadistic chuckle echoed through the garden. I pushed against him with all my might, but he was too strong and guided me back until I collided with an apple tree.

"Get off me!" I screamed, trying to break free from his grip.

He pressed closer, inhaling the scent of my neck and trailing his nose to my ear. The smell of his body, like a wet dog, made me nauseous. His hot breath and the rotten smell of meat only added to my discomfort.

In a twisted attempt to seduce me, he whispered in my ear, "I can have you here, in the garden or the woods..." He forced one knee between my legs, and then his filthy hand began lifting my skirts and violating my personal space, leaving me feeling vulnerable.

"NO!" I cried out from deep within as I pushed him away.

He stumbled back, tripping over debris and pulling me by the arm towards the berry bushes. My voice shook with fear as I tried to find something to defend myself with. He spun on his back, knocking me off my feet with one strong swipe of his hand. I crashed onto the ground, winded.

Hunter loomed over me, a dark glint in his eyes as I struggled against him. His hands pinned mine down to the soft dirt. "I can smell the fear you have for me," he taunted as his lips traveled from my collarbone down to the top of my breasts, nipping at my clothing.

I thrashed and squirmed beneath him, my body fighting against his oppressive weight. Suddenly, a sharp sting across my cheek jolted me with intense pain, causing my vision to blur for a split second. With a sickening realization, I felt the fabric of my dress tear and rip apart, exposing my vulnerable flesh to his lustful gaze. Through the ringing in my ear, I couldn't make out his taunting words as he held me down with brute force.

As I tried to push him off, he laughed maniacally, his eyes widening and pupils dilating into dark pools of madness. At that moment, I knew I was at the mercy of a deranged predator who took pleasure in my suffering. I gritted my teeth and counted to four, trying to regain control over my body before it was too late. The wide-eyed look in his crazed eyes set my nerves on edge, and I knew that this nightmare was far from over.

A sudden boot to the face sent him flying. In that split second, I saw his expression change from desire to shock, then pain. Dress skirts flew up and covered my face as blood spurted from his mouth. I was hit with dirt particles and the wind from Amara's swift kick.

Her quick action gave us a momentary reprieve, but Hunter was already getting back up and ready to attack again. That is until he faced an imposing figure standing behind Amara.

Reynard stood like a towering wall, blocking the entrance. His massive and muscular frame exuded an aura of danger, making it clear that he was not to be trifled with. Any stranger would mistake him for the leader and assume he took pleasure in wielding violence. His eyes narrowed into venomous slits. His brows furrowed with disgust as they landed on Hunter. He gripped his electric stick in his hand, its switch flipped to "on" and sparks crackling with deadly energy.

"Explain yourself," Reynard demanded in a deep, serious tone.

Hunter wiped his bloody lips and raised his hands in defense. "Just having some fun. Right, Liz?"

My voice trembled with anger as I snarled through gritted teeth, "You vile, twisted monster." My loathing for him intensified with each passing second, consuming me like a fiery inferno.

Hunter's smooth and cunning words slid out as if this were a casual conversation. "She practically asked for it."

Amara was livid and lunged at Hunter, shouting, "You're lying!" But before she could make contact, Hunter grabbed his electric stick and swung it towards her chest.

I moved to intervene, but I was too late. Amara stumbled backward, gasping for air as I caught her.

Reynard jumped in to restrain Hunter, pinning him against a nearby tree with a firm forearm against his throat. "Our weapons are not meant to be used like this!" Reynard's voice boomed. "Stand down! That's an order!"

PORCELAIN TUB

Amara sat up from my lap, coughing and padding her chest where the strike had left a black burn mark. We checked for blood or an open wound, but she was in the clear. I let out a sigh of relief as I examined her, grateful that the damage wasn't worse.

I heard the gurgling sounds behind me. Hunter struggled to breathe as Reynard held him against a tree with his forearm pressed against his throat.

"What are they to you?" Hunter's voice weakened as he struggled for air.

Reynard ignored his question, watching Hunter's skin turn blue and his eyes roll back in his head.

Amara slowly got to her feet and approached them, gently placing her hand on Reynard's arm, constricting Hunter's airway.

"Rey, it's me. I'm okay," she said with gentle ease. "Let His Grace decide what should be done."

Reynard released his grip on Hunter's throat and watched him fall to the ground like a rag doll. Hunter gasped for air and coughed, trying to inhale life back into his lungs.

Reynard turned to Amara, cupping her small face in his big hands. Gazing at her with tenderness, he felt like she was the most precious being he had ever seen. Then he kissed her forehead.

As I gathered myself, still in shock and processing the intense experience I had just been through, my eyes fell upon Reynard and Amara standing together. I felt overwhelming gratitude for their quick and decisive actions at that moment.

Reynard's gaze turned towards me, his face a mixture of concern and relief as he took in my state. His strong jawline was set, his piercing blue eyes reflecting the emotions he was trying to conceal. Despite his composed exterior, I could sense his urgency and protectiveness.

Amara stood beside him, her chestnut hair cascading down her back in perfect waves. Her stance embodied calm and strength. Together, they were my rock in this chaotic moment.

"Are you okay?" Reynard asked me.

"Mentally, no. Physically, I'll survive." I struggled to keep my body from trembling, but it was more complicated than I thought. He helped me stand and led Amara and me toward the entrance.

As Reynard opened the door to the outside world, the sweet scent of fresh grass and blooming flowers enveloped me, filling my nostrils with a sense of freedom. It was as if I had been holding my breath all this time, and finally, I could exhale.

The other people on the grounds went about their daily routines, unaware of the terror that had just unfolded inside the greenhouse. But when they saw our distressed faces, they became curious and concerned.

As Hunter coughed and spat behind us, Reynard's muscles tensed, his fingers twitching at his side in anticipation. The air enveloped tension but also a subtle undercurrent of determination and strength.

"Stay here," Reynard commanded. He went back inside, and before the door closed, I caught a glimpse of Hunter on his knees, hands stretched out and begging for forgiveness.

Wallace and Marshall charged out from behind the castle, brandishing their electric sticks. As they passed by other villagers, they gathered attention and followers who offered to help. This was what I had been trying to avoid.

Marshall's small eyes narrowed in annoyance. His lips pursed in a slight pout. "In there?" he pointed with his electric stick. I nodded.

Wallace lagged a few steps behind, eyes scanning my rumpled dress and tangled hair. It appeared as though I had just emerged from a brawl with the barnyard animals. Slowing his pace, he cautiously approached me while I clung to Amara. He reached to touch my face, but I pulled away, holding onto Amara even tighter.

His concerned eyes couldn't help but travel down, taking in my torn top dangerously close to exposing my breasts. I tried fixing it, hoping pressing the fabric against my skin would somehow repair the shredded seams.

The door to the greenhouse swung open, revealing Hunter with his hands tied behind his back. Enraged, Wallace marched over to confront the situation.

The voices from the other villagers grew louder and closer, muttering words of judgment and pity. I could feel their eyes on me, weighing me down with shame. In the distance, I saw Angela and Mother rushing towards us, their skirts swishing as they ran up the hill.

The small crowd of ten or so gasped at the sight of Hunter being led out, bloodied and bruised. I refused to look in his direction, determined not to give him any satisfaction in seeing how much he had hurt me.

Mother rushed towards me with open arms, embracing Amara and me. A wave of emotion ran through me, and I didn't realize how Mother's embodiment made me feel safe as I exhaled, clinging to her.

"Are you okay?" Mother's words exasperated, needing to catch her breath.

"What happened to your dress?" Angela inspected the fabric and noticed Amara's burn mark.

Mother draped her shawl over my shoulders. "Angela, take Amara to the medical facility. I'll take Liz." She led me down the hill and into the castle.

"Come on, let's get you cleaned up," Her grip tightened over my shoulders as she led me down the hill.

MOTHER WANTED me to feel safe, so she took me to her private quarters. She motioned for me to sit on a bench in her luxurious bathroom, adorned with soft pink hues and Italian marble. As she knelt before me, she examined my dress and dirty hands.

With her regular frumpy and sour face, Johanna entered the room with extra towels and washcloths. Her small mouse face never showed excitement, but today, she gasped at my appearance.

"Run the bath, Johanna," Mother commanded without looking back. "And bring some fresh milk and lavender cream."

Johanna scurried off to fulfill her tasks, avoiding eye contact with anyone.

With Mother's help, we peeled my clothes from my body. I felt exhausted, and my body ached from head to toe. Her eyes watered as she saw my drastic weight loss and recent bruises. Trying to compose a smile, she helped me to my feet. She guided me over to her bathtub.

Johanna returned with a pitcher of milk. Before she could pour a drop into the tub, Mother excused Johanna, taking the pitcher to pour the milk into the steaming water. Its white embrace softened the steam.

"Liz..." Mother's voice remained calm and neutral. "I only want to ask you one question, okay?"

"He didn't rape me," I strained to reply.

Mother closed her big brown eyes, relieved as the tension left her shoulders. Nodding at me, she guided me into the tub and helped me relax in the warm water. She stroked my hair, scooped the pitcher into the water, and poured it onto my head.

"He will be punished for this," Mother's voice sounded distant.

Then her tone softened as she stroked the back of my head, asking if I needed anything - food to eat or any specific requests. Each time, I replied with a simple shake of my head. I asked to be left alone.

She respected my wishes and left me alone with my thoughts. The click of her heels on the cold marble floor reverberated like gunshots in the spacious bathroom. Still, even their sharp echoes couldn't drown out the haunting images burning in my mind of how Hunter's hands grasped my body, the sound of fabric ripping apart, the pressure of his weight crushing me, the searing pain across my face, and his hot breath assaulting my skin. The scene played on an endless loop, tormenting me with every detail.

The ghost of his touch still lingers on my skin, a slimy residue that I can't scrub away. I can almost feel his hands gripping my shoulders, digging in with a force that leaves bruises and imprints. The putrid scent of a wet dog fills my nostrils as I try to catch my breath, but all I can smell is him. His stench suffocates me even over the faint scent of lavender from the water.

My trembling hand reaches up to the spot where his rough knuckles collide with my cheek, the pain still throbbing like a thousand needles pricking at once. Strands of hair cling to my face, matted with dirt and grass from our struggle. I can't escape the memories or the physical reminders of what he did to me.

You smell him because his scent is in your hair.

I collapsed, my back slamming against the unforgiving porcelain tub. The water rushed like a raging river, enveloping me in its suffocating embrace. I couldn't escape or breathe as it rose higher and higher, drowning me inch by inch. Hunter's image burned into my mind like a searing brand.

I kept my eyes open, hoping the milk and lavender would cleanse my tainted thoughts. But all I could see was his cold, malicious face reflected in the swirling water.

I plunged into the water, holding my breath for as long as possible. The scent of lavender burned my eyes, but I welcomed the sting as a sign of cleansing.

As I submerged deeper, I could feel all the pain and trauma being washed away. But was it being cleansed or just buried deeper within me? I fought against the urge to resurface, knowing that if I gave in, all the agony and suffering would resurface with me like a tidal wave. I had to stay under until every last bit of it was gone, even if it meant drowning in the process.

The milk above me seemed to split apart, like clouds parting around the sun in the sky, revealing a small opening. Through it, I could see Brant standing over the tub, peering down at me with one hand outstretched and saying something. But his voice was muffled by the liquid around me. I exhaled all my oxygen and watched the bubbles float to the surface. Brant remained there, waiting for me to resurface.

I sat up and coughed, choking out the water and catching

my breath. My eyes scanned the room, but no one was around. Alone and afraid, I hugged my knees to my chest. The shame of not feeling strong enough to fight back weighed on me, filling me with anger and self-loathing.

Tears streamed down my face as I allowed myself to feel the emotions that had been plaguing me since the first incident. Despite being alone in the grand luxurious bathroom, the memories were suffocating, and the walls were closing in and around me.

"It's dangerous to be alone in your thoughts like this," Brant's voice echoed, striking a chord within me. I conjured up an image of him sitting on the windowsill, watching over me with a protective gaze. I relied on his projected presence to overcome these difficult moments, creating an unhealthy pattern.

"No more dangerous than being trapped behind these walls," I replied dryly.

Brant leaned down, resting his elbows on his knees. "You need to tell them what this is doing to you," his voice close to my ear as if I could feel him right next to me.

"Why?" I snapped, turning my head towards him.

Anger bubbled up inside me, and I gripped the sides of the bathtub. Anxiety filled my chest, my heart racing as blood rushed to my head. The once soothing water now failed to calm me.

But Brant's eyes met mine with a sadness reflecting my mental state.

"You need to play their game. It will help you survive, and then you can escape and return home to me."

I hated that he was right, or at least that my projection of him held a truth I couldn't deny.

INTERNAL STRUGGLE

Johanna entered the room carrying a steaming pitcher of water, its handle wrapped in a towel to protect against the scalding heat. As she moved to pour it into the tub, I cleared my throat and asked for a towel, indicating that I had been in the bath long enough. I didn't want to seem ungrateful.

She looked at me, her expression implying that she thought I purposely waited for her to carry the heavy pitcher. Exaggerating her exhale, Johanna set the pitcher aside and perched on the tub's edge, her hands folded in her lap.

"Are you finished with your pity party?" Her tone was direct and tinged with exhaustion, as if she was tired of catering to my needs.

"I'm sorry?" I responded, surprised by her sudden sharp tone.

She took a sharp breath and sat up straight, keeping her stern gaze fixed on me. "Since you arrived here, everyone has been walking on eggshells around you. I can't understand why," her voice dripping with disdain.

Before I could defend myself, she went on pacing around in a small space with her hands on her hips, clearly disapproving.

"We all know your story. You mope around crying about how much you miss the outside world, and don't get me started on how you constantly draw attention to yourself." She pointed a finger in my direction. "You should be grateful and appreciate a place like this exists, and fate allowed you to be among us."

My initial shock transformed into frustration. I turned towards the empty pitcher next to me and, without hesitation, grabbed it by the handle and hurled it in her direction. She leaned over as she dodged the empty pitcher as if she had predicted my reaction. Her expression wasn't one of surprise but annoyance.

"Do you think being kidnapped and taken away from my family is fate?" My disbelief was evident in every word. "You're even more delusional than the others."

Johanna remained unfazed, crossing her arms as we exchanged words. She glanced down at the shattered glass, her steps crunching on the broken pieces as she approached me.

"If you want to play the damsel in distress, be my guest," she sneered. "But sulking in this tub won't get you anywhere." She waved me off dismissively, her tone dripping with contempt.

Her casual remark struck me harder than Hunter's backhand. I couldn't believe what she had just said. Anger surged through me, tightening my hands on the tub's edges and grinding my teeth together.

She planted her hands on her hips and continued, "You can either keep wallowing in self-pity or pull your head out of your ass and take control of your destiny."

"How dare you—"

"No one is coming to save you, Liz," her annoyed tone pulsed through my body. "They won't find you here, and it's clear that you're incapable of getting yourself out. Stop playing the martyr and accept your fate."

Before I could respond, we were interrupted by Mother clearing her voice from her sitting room. Johanna was embarrassed; she straightened and bowed her head, but not before giving me one last disdainful look.

Mother walked in, holding a soft cotton robe in her arms. As she took a few steps forward, she heard the crunch of broken glass under her heels.

What happened?" She stepped back and saw the pitcher shattered on the floor.

Johanna and I exchanged a meaningful look, waiting for one of us to confess to Mother.

"Ladies?" Mother's gaze shifted between me and Johanna, waiting for an explanation.

"I got angry and threw it," I admitted.

"Johanna, please get the broom," Mother instructed without asking for more details.

I SAUNTERED into the sitting room, my new clothes still clinging to me with their crispness. My damp hair stuck to my neck as I walked, each step a painful reminder of the event in the greenhouse. Mother stood by the fireplace, her kind eyes welcoming me like a lost puppy. She motioned for me to sit across from her as sour-faced Johanna lingered by the door, her hands clasped in front of her. Her disapproving gaze never left me as I took the offered seat, and Mother poured me a steaming cup of tea.

I lowered myself into the plush armchair, admiring the cream and floral pattern. The crackling of the fireplace filled the silence. My eyes focused on the fireplace screen's vine design to catch stray embers. The orange and yellow flames on the burning log aligned the top like a perfect dancing symphony.

A slight knock on the door caught everyone's attention. Mother nodded to Johanna, and when she opened the door, Amara pushed her way in, making a beeline for me. I stood to meet her, and she wrapped her arms around me as if we hadn't seen each other in years.

Angela entered and gave a respectful nod to Mother before gently placing a hand on Amara's back. "I told you she was safe, "her caring eyes smiled at me as if the sight also reassured her for herself.

Amara let go of me but kept her hands on my arms as she looked at me with a mix of sadness and urgency. She needed to tell me something, but the words remained unspoken.

"Are you hurt?" I asked, noticing the burnt fabric still clinging to Amara's chest from where Hunter's electric stick had struck her.

She brushed off my concern. "Nothing I can't handle."

"This one is tough," Angela chimed in. "He did more damage to her clothes than her skin."

"Now that we're all here," Mother began, directing her attention towards us, "I need the four of us to discuss the incident before I take this to His Grace."

"He doesn't know?" I interjected, shocked.

We settled into the rolled arm couches, finding just enough space for each of us. The cushions were still firm as if they hadn't been used. The fabric resisted but gave in to our weight, providing a slight sense of comfort.

Mother spoke up, her tone gentle, as she understood the severity. "I had asked for more time with you." Her sad eyes were on me. "Without a second thought, he wanted you to take as much time as needed."

I felt safe in her presence, yet I couldn't shake my guilt for burdening her with my troubles.

The three of them began the discussion while I withdrew from their words. Brant's voice broke through from across the room. The flickering fire cast an ethereal glow on his tanned skin, turning his green eyes into hazel orbs. My focus shifted between his comforting presence and the distant voices of Mother, Angela, and Amara.

Brant stood tall and robust in Watchmen attire, fitting in seamlessly. I was intrigued that I pictured him this way, but his imagined presence provided a sense of calm during this turbulent time. Even though I knew he wasn't physically there, these moments of escape into my mind were a welcome break from the harsh reality around me.

"You won't know unless you take the risk," Brant said with a shrug. "You have to start somewhere and stop being a lone wolf. It's not working."

Despite my initial resistance, I had to admit he was right. Playing it safe had gotten me nowhere. It was time to take a leap of faith and see who I could rely on. Loyalty meant everything to the Faithful - practically the foundation of their existence. And now, I needed to put that to the test.

In an instant, Brant disappeared from where he had been standing. Mother looked at me with concern, sensing something was amiss. Gathering my courage, I declared that I needed to tell her everything. And so, I began recounting every detail from my first encounter with Hunter in the tower on the first day, when he taunted me with his electric stick, and every interaction since then.

MY STORY

I recalled the details of when I left Aldrich's tower after taking his test on the tablet and was attacked by Hunter shortly after I left. I shared the details of my attack, such as an out-of-the-body experience. I was relieving every painful memory in the seconds they happened. I shared how he pressed me against the wall, what he said in my ear, and how he slipped away without anyone noticing.

I left the part where Reynard and Amara found me in the women's showers. I didn't want Mother to get him in trouble. I was still conflicted about who to trust.

Mother chimed in, remembering the footage and asking Zak to investigate it further, sensing something was wrong. The memory of her distress was still vivid in my mind. I lied then, telling her I was chasing Aldrich's cat, Shadow. I even shared how I wanted to electrocute myself and grab hold of the fence, but Zak was there for support.

As I continued, I opened up about feeling safer in the weeks following the incident. Hunter's behavior had changed, possibly due to being reprimanded or perhaps from increased scrutiny.

"Now I understand what he was doing," I concluded. "He was stalking his prey."

With no holding back, I recounted today's incident in full detail, baring my emotions and making them understand the depth of my pain. I described how his touch made me recoil.

Angela shifted while Amara sat back on the couch with her arms crossed, her gaze fixed on my feet. However, Mother remained absorbed in my story, her unwavering attention speaking volumes about her concern for me.

Tears threatened to spill from my eyes as I confessed to Mother, my voice heavy with emotion. "I'm sorry for not telling you sooner," I choked out. "This new reality is hard for me to accept. I've rebelled and lied, desperate to find a way back home."

Mother embraced me, offering comfort and understanding. "I am sorry that you have endured this pain. My heart breaks for you," her voice cracks.

"Mother, what will you tell His Grace?" Angela's question hung in the air.

"Everything," Mother replied. "He needs to know the real monster he brought into our safe space."

A wave of relief washed over me so vigorously that I almost collapsed if I hadn't been sitting down.

"Thank you," I whispered, my voice trembling.

"After speaking with His Grace, do you think he will understand and let Zak out of the locker?" Amara asked.

Her question jolted me back to reality, and my heart raced. "What's happened?" The heavy burden in my chest weighed on me. "Why is Zak in the locker?" My voice rose with concern.

"He shouldn't be punished for standing up for Liz," Angela stated as if I wasn't there.

"Amara," I snapped, frustrated, "can you please tell me what's happening?"

Mother stood up. "I need to see his Grace. You ladies wait here. I'll be back as soon as possible." With that, she left the room. As Johanna opened the door for her, Mother's footsteps hollowed as they clicked further and further down the long hallway.

"Johanna, could we have a moment alone?" Angela asked.

Johanna turned her sharp eyes towards Angela, but they softened when she realized the significance of the request. "Of course," she said, bowing her head before exiting and closing the door behind her.

"Don't let her get to you," Angela warned me.

"I'm afraid it's too late," I admitted, still stinging from Johanna's harsh remarks.

"She's just jealous because Hunter doesn't pay attention to her anymore," Angela stated matter-of-factly.

"What?" Amara and I exclaimed in disbelief at the revelation.

"She's had her eyes on him since day one," Angela explained. "Then, the day he met you, there was a shift." She crossed her arms. "His demeanor changed with her," she shrugged. "We all see it at our dinner. He won't talk to her and makes excuses to leave early."

"She can have him," Amara stated with a wave of her hand, speaking for me.

"Hunter is like a chameleon," Angela's eyes held an intense sadness. "He truly believes he can do whatever he wants without facing consequences." Her hands clasped at her lips. "He's been roaming the village for months, eyeing us like pieces of meat."

She stood her hands at her waist, pacing the room, taking the truth like a painful memory. "In front of His Grace and Mother, he's been the perfect Faithful, always taking on more responsibilities and standing by their side." She smirks at Amara, "But Reynard has put him in his place a few times."

Angela crossed her arms. "He's a typical narcissist. He thinks he's entitled because of his position as a Watchman." Her lips pressed together to hold in her anger. "It disgusts me." Her Bronx accent was thick as she explained further. "They make excuses for him, ya know. That's why some of us are watching him," her gaze bearing down on his. "I don't want anyone to get hurt. I...I know he'll be the death of someone someday."

"Like Zak," I pressed, trying to stay focused on our original topic despite all the distractions. "What happened?"

Angela and Amara glanced at one another as though they were telepathically discussing who should tell me the details of the situation.

"We weren't there," Amara shared, looking at Angela for confirmation. "But, from what Reynard shared later," Amara explained. "Hunter was left in His Grace's study. He had been bound at the wrists, leaving him defenseless."

So far, I didn't see anything wrong, "go on."

"His Grace walked in, and Zak was beating him, using Hunter's weapon, the electric stick...thing…it wasn't on, but Hunter was bloody. Zak confessed after feeling enraged after hearing the rumor about what happened in the greenhouse." Amara explained.

My stomach turned. Zak had gotten himself caught, or in the moment, he wanted to keep beating Hunter until he had no breath left.

I looked towards the fireplace, mesmerized by the dancing flames. Angela had thrown in a cedar log, rekindling the dying fire. The crackling sound and warmth emitted heat like a soft blanket draping over us.

As Reynard entered, offering to take us to a private dinner across the hall, my thoughts were in turmoil. My body may have been hungry, but my mind consumed the day's events. I was exhausted, and my muscles ached; food was the last thing on my mind. Despite my physical needs, I couldn't bring myself to join them for dinner.

It took some persuasion, but Angela and Amara left with the promise of bringing me food. As soon as they were gone, I sighed in relief. I didn't want to face anyone right now.

The thought of being the center of attention, everyone whispering and staring at me over what happened, filled me with dread. I only wanted to sink into the cold, solid stone beneath my feet and disappear from the world. Away from all human contact and scrutiny.

I couldn't stop thinking about Zak, locked away in that desolate cell. My heart ached for him, knowing he was suffering because of me. A part of me felt grateful for his actions - defending my honor and standing up to Hunter. But then the guilt would wash over me, knowing I shouldn't feel grateful for violence.

It scared me how much I enjoyed hearing about Zak's fists flying as if it were a form of karma. But deep down, I knew this wasn't who I was - someone who condones violence. Yet, a darker part of me wondered if I would have just sat back and watched with a smile if it had happened before me.

Brant appeared and lounged on the opposite couch, staring into the flames. "Someday, you'll have to face them all again," he commented.

"Not tonight," I asserted.

Brant leaned forward, resting his elbows on his knees and clasping his hands under his chin. "I worry that you'll get lost in your thoughts," he muttered.

"Like how I am now?" I retorted.

"Hmmm." He stood up, propping an arm against the fireplace mantle. "You have to play their game."

"How long?" I sighed, feeling the exhaustion weighing me down. I didn't want to participate in this facade.

"Until you're back home and in my arms."

His gaze filled with longing pierced through me, stirring a yearning in my heart. I placed a hand over my chest.

"I don't know if I can do this," I admitted.

"Do you mean playing the role or coming back to me?" His question hung heavy in the air.

"Both. And what if Mother brings up the procedure again? Can I honestly go through with carrying a baby and then giving it away? How would you feel about me then?"

Brant straightened up, furrowing his brow. "Do you still think I want another child?"

I blinked, closing my eyes for a moment before opening them again. Brant had left while I was lost in thought. I forced myself to face the harsh reality that my subconscious was trying to make me confront amidst the chaos of my life. Brant was right. Being alone with my thoughts wasn't something I excelled at. I needed some fresh air. Standing up, I smoothed out the wrinkles in my dress from sitting.

The walls seemed to close in on me as the room grew darker, like a vice. Panic set in, and I took deep breaths as I approached the door. The worn, wooden panels creaked as I pulled it open, revealing Wallace standing on the other side. His tall frame filled the hallway, his stance rigid and alert as if he were on guard duty. He took quick steps towards me, his hand reaching out as if he wanted to touch my face, but then he hesitated, realizing that I didn't want to be touched, and retreated his hand back to his side with a regretful expression.

"I've been worried about you," Wallace said, stopping a few steps away.

The gentle concern in his voice was like a warm embrace, offering comfort and understanding. I was grateful for his caring nature, but my hesitation and the slight crack in the door spoke volumes - he wasn't welcome to enter. The barrier between us was not just physical but emotional as well. My closed-off stance conveyed the message that I needed space.

"Is there any way you can go get Amara?" I asked.

He looked down the endless hallway and hesitated before considering the idea.

"I'm not supposed to leave my post. Liz, I wish I had known about--"

"I need her," I interrupted.

There wasn't enough time. Mother's heels were coming back down the hallway. I shuffled back and closed the door in Wallace's face.

KEEP THE FIRE BURNING

As Mother swept into the room, her presence seemed to wash away my sudden feelings of suffocation. Moments ago, the walls felt darker, as if they were closing in on me, but they now seemed to brighten with her arrival. She was like a breath of life that I needed, but I couldn't help but wonder how the discussion between her and His Grace went.

"How did His Grace handle my story?" I blurted out, unable to contain my worry.

"He believes you," she reassured me, though her words lacked conviction. "He's just contemplating the appropriate course of action."

"What will happen of Zak?...of Hunter?" I pressed.

"His Grace is deeply disturbed," Mother walked toward the fireplace. "He is trying to process the information," her voice measured. "When things don't align with his expectations, it's as if...he malfunctions."

The idea seemed absurd. While I could appreciate the concept of offering perspectives, the notion of someone being so oblivious seemed far-fetched.

“Malfunctions? Seriously? Is he a cyborg now?” My tone carried a hint of irritation, my sympathy waning.

Mother dismissed my comment with a look that suggested I was the one with the outlandish perception.

"What kind of punishment will Hunter receive?" I pressed when she hesitated to answer. "Surely His Grace sympathizes a Faithful when defending an innocent person? You said yourself that Hunter should be punished." I pointed out. Hoping that my sudden change in tone and word choices meant I was trying.

“Zak isn't a Faithful yet," she corrected. "His Grace is struggling with the guilt of his actions. Knowing that someone like Hunter was able to harm you in this place has embarrassed him. It's a heavy burden for him to bear.” Mother's tone sounded forced, as if she was reciting what was expected of her.

I sensed there was more beneath the surface. Part of me wanted to hear that Hunter would be punished and banished from these walls or locked away until his dying breath. This moment felt like a turning point in my story, and not knowing how it would all unfold left me uneasy.

I clenched my hands to control my rising anger. I knew snapping at anyone wouldn't help, but playing their twisted game was becoming increasingly difficult. In my mind, Brant's voice reminded me to do whatever it took to escape and be reunited with him.

“What is going to happen to Zak?” I asked, still worried about him.

“Both of them will be lashed.” Mother stated with unsettling ease that it was a routine occurrence.

“What? Zak didn’t do anything!” The disbelief in my voice reverberated through my chest. “Please tell me you spent all that time trying to convince His Grace otherwise.”

Mother raised her hand, her eyes sharp, a warning to

watch my tone. “Zak still attacked a Watchman. He will receive five lashes and Hunter ten.”

My mouth fell open. I couldn’t fathom how Zak, who had defended me, was now being punished while I escaped a brutal assault.

“Is that all?” I hissed through clenched teeth.

“No, it’s not,” Mother snapped back, her voice dripping with venom. She leaned close and hissed, “His Grace wants to humiliate Hunter. We were carefully plotting the next step.” Her hand clenched the mantle, and her nails left indents in the wood. “Hunter has evaded detection for too long. Either he’s adept at manipulating the system or has help from others.”

The mere suggestion sent a jolt of terror through my entire body. It felt like an icy finger traced its way down my spine, leaving a trail of goosebumps in its wake. The thought alone made my heart race and my hands tremble.

As Mother's gaze lingered on her hand gripping the mantle, I could see the turmoil in her mind. She took a deep breath and forced herself to stand tall once again. With a hesitant release of her grasp, it was as if she was trying to rid herself of the dark thoughts that plagued her.

"I have one question for you," she began, "will you choose to play an active role in His Grace's plan, or will you resist?"

“You want me as bait?” I realized the adrenaline rush, both exciting and terrifying. Half of me was eager to turn the tables on Hunter, to outsmart and humiliate him. But the other half feared a repeat of today’s event, worrying whether I would be able to defend myself if things went awry and he attempted to harm me again. The thought of enduring another ordeal like today seemed unbearable.

Mother shook her head. “He wants you and Nellie as bait.”

“Isn’t she a bit unstable for this?” I voiced my concern, my mind haunted by the possibility of something going wrong.

My role in His Grace's plan was vague and undefined, yet I couldn't escape my promise to Mother that I would help somehow. I couldn’t ask about Nellie's part and agree not to discuss anything with His Grace. The less I knew, the better off I would be—or so she said.

But what about Zak? He was caught in this mess, which weighed heavy on my conscience. Despite my guilt, I couldn't help but ask to see him.

Mother's sharp gaze met Reynard's without hesitation at the sound of a knock on the door. I followed her lead and turned to see him standing there. His posture was rigid, his expression unreadable as he awaited further instructions from Mother.

Before he could speak, she ordered him to escort me to the locker so I could check on Zak myself. I couldn't shake off the feeling that something was brewing beneath the surface. The tension between us was noticeable, and I feared what chaos it might unleash.

Reynard's face scrunched with unspoken questions, but he pushed them aside as if nothing else needed to be said. My heart raced at the thought of others seeing me, judging me, or wanting to ask me questions. Anxiety swelled in my chest like a tidal wave.

"There is a secret passage we can take," Reynard said as if he had read my mind.

As we made our way to the locker, Reynard and I kept our voices low, mindful of the prying eyes and ears around us. We walked in tight quarters down the long hallways as if we were walking behind the stage of a movie set. His long strides almost forced me to jog to keep up, but my mind was racing too fast for my body to match. My instincts were my only guide, but I couldn't shake the sense of chaos and mistrust that seemed to surround me. This was my life now, and I wasn't sure who I could mold myself to be to survive.

Rounding the last corner, stepping out into the warm air from the hot day, Reynard cleared his throat before addressing me.

"Are you sure about this?" he asked.

I felt a surge of confidence unlike any I had felt before. I believed I could make a difference in my situation now that I was part of something bigger—a purpose guiding me forward.

"How did Zak get access inside His Grace's study?" I said we had fewer people around who were too far away to hear anything.

"The less you know, the better." He quipped.

I felt a pang of unease, "Reynard…" I sighed, feeling disappointed at the outcome. "Zak could be lashed for this." We stepped onto the bridge.

He remained resolute. "He was aware of the risks."

We arrived at the locker's entrance, and Reynard raised his electric stick to the keypad. When the green light to the door signaled he was allowed entry, I was again welcomed with the musty odor as the door opened.

My heart raced as we stepped inside. Zak was confined in the first cell on the right, his piercing blue eyes staring back at me through the bars. A rush of emotions flooded me - fear, anger, relief, and sadness. The cell door creaked open, and I stepped closer to my friend, who looked worn and beaten but still held onto a spark of defiance in his gaze.

Zak's fingers wrapped around the bars when he spotted me, hauling himself up from the ground.

"I'll leave you two alone and check on our other cellmate," Reynard announced, stepping away.

Zak's expression brightened at my presence, the door

casting a moonlit glow between us, illuminating his sharp features.

A smile spread across his face. “I’m glad you came.”

I reached out, my hands grasping the cold metal bars beneath his. The icy touch sent shivers down my spine, a stark reminder of the wretched conditions he was enduring in this place. The rust and grime on the bars told a story of confinement and suffering that I could only imagine. My heart ached for him, trapped behind these unforgiving bars.

“Why did you risk being caught?” I asked.

“At that moment, I didn't care,” he replied with a shrug. “Someone needed to teach him a lesson about disrespecting women. And I swore to keep an eye on you, to defend you.”

“No, you said you’d help me…” I leaned in closer, whispering, “escape.”

A hint of amusement flickered across his face. “And isn’t that another form of protection?”

I returned a smile; he was stubborn, but I am thankful to have him in my corner. Even when we were abducted together, he had been fiercely protective of me. I remembered how he had risked his safety twice to try and help us escape - the first time from the back of a van and the second time from the cargo area on the train. Each time, he took the brunt of the attacker's blows and yelled at me to run. But I couldn't leave him behind.

As I recounted this, tears began to well up in my eyes. "You could be lashed for this," I said, my voice shaking.

Zak shook his head and placed his hands on my forearms. "I don't care about that. I couldn't allow him to think for another second he could abuse you." His gaze was unwavering as he met my tear-filled eyes.

I couldn't hold back the tear, and it escaped to run down my cheek. "I shouldn't have been alone."

Zak's expression softened. "You're not going to start

blaming yourself." He wiped away a tear with his thumb. "I stand by my actions and would do it all again if it meant protecting you."

I wanted to share with Zak my discussion with Mother, but I couldn't risk being overheard by hidden cameras or unseen guards.

Reynard's heavy footsteps were coming closer in our direction. My hands clenched tighter around the bars.

"I promise I'll fix this," I blurted out before he could hold me back.

"Wait, Liz..." His eyes widened with worry as he reached through the bars towards me. "What are you going to do?"

Reynard appeared in front of us. "Time's up."

"Wait, no...Reynard...she's..." Zak grabbed onto the bars, panic creasing his face. Then, he calmed as if he changed his mind and trusted me. "Just watch out for her."

"I already have a plan," Reynard assured him with a smirk as he led me away.

As Reynard and I walked away from Zak, the sound of the locker door closing was deafening. My heart ached as I watched his deep blue eyes disappear into the darkness.

As we leisurely made our way back to the women's tower, the sky was painted with hues of dark blue with a thin layer over the mountain of pink and orange. The sun had set behind the mountains, casting long shadows on the ground. Most of the Faithful had already retired for the night, their homes glowing in warm light.

Our stroll was unhurried, allowing us to breathe the crisp night air. The cool breeze brushed against our skin, carrying the scent of fresh pine from the surrounding mountains.

It was a refreshing and invigorating sensation, like inhaling pure oxygen. The fragrance of pine trees enveloped us, reminding me of those little pine tree-shaped car air fresheners. But this was far more real and enchanting than any artificial scent could ever be.

I sometimes thought I heard hushed discussions and curious glances from windows as curtains drew closed to avoid detection. The whispers carried in the breeze, making it clear that everyone was aware of the attack. I imagined the village could be split into two. One side could agree that Hunter was in the wrong, and the other side, like Johanna, could believe I was portraying the damsel role and got what was deserved. The knot twisted in my stomach like a sharp pain. Then, I realized I was hungry.

Reynard's advice was to ignore the stares and keep moving forward.

"I'm trying," I replied, but it was difficult not to feel self-conscious under their gazes.

It was as if they were judging me, like I should be branded with a red letter 'A' on my chest, just like the character in The Scarlet Letter.

We reached the front entrance and stopped. Reynard reached for the handle, hesitating, "I'm grateful that Wallace and Marshall showed up when they did. When I saw Hunter and his actions towards you, all I could think about was making him hurt. I wanted him to feel the same pain he caused you. And I'm sorry about Zak; there are some things a man has to do."

"I appreciate your support today," my response was swift, not wanting Reynard to misunderstand my situation. "Please know that I want to help in any way I can."

Reynard opened the door and bid me goodnight with a twinkle in his eye.

"I'll pass along your kind words to Amara," I replied with a smile.

IGNORANCE

When I opened the door to my room, I saw that the candle on my nightstand was on its last flicker before burning out. It was as if it had waited until I entered before flickering its last bit of light.

The twins were sound asleep in their beds, chests rising and falling in sync. Amara lay in her bed, wrapped in her comforter, still recovering from the traumatic events of earlier today.

I opened my drawer and retrieved my nightgown, trying not to disturb anyone with the rustling fabric. After removing my top and loosening my skirt, I slipped into bed and let out a sigh of relief as the cool sheets enveloped me. Another day gone in this strange place, filled with guilt and uncertainty about our fate.

As I emerged from the fog of trauma, my body ached, and every movement was a painful reminder of what had happened. As I stretched my arms, I winced at the bruises on my arms from Hunter's violent hold on me.

I was feeling the bruises on my thighs when he needed them to move in the direction he wanted. My hand reached down to feel how it was sensitive to the touch. Earlier, in the bath, I had tried to ignore the evidence of his abuse, but now, in my bedroom, I couldn't escape it.

I straightened up in my bed, shaking with emotions I had been repressing to keep going. It was a tidal wave of pain and despair, leaving me feeling alone.

All I wanted was my family, especially my sister, by my side. She always knew how to encourage me and stay strong during challenging situations. Her words were like a lifeline, but she wasn't here now when I needed her the most. As I thought back on all the times I had imagined Brant next to me, It only made the ache in my chest worse that I couldn't conjure up the memory of my sister.

I felt a gentle hand on my foot and gasped in surprise to see Amara standing beside me with a pained expression. I hadn't heard her come down from the bunk bed above us. She knelt beside me, taking my hands in hers.

I saw the deep red and purple mark on her chest where the electric stick had struck her. I brushed back the top of her gown with shaking fingers to reveal more injuries beneath. My heart broke for her and for everything we had both endured at the hands of our abuser.

My voice caught in my throat as I tried to apologize. I fought back tears, not wanting to disturb the sleeping twins nearby. My whole body shook with emotions that I couldn't control.

Amara's grip tightened around my hand, providing a comforting anchor. "Don't be sorry," her eyes she murmured. "I've been through worse, especially with people I thought loved me."

"I don't know if I can do this anymore," I admitted, feeling defeated.

"You can do it," she urged. "You're stronger than you think." Amara's lips turned up, seeing the change in my eyes.

"Each one of us has had to become someone else to survive. You're not alone in losing your identity - some of us lost it at a young age and had to learn how to move forward." Rising to her feet, Amara bent down and planted a kiss on the top of my head. "Get some rest," she whispered. "Tomorrow is a new day."

IN MY DREAM, I stood in a luxurious hotel room overlooking the city of Seattle. The warm sun bathed everything in a golden light, and I could see the famous Space Needle in the distance, with the Pacific Ocean beyond.

A tiny bundle swaddled in a soft cotton blanket was as light as a feather in my arms. The sleeping baby stirred and stretched her fingers toward me, a sweet smile on her face. My heart overflowed with love and pride. This was my child, my miracle.

Behind me, Brant's footsteps approached. He leaned down to kiss our daughter on the forehead, and one of his hands rested on my lower back in a comforting gesture.

"Do you know what you want to name her?" his soft tone didn't want to wake her.

I shook my head, unable to tear my gaze away from our daughter's peaceful face.

"Don't forget who the real father is," this voice sent a shiver down my spine.

As I turned to see Hunter behind us in his Watchmen uniform, his sly smile fixed on me as he held out his arms.

"Let me hold my daughter," his eyes fixed on the baby in my arms.

I held my baby tighter to my chest, taking a step back. She was nestled and sleeping, and my eyes did not want to tear away from the image of her pouty lips making the perfect heart shape. Thinking about handing her over made my heart pound. The fear of him in this space was building, and my eyes never left Hunter's. His arms were raised to reach out for the baby.

"She's not yours," I snapped.

Hunter's eyes gleamed with amusement as he replied, "She doesn't belong to you."

Panic surged through me as I turned to Brant for help, but instead saw His Grace standing in Brant's place. Fear gripped me as I realized this wasn't just a dream but a nightmare unfolding before me.

Before I could react, His Grace reached for the baby, ripping her from my arms and his elbow blocking me from trying to take her back.

He handed her to Hunter, and the ear-piercing scream from her tiny lungs ripped at me. His sly smile and cooing as he tried to calm her made me scream in terror, trying to get past His Grace.

I was pinned to the wall, His Grace telling me this must be done. I watched Hunter turn away from us and walk out of the room.

MY BODY JOLTED AWAKE, my heart pounding against my chest. I sat up, trying to catch my breath and calm the panic inside me. The nightmare felt too close to reality.

Taking a deep breath, I swung my legs out of bed and attempted to shake off the lingering unease from my dream. I needed to focus on moving forward, facing everyone after what they had seen yesterday. But first, my goal for today was to get Zak out of that locker.

In perfect timing, Yasmin entered the room. We paused, meeting each other's gaze for a moment. A wave of relief washed over me at the sight of her familiar face. Her eyes glistened with tears as she hurried over to hug me. She apologized for not being there for me and expressed guilt for not finding out until this morning.

I hesitated, unsure if I was ready to discuss the assault yet. But as she squeezed, I couldn't resist hugging her back and welcoming her comfort.

"How are you feeling?" she uttered, brushing a stray strand of hair from her face. "Wait, I'm sorry, that's stupid. Ignore my ignorance. What can I do for you?"

"Can you get me a pill to forget this nightmare?" I attempted to make a joke, trying to ease the tension she wore on her face.

Yasmin's expression turned serious as she considered what herbs might help with such a request.

I reassured her that I was kidding, my hand resting on her shoulder.

"Do you want to talk about it?" Her tone was evident out of respect and pure curiosity.

I shook my head. I was still uneasy, and the memory of my dream formed a knot in my throat. I would become an emotional mess if I uttered a word. My fingers fumbled through my drawer for some clothes.

"What is everyone saying?" My curiosity was getting the better of me.

"That Hunter attacked you. It has everyone on edge this morning. You shouldn't be alone," she said.

"Why is that?"

"Because being alone gives you dark thoughts or bad dreams." Her voice was distant, lost in her thoughts.

"Like the one I just woke up from. A silly dream." I ruffled through my clothes, trying to find the top of my skirt.

Yasmin clicked her tongue in disappointment. "I wish I had my dream book with me. It could help us figure out what your dream means." She tapped her index finger on her lips. "But let's try this—can you remember three things from your dream? It might give us insight into what you're going through or any hidden meanings."

Sighing, I pulled up my skirt and tried to push the dream out of my mind. "It's nothing." I tried to play off, but Yasmin's words lingered.

"Don't stress," Yasmin was confident, as if reading my mind. "Pay attention to these signs from the universe and your emotions. They're trying to tell you something. What do you have to lose by exploring it?"

Who was I to argue with her logic? Johanna's words about not playing the victim hissed in the back of my mind, and Amara's advice last night on focusing on moving forward were signs I needed to pay attention to.

I conceded with a sigh, tightening my skirt. "In my dream, I held a baby girl. I was in a tall, high-rise building in Seattle. She was mine - Brant and I were discussing what to name her."

Yasmin's eyes brightened as she sat on her sister's bunk bed, listening. "Go on," she urged.

"The thought of having a baby with Brant warmed my heart." My arms slipped through my cotton shirt to tuck and tie at the waist.

Yasmin nodded. "Interesting. Your dream is trying to tell you something about your future or your desires.

I almost wanted to leave the conversation then to have a happy memory and not admit the rest. Admitting the rest of my dream would have built that fear rising in my chest and made breathing hard. I was distant from Yasmin and our conversation because I didn't want to share.

I focused on the burned candle on our dresser. Hunter's haunting words that the baby was our child and how he cooed to soothe her and walk away from me made it difficult to shake off the feeling of facing the reality of a strange premonition.

"Liz?" Yasmin's concerned voice and simple touch on my shoulder snapped me back into reality. "Where did you go?"

"I could hear Hunter's voice behind me as he told me it was our baby," my voice went dry, "Somehow, Brant was gone, and then His Grace snatched the baby out of my arms and handed her over to Hunter." My hand rubbed over my heart, trying to soothe the pain that was not real.

Yasmin's expression grew wide with shock. "That is a nightmare," she said, concern evident in her voice.

"It felt so real," I said, my voice trembling.

It wasn't the first time I had a dream like this. The memory of being in the backseat of a car, looking out at the endless desert, still sticks with me. It was a dream from my younger years, with two silent men in the front seat.

Suddenly, the car screeched to a stop, kicking up dust and dirt. One man dragged me out by my arm, but I resisted and didn't want to leave. They abandoned me in the blistering heat of the desert sun.

It took me a whole day to calm down and convince myself that my nightmare wasn't a prophecy and that everything would be okay. I haven't shared the story with anyone besides my sister because she would have the same type of dreams and an open mind that the universe was trying to tell us something.

Sometimes, the feelings and emotions were too real to be just a dream. My sister and I even tried Googling its meaning, but the results ranged from fearing being alone to predicting an upcoming journey. Since then, when I wake up from unsettling dreams, I push through the day by reminding myself that it is all in my head.

Yasmin's eyes widened when I looked in her direction. She crossed her arms as if a chill descended in the room.

"What?" I asked.

"You don't see it?" She looked at me like I was the crazy one.

"See what?" I tied my apron on, completing my attire for the day.

Yasmin was searching for the right words. She was careful. "That was not a nightmare but a premonition. You just experienced being taken, brought here, in a way alone, because you don't have your family."

Her words made my mouth go dry. "That dream was many years ago."

"True, but let's dive into this one you just woke up from," she started, as if ready to solve a case. "It's possible that dreaming about someone taking your baby could symbolize feeling neglected, or..." She was trying to recall. "It could also mean lacking love and acceptance in some aspect of your life," she promptly stated.

"That covers everything I've been through here," I remarked, my sense of sarcasm coming alive.

Yasmin smiled at me, "It's good to see you smile." She came over and took a seat next to me. "Dreams can hold deep-rooted meanings. Your spirit is trying to guide you. It's like ignoring your instincts. Do you trust your instincts?"

"Yes, of course."

"Then why ignore them?"

A familiar feeling of unease began to gnaw at my insides as I hung onto every word she spoke. It was the same sensation that had coursed through me in the Chihuly Gardens right before I was violently taken by force.

The women's side of the small restroom building was locked, so I ventured into the men's side. My heart raced as I tried to remain inconspicuous, aware that I was trespassing in a place I shouldn't be.

And then, the sound of a van pulling up outside shattered the silence, followed by the screeching of its doors as they were flung open. My instincts were on high alert, warning me that something was wrong.

My mind tried to rationalize and push away the fear, but deep down, I knew it was a warning. I thought I had learned my lesson that day, but I am now paying the price for ignoring my instincts.

HIS STORY

I made a rash decision this morning before breakfast, and before I knew it, I was standing outside His Grace's study. My palms began to sweat, and my heart raced. I took a deep breath before knocking on the door.

When His Grace opened the door, a surprise flashed across his face. "Liz? What are you doing here?"

I swallowed hard. "May I come in?"

He stepped back to let me in, and as I entered his study, I saw Mother sitting in one of the plush armchairs by the fireplace. She set down her teacup and greeted me with a warm smile.

"It's so wonderful to see you," she said, coming over to hug me.

I stood between them, and it felt awkward. "I just want to make this quick."

"You can stay for tea," His Grace offered in a kind gesture.

I shook my head. "No, thank you. I need to talk to you both about something important."

With a graceful sweep of his hand, His Grace invited us to sit at the quaint round table tucked into the corner of the room. From our vantage point, we could see the sprawling landscape below and the charming houses on the gentle slope of the hill. As he moved to guide me to my chair, I flinched, avoiding his touch. His expression shifted from optimistic to embarrassed as he recoiled and gave me space.

"Liz, I'm so sorry. I didn't mean--"

"Zak stood up for me yesterday. Now it's my turn to do it for him," I interrupted. "He doesn't deserve to be punished for defending himself against a monster."

Both His Grace and Mother exchanged glances before returning to me.

"If Hunter had attacked Mother, would you allow him to walk away freely?" I tried to sound confident but couldn't tell if it was convincing enough.

As I stood before His Grace, I could feel the weight of his gaze as our eyes met. On one hand, he seemed to understand the turmoil and fear that consumed me, or so I thought. Then, he seemed to dislike being bothered about this as he took a moment to answer.

"I guess not," she murmured, his gaze shifting to the floor.

My hands clenched at my stomach, trying to gather the courage to speak without stumbling over my words. "Zak has been my protector ever since we were kidnapped. He's a dear friend, and after all that I have suffered at Hunter's hand, I beg you to please...set Zak free."

His Grace hesitated, considering my request. Just then, Mother stepped forward, blocking my view of him.

"Liz, I want to thank you for supporting Zak." Mother's voice lacked its usual comfort. "We are considering any other man who has a strong desire to protect could behave the same way." She sounded more like a corporate boss, trying to weigh the options and not say anything that could cause legal trouble. "In fact, His Grace and I were discussing what we might require from you." Her words held an assertiveness as she blocked my vision from seeing His Grace, her eyes wide as if silently urging me not to bring up this topic.

"I'll do whatever it takes," I interjected, serious and determined.

After waking up from my dream this morning, I needed a purpose, something to distract me from the trauma I had endured from Hunter.

"Liz, we can't reveal everything to you. It's for your safety and the success of our plans." His Grace's voice spoke up before Mother had a chance to rebuttal.

He came into my view, his gentlemanly touch pulling a chair out for Mother and me. He waited to be the last one seated.

The realization hit me hard - I had no bargaining power. And now, it was becoming unclear whether this was for my benefit or theirs. The thought of volunteering myself with no leverage or angle left me feeling vulnerable.

"Will Zak be set free?" I blurted out, desperate for confirmation.

His hesitation was palpable as he exchanged glances with Mother before responding, "He will be set free."

My shoulders relaxed in relief, but then another thought crossed my mind. "Will he be lashed?"

The room fell quiet as His Grace's gaze turned to me. His eyes had no emotion, making it difficult to decipher his intentions.

After a tense moment of silence, he spoke. "If you're fully committed, Zak won't suffer any consequences."

"I'm all in." My lips speaking before my mind had a second to ponder, "I'll do whatever it takes to spare Zak from punishment."

But then His Grace held up his hand and requested that I comprehend their expectations before I agreed.

"No need," I briskly assured him, eager to make the deal

official. "I promise not to resist or attempt to run away." I extended my hand for us to shake and solidify the agreement. In this dystopian world, all I had to offer was my word. He took my hand in his firm grip. Our eyes met as we sealed the confirmation of our agreement.

"Thank you." I stood up and curtsied to both him and Mother before taking my leave.

I'VE BEEN stuck in the women's tower for two days now, avoiding all human contact. Amara and the Twins have been trying to provide support, but I prefer the solace of my room. From my window, I can hear the laughter and chatter of the female villagers going about their daily lives as if nothing has changed.

In the mornings, I listen to the women passing by my door, unaware I am leaning against it on the other side. As I reached for the doorknob one morning, I overheard their conversation.

"Has anyone seen Liz?" One voice asked.

"I'm sure she's hiding in the locker with all the other crazies," another chuckled at my expense.

"It's a shame what happened to her," a third voice commented.

"And rumor has it, she asked for it," the last voice laughed dismissively as they descended the stairs.

Frustration and sadness overwhelmed me, and I retreated into my room. The twins and Amara came in with breakfast, but they knew something was wrong when they saw my face.

"Liz, what did they say?" Amara asked with concern.

She knew all too well what they were saying. But I didn't want to talk about it. It was Sunday, which meant we had to dress up for church.

Amara didn't hide her disappointment. She expected me

to share, but what difference would it make? We still had to go through the motions and attend service like everything was normal.

"Let's just eat and get ready," she gestured towards the fruit bowls.

We were dressed in our cream-colored Sunday dresses. As Amara worked on my hair, weaving a ribbon through it, I couldn't shake off the feeling of being a mere shadow of myself. It took me a few minutes to walk through the bedroom door and reach the railing. There, I saw the twins on the bottom floor, smiling across their faces, waiting for me to build up the courage to walk to the church.

"I wish we had hard alcohol." Amara leaned into me. "This will take a lot of courage, and I'm proud of you."She said, resting a hand on my back.

As we headed towards the church, I saw the Faithful gathered outside, chatting and laughing. Despite their normal behavior, my chest tightened with anxiety at the thought of facing them all.

My hands fumbled and squeezed so tight my fingers were losing their feeling from the blood loss. I needed this to distract me as my cheeks flushed with embarrassment.

As I approached, I could feel their curious glances and judging eyes and hear their hushed tones whispering words. Amara intertwined her arm with mine, walking with me with enough courage and strength for the both of us.

As the doors opened, a stream of people filled the room. Amara and I followed suit, dipping our fingers in the fountain at the entrance before pressing them to our hearts and taking our seats in the back row. I glanced at the men's side of the room, hoping to catch a glimpse of Zak.

The trumpets blared through the speakers, causing my heart to skip a beat. We all rose to our feet as His Grace strode down the aisle, and we curtsied while the men bowed their heads.

Amara leaned over to me. "I don't see Reynard," she whispered, scanning the room with her eyes.

I couldn't ignore that Wallace and Marshall were missing from the room. As His Grace took to the podium and instructed us to sit, I noticed his intense expression. This made the rest of us uneasy, causing a ripple of movement throughout the pews. The shifting gazes of those around me distracted me from listening to His Grace's words.

"In your previous life, this day would have been marked as a day of worship," his Grace started. "But now, we acknowledge that one among us has betrayed our trust and violated innocence. How can we preach love and devotion when such actions occur?"

All around me, eyes started darting in my direction as his words hung heavy. I wanted to disappear into my seat and be left alone, but Amara squeezed my hand reassuringly.

"Our purpose as Faithfuls is to live by our standards, not society's," His Grace continued, gripping the edges of the podium with both hands. "We trust in nature, in our hearts, and we will overcome this betrayal together." The Faithfuls in the front row bobbed their heads in agreement with His Grace's words. "How should we handle those who break our laws, manipulate, and act violently?"

The first few rows of Faithfuls jumped, shouting for justice. It was challenging to make every point of the argument, so I tried to stay composed and listen in.

"Starve him!" Someone shouted.

"Keep him in the locker!" Another voice shouted with cheers and applause.

"Strip him of his title!" a woman shouted. More cheering and applause erupted from the comment.

His Grace motioned for the crowd to quiet down before speaking. "Bring them in."

A back door behind the stage opened, and Reynard emerged, dragging Hunter out by his chains and shackles. Despite the bruises healing on his face, he still looked rough and worn from his recent stay in the locker. The murmurs in the crowd grew louder as Hunter was brought onto the stage and shoved to the ground in front of His Grace.

The room fell silent as His Grace stood next to Hunter. "Hunter, you have been brought here to be judged and sentenced by myself and your peers." He addressed the crowd. "You attacked a woman who shall remain nameless."

Despite His Grace's efforts to protect my identity, many people turned their heads to look in my direction as if they needed confirmation from me. This was an excellent distraction to keep me from rolling my eyes.

"You attacked her, ripped her clothes, and tried to force yourself upon her. Did you not?" His Grace asked, turning his direction to Hunter for an answer, who remained silent. "Fine then, how do you plead?"

With knees planted on the stage, Hunter glared at the surrounding crowd. His annoyance was noticeable, and he looked embarrassed at being displayed like this. Even in the last row, I saw the eyes of curious onlookers bearing down on him like he was a caged animal in a zoo. Hunter gritted his teeth, trying to maintain his composure in the face of scrutiny.

"Guilty," Hunter spat out, his voice hoarse.

Gasps filled the pews as people reacted to the admission. I was surprised and assumed he would try to debate the matter, trick His Grace and the audience, and plead innocence.

As His Grace returned to his podium, his eyebrows raised

in surprise at Hunter's response. "Guilty, you say? And why is that?"

"I have not laid with a woman since our arrival," Hunter continued, his voice filled with desperation. "I was weak and allowed impure thoughts to fester."

"You have spoken your truth," His Grace affirmed before signaling Reynard to move Hunter to a chair on the left side of the stage.

Just then, another door opened, and Wallace appeared with Zak, also in chains and shackles. Zak seemed more presentable than Hunter, but the fatigue and dark circles under his eyes showed the toll of his recent incarceration.

My stomach churned with a sickening mixture of guilt and fear as I watched Zak on stage. His tense posture and clenched fists revealed the weight of his nerves, and I couldn't help but feel responsible for adding to his burden. My lip trembled, but I forced myself to bite down hard, desperate to maintain composure.

The clanking sound of the heavy metal cuffs and chains echoed off the wooden stage as he stood near His Grace, also on display. It felt like we had been transported back in time, where humans were bought and sold, and Zak was nothing more than an item up for sale.

"Zak," His Grace's voice boomed through the microphone, "you are not yet a Faithful, but you defended Liz's honor. Can you tell us how you learned of the incident?"

"I was with Wallace and Marshall when they received a message from Reynard over the radio. He said there was an attack at the greenhouse, and Hunter was involved." Zak's husky response echoed throughout the church.

His Grace nodded solemnly before continuing, "And why did you feel compelled to defend Liz's honor?"

Taking a deep breath, Zak remained confident, "It was the sound of Reynard's voice. I knew something was wrong. I followed, then saw Angela escorting Amara. Her face was red, and she was emotional. I overheard Liz's name..." His eyes scanned the crowd as if trying to see where I was sitting. "I saw the burn mark on Amara's clothes. I asked what happened, and Amara told me that Hunter had attacked Liz and nearly raped her."

Together, the crowd held their breath in shocked silence. The onlookers' whispers and murmurs filled the air, each word hinting at suspicion and judgment. My name floated on their lips, accompanied by their versions of the story. I was able to drown them all out and keep my focus on Zak. His confidence gave me strength. Hearing him defend his actions and be willing to be locked up was more than anyone has done for me.

His Grace asked the crowd to stay calm and continued, "And what did you do next?" His Grace asked.

"Honestly, your Grace, I can't recall much after that." Zak's knuckles were turning pale as he spoke.

Hunter, who sat smirking in his chair, could see the tension in Zak's jaw and his rigid posture as if he were ready to pounce if given a chance.

His Grace strode over to Zak, hands on his hips. "You meddled yourself in a situation that was being handled. I understand Liz is your friend, but Hunter is still a Watchmen. Reynard had this under control, and you chose to engage in physical violence."

"What he did to Amara and Liz is unforgivable!" The words seared out of Wallace from the side of the stage with a fiery determination, his voice ringing solid and unwavering. If I hadn't known better, I would have thought Wallace was waiting for the right words to tear Hunter apart.

"I concur," one man shouted.

"Make him an example," a woman followed.

The crowd was agreeing with one another, fueling Wallace's adrenaline.

"Watchmen or no Watchmen, Your Grace," Zak raised his voice, unphased by the crowd's reactions. The hushes and soft tones from the crowd were eager to have him finish. "I am willing to accept whatever consequences may come."

"It's not just up to me. It's also a vote from the people," His Grace announced.

"Here, here!" Someone shouted.

Sitting in a forum filled with other people always made my heart race. I was used to the guidance counselors at school or public forums where parents and educators would gather. The discussions were always the same, just like in this room. Someone on stage would present a problem, and the crowd would offer their opinions.

But ultimately, one person had the final say: my Superintendent. She would listen to everyone's input, and someone like me would take notes, but there was already a predetermined answer. School forums had to follow state laws and regulations, making it difficult for any real change to happen based on the opinions of those in attendance.

A wave of adrenaline swept through the crowd as the words were spoken, and I could feel its effects. The people in the audience felt empowered, thinking they had a voice. Little did they know that His Grace already had a plan in motion, rendering their opinions meaningless.

Despite their vocal votes and nods of approval, it was clear that their voices would be disregarded. They just wanted to believe that they had some influence, but it remained to be seen which path His Grace would choose to follow and approve.

"We cannot solve our problems through violence," His Grace continued, speaking to the Faithful in the first few rows. "These outsiders do not yet understand our ways. We must show them compassion and teach them our peace-loving ways. While I do not condone Zak's actions, I can understand his innate instinct for protection."

Doctor Ferrarius stood up, holding his brown flap cap as he addressed His Grace. “Zak shouldn’t be punished. He’s already been in the locker,” he declared, garnering nods and murmurs of agreement from the audience.

Mother joined His Grace on stage. “What are your thoughts on punishment, Your Grace?” she asked, clasping hands and displaying a concerned expression.

After silence, His Grace's gaze swept over the crowd and settled on the two men being debated. “Both are to receive lashings.”

A visceral divide rippled through the room, splitting the audience into two factions. Some vehemently dissented, while others agreed. Their conflicting emotions created a charged energy that made Amara and I cover our ears to block out the cacophony of voices. The tension was palpable, threatening to boil over at any moment.

“Alright...alright..." His voice raised over the crowd, booming into the microphone. He turned in Zak's direction and pointed at him. "Your only warning. You are free to go.”

The crowd applauded, relieved for Zak's reprieve. But when His Grace walked over to Hunter, his demeanor showed no sympathy. The heavy thud of his boots echoed in the room as he faced Hunter with a stern expression.

“Are you willing to accept your punishment?”

Hunter's face contorted into a sour expression, though it was difficult to tell if it was from defiance or the bruises and swelling on his face. Either way, he didn't seem afraid of what would come.

“I am,” he replied without hesitation.

“Good,” His Grace nodded, motioning for Reynard to take Hunter away without further discussion.

MEET & GREET

With a sharp click and metallic clatter, the handcuffs and restraints that had kept Zak bound dropped to the stage with a resounding thud.

He flexed his hands and stretched out his cramped limbs, relishing being free from their grasp. His Grace stood beside him, resting a hand on Zak's shoulder, basking in his victory.

The audience rose to their feet in jubilation, cheering and applauding as Hunter was hauled away.

I noticed how His Grace masterfully manipulated their emotions, making them believe they were responsible for Zak's release and reveling in their adoration. I remained unmoved, refusing to be deceived by his cunning tactics.

"Zak, these people have accepted you and your honor," His Grace proclaimed. "What you did was heroic, yet not the Faithful way. Let there not be a next time."

Zak nodded and walked off the stage. He made his way down the aisle to the back of the room, and as his eyes followed him, he received thanks and pats on the back.

I couldn't tear my gaze away from him. I wanted him to

see my eyes and how remorseful I was. Did he feel relieved, ashamed, or guilty?

I couldn't help but feel a twinge of guilt. But then Zak's eyes shifted towards me, and my burden of this emotion lingered like a dark cloud. As he blinked, his expression softened, and I found myself feeling relieved yet conflicted.

Could things be okay between us after what had happened?

Amara's gentle nudge reminded me of the gravity of the situation.

His Grace was speaking, and I needed to pay attention. As I turned my head, I saw the others and felt a rush of conflicting emotions. I couldn't forget that cameras and the judgmental eyes of the Faithful and others were watching us. I couldn't afford to let my guard down in this scrutinized environment.

His Grace's hand rested over his heart, and he spoke with conviction.

"You inspire me. I know this path was not your choice, but I chose you." His voice boomed through the speakers and echoed off the walls as he stepped down from the stage, his boots echoing down the aisle.

People rose reverently, reaching out to touch his hand or the hem of his flowing robe as he passed. The thunderous applause filled the room, showing how much the audience was under his spell.

As His Grace led us outside to mingle with one another, I kept my eyes fixed on Zak, hoping for a chance to speak with him.

The Faithfuls were allowed to exit first, followed by the women and then the men. I caught Zak's gaze, and then, looking down, I was startled to notice the bruising and raw skin on his wrists.

I gestured to where I would be standing, and he gave me a quick, visible nod to show he understood. Amara discreetly slipped away from the crowd and navigated through the crowd towards the food and drinks.

She moved with determination, searching for something —or someone. She almost collided with a Faithful, but then she spotted Reynard and straightened up.

A small smile played on her lips as she spotted him. He was also scanning the crowd, most likely searching for her. She made her way towards him, surprising him with her appearance.

My view was obstructed by tall Faithfuls that towered over me. The sky above us was dark and foreboding, casting a somber mood over the lush green grass below. Gray clouds threatened to pour rain on our gathering, but it didn't dampen the spirits of those around me.

That is until I heard my name being called. I saw Zak surrounded by adoring fans, all vying for his attention.

Amara waved me over. I approached with caution and, catching Zak's wrists again, the bruising and open wounds from the handcuffs that marred this skin from being held captive in the locker. Despite their praises and compliments, he seemed tired and drained, wanting nothing more than to escape this chaotic scene.

"Can we please get out of here?" he asked me in a low voice, his exhaustion evident.

Reynard must have heard as he asked the gathering crowd to make room, led the way, and had Zak follow.

Amara and I were close behind, walking toward the forest, and before I knew it, the crowd had moved on as His Grace made his way over to them to speak and welcome conversation.

Reynard dodged past the fire pit and led us toward the dense forest. I hurried to keep up, hoping no one would follow us as the crowd seemed to gather around the food and drinks.

The conversations drowned out behind us as the pulsing hormones and flirtation filled the air. Everyone seemed to lose their focus on Zak's heroic moment and start their conversations as they courted one another.

Zak stopped behind a towering pine tree and rested against its rough bark. He let out a deep sigh that seemed to release all of the tension in his body.

Reynard nodded toward Amara and gestured for her to follow him to the lively crowd. She went with him, leaving me alone with Zak in the peaceful solitude of the forest.

As I studied him, I couldn't help but notice how worn out and weary he looked, with dirt smudges covering his face and clothes and sweat glistening on his skin.

The familiar scent of pine needles floated through the air, mixing with the earthy smell of damp soil. A slight breeze drifted by, reminding me that we were still in the cool embrace of the woods. I rubbed my arms to generate warmth, wishing the crackling fire pit was within reach.

"That could have gone wrong instantly," his exasperated breath blew out his mouth as though he held his breath the whole time we were in the church. His gaze looking at me with deep concern. "Are you alright?"

I couldn't meet his gaze, knowing that facing him would bring tears to my eyes. Admitting the incidents to Mother had been hard enough.

"I'm managing."

I knew I would share with him, but I needed to focus on moving forward. Deep down, I feared that once Zak knew the truth, he would seek revenge against Hunter, possibly even taking things too far. It was a difficult internal battle between my desire for closure and fear of potential consequences.

He pushed himself off the tree and stepped towards me. "Has Hunter attacked you before?" his eyes watched my behavior. I shifted, avoiding his question. "Hey." Zak's voice was soft as he turned me to face him. "It's just me."

Taking a deep breath, I could only shake my head and bite my lip to hold back the tears.

Zak reached for my chin and tilted it up to meet his gaze. The muscles in his face tightened as he looked upon my face, waiting for an answer, those piercing blue eyes drawing me in.

"I don't want you to go through this alone," his vow low.

"But I don't want anyone else hurt because of me," I replied, thinking about all the chaos and danger that seemed to follow me wherever I went.

Without warning, the noise of breaking twigs caught our attention from behind. We spun around to see Aldrich approaching with a woman at his side.

She stood as tall and slender as he did, her long blonde hair framing her face on both sides and parted down the center. Her thick, straight locks covered her features, making it difficult to identify her. She avoided eye contact and was too timid to approach us alone.

"Sorry to interrupt," Aldrich said with a smile, "but I wanted you two to meet my sister, Nellie."

I hesitated, surprised to see how put together she looked compared to her usual rugged appearance from behind bars in the locker. I recognized her wild side when she looked up at me with big blue eyes. I put my hand out to greet her.

"Nellie," I was being polite.

Instead of shaking my hand, her gaze was fixed on Zak. Her mouth beamed, and she took his extended hand. Nellie's gaze was drawn to his long, slender fingers. She took his hand and studied him with intense curiosity. Her fingers wanted to trace the wounds and bruises on his wrists.

Aldrich noticed Nellie's fascination and pulled her away.

"Sorry, she's been out of touch with people lately." His worried gaze met mine.

Nellie turned to Aldrich as he spoke, her eyes lingering on Zak. "Are you the same Zak in the locker with us?"

"I am," Zak replied.

She broke eye contact with Zak and looked at Aldrich with an inquisitive expression. "For her?" she asked, pointing in my direction.

Not sure if he should be offended, Zak shifted under Nellie's scrutiny.

"Let's meet the others," Aldrich said, turning his sister's body back toward the crowd. "There are plenty more people to meet."

Nellie waved her fingers at Zak as she said her goodbyes before joining the other guests. As she introduced herself to new faces, her eyes drifted back to Zak, almost as if he had entranced her.

I knew that look all too well—the same way Hunter looked at me.

MOTHER'S STUDY

My heart sank as His Grace's announcement echoed through the surround sound, forcing us to part ways. Our courting hour was over, and I longed for more time with Zak, but Mother stood in the yard, waiting to gather the women, and I knew she would be searching for me.

I sat in the crowded dining hall, flanked by my protective friends, the twins, and Amara. They knew I wasn't ready to face anyone else yet, not after what had happened.

As the whispers from others reached my ears, I could tell they were discussing me. Their voices were sympathetic and filled with pity as if they understood how wrong I was and how brave I was for just sitting among them.

But I didn't want their sympathy or apologies. Their well-meaning words felt like acid on my already raw emotions. I needed time to process and figure out how to move forward, but it was almost suffocating to be surrounded by their concerned gazes and unwavering tones.

I tried to distract myself from thoughts of Hunter and his

arrogance on stage. Yet, every time I closed my eyes, his face appeared, and his smirk taunted me.

I no longer feared him, knowing he was locked away, but the memories still haunted me. Esther's hand on mine snapped me back to reality, but I couldn't shake off what was stirring inside me.

"Are you planning on feeding the birds?" she asked, gesturing towards the crumbs that had fallen onto my napkin.

Embarrassed by my absent-mindedness, I balled up the napkin and excused myself from the table. I couldn't handle any more questions or judgment from those around me. Escaping into the noise and chaos of the surrounding conversations, I went to Mother's study - where I felt safe.

As I went to knock on the door, it cracked open before my hand could make contact. A strange sensation washed over me, so I pushed the door open against my instincts. The study was orderly, and the fireplace had a faint crackling that needed tending to. I added another log to keep it going.

A faint noise drifted from Mother's garden. My curiosity was piqued, and I slowed my pace to approach the window. I could hear passionate moans and giggles coming from nearby, but as I listened closer, I realized I was mistaken about the location. The sounds were coming down the hallway and getting louder by the second.

Feeling like an intruder, I hid behind the couch just as Mother and His Grace burst into the room, entwined in each other's arms. My face flushed with embarrassment as I listened to their intimate whispers and clothing being ripped off. I covered my ears as they neared my hiding spot, wishing I had never come here.

But then they started talking about something unrelated to their lovemaking - how everyone in the village adores them and how their reign will bring prosperity.

Mother panted as His Grace's lips sucked and kissed her skin. Their giggles filled the room as I heard the rustling of Mother's skirts.

"They see you as their savior," she whispered, her lips against His Grace's skin.

They stumbled back onto the couch, which scooted along the stone floor and knocked me over. I caught myself from falling on my face and slowly turned to see Mother gripping the back of the couch, her eyes widening in surprise at my presence. She jumped up from His Grace's lap, scrambling to cover her exposed breasts.

"What are you doing here?" she exasperated, straightening her clothes and giving me a stern look.

As I stood up, I felt guilt wash over me. It was like being caught in my parents' room as a child, and I knew I had some explaining to do.

Their expressions shifted from shock to annoyance, and I couldn't bring myself to look them in the eye. I had ruined their intimate moment.

"Sorry, I panicked. I was looking for you," I stammered.

"Another time," His Grace said, leaning in to kiss Mother on the forehead before leaving the room.

“Please don’t leave on my account,” I implored, uneasy at my unfamiliar choice of words. But as I stood surrounded by luxury and formality, I felt transported to a different era.

I felt like I was losing my identity and becoming a part of this otherworldly realm.

"Your Grace, please," I pleaded, my voice trembling with urgency. "I will take my leave and speak with Mother tomorrow regarding Nellie."

I held my breath as the door creaked open, anticipating his departure. But he stopped and turned back to me with a curious expression.

“Nellie?” He asked, his voice laced with concern.

Mother's eyes narrowed at me, but I couldn't stop the words from tumbling out. "I've been worried about her mental health."

His gaze shifted between me and Mother, analyzing our reactions. She tried to hide any signs of deception, but I could tell she was struggling.

Without warning, he stepped forward and placed himself between us, studying our body language. We were standing far enough apart, and he made it challenging to exchange whispers or glances. It was clear that something was amiss.

What I have gathered this far from my perception is that His Grace was a man who needed to be in control and know everything about everyone. His gaze made me nervous, and the tension in the room was suffocating. I felt uncomfortable under his scrutiny, trying to avoid eye contact.

This brought me back to when my brother-in-law joked that I could never be a spy or hold a secret. I had a horrible poker face, and every time he gave me the same stern look His Grace was giving me now, I would crack under pressure.

"You are aware of her condition?" His Grace's voice cut through the silence. He scratched at his beard and shook his head disapprovingly. "Why?" His tone was harsh and accusing.

"Your Grace," Mother interjected, her voice sweet and comforting as she smiled at him. "Nellie needs a friend, and Liz has the experience and the right temperament for this."

But His Grace's eyes remained fixed on me, unimpressed by Mother's words. "Of all the psychiatrists and mental hospitals available, you think you can do better? Do you even understand what you're getting yourself into?" His condescending behavior didn't frighten me, but I was confused because I was missing something.

My mind was racing as I tried to figure out my next

move. Mother and Aldrich worked together, but His Grace remained unaware of their schemes.

Should I play along and continue to hide what I knew? Or should I risk exposing everything and betray Mother?

My head shook in confusion as I struggled with the conflicting thoughts. It was a delicate balance between loyalty and self-preservation.

"And do you have any qualifications beyond being a teacher? I don't recall seeing those credentials on your file." His Grace's voice dripped with sarcasm.

My anger burned bright, fueled by every word that escaped his lips.

"It's common sense that nobody in their right mind should be subjected to this cold, dark, and degrading environment. To treat anyone like an animal is despicable." My voice rose with each syllable, laced with a fiery passion.

He let out a derisive snort and sucked in air through gritted teeth, unimpressed by my words. "A teacher and a psychiatrist. How intriguing."

Mother stepped between us, her hands held up in a futile attempt to calm the rising tension.

"We all know how difficult Nellie's arrival has been," she was careful with her words. "Liz is only trying to help." Her voice almost pleaded as she tried to diffuse a situation she saw stirring in him.

She reached out to touch his arm, but he recoiled and turned to face me instead. He got within a foot, and I saw the hesitation on his face, wanting to get closer and invade my personal space. I'm sure the memory of what I had been through flashed in his mind, and he kept his distance.

"This was your idea, wasn't it?" He accused, jabbing a finger in my direction. "You despise being here, reject our ways, yet suddenly you want to play savior?"

I clenched my jaw and remained silent, refusing to engage in his blatant provocation. Mother circled back around to stand next to him.

"No, your Grace. It was my idea," she said in a soft voice. But her words fell on deaf ears.

He whipped his head towards her with a ferocity that made me cringe. "Why?" His demand was sharp and cutting like a blade, ready to strike any moment.

"Because Liz needs a distraction, a way to reform Nellie," she was trying to make him understand. "With her background, patience, and understanding nature, I thought she would be a good fit."

He let out an exasperated sigh through his nose. It was unclear if he believed Mother or was annoyed by her persistence.

He scoffed, "with the trouble she has already caused among the Watchmen, I can't allow her to influence Nellie," he said with disdain.

As I listened to his words, anger bubbled up inside of me. My ears burned with heat, and my body trembled with rage.

"What you've done to her is wrong!" I yelled, unable to contain my anger. "Hunter tormented and almost raped me!" My voice felt unrecognizable as hostility fueled my words.

"I didn't ask for his hands to touch me or press me against a wall and force himself on me!" My hands were balled up into fists, my nails digging into the palms of my hands, feeling the warmth of blood. I didn't even feel the pain, my inner turmoil speaking through me.

His Grace's expression remained unreadable. His hand reached for the doorknob as if ready to escape my wrath. I could see confusion in his eyes, trying to piece together the bits of information he had been given.

But did he know everything? Did Mother and Aldrich

keep him in the dark, or was he an expert at hiding his emotions behind a stoic facade?

With one final look at Mother, he spun on his heels and stormed out of the room, the door slamming shut behind him. Silence engulfed me as I stood, and I felt even more trapped.

GARDEN WALK

I could feel Wallace's gaze as he escorted me back to the women's tower at Mother's request. My mind was buzzing with the intense conversation I had just had with His Grace, and I needed some time alone to process it all.

The frustration and powerlessness I felt during that meeting were still swirling inside me, threatening to consume me. It wasn't who I wanted to be, but in that moment, it was all I could feel - a mixture of hate and anxiety.

Wallace slowed his pace as we passed by fewer and fewer people. He turned to me with a concerned look.

"Liz, can we talk?" He seemed a bit shy and relieved when I didn't dismiss him.

My heart sank, and a lump formed in my throat because I was not ready to discuss or explain how I felt. But before I could answer, he spoke up again, his voice sincere and tender.

"I know things have been tough for you, but please know

you have friends here. I consider you my friend, and maybe one day..." His words hung in the air, unfinished.

He reached out and grazed my hand; he was testing his boundaries with me; as his fingers grazed over again to lift to his mouth to kiss it, I pulled away.

"Wallace, I can't do this," I spun on my heel and marched towards the women's tower, trying to distance myself from the awkward moment.

Behind me, I could hear him cursing under his breath, being at odds with his actions. Part of me wanted to turn around and face him, but that meant I had to explain myself, which I was not in the mood for.

"Do you not want me to fight for you?" he called out after me.

I stopped abruptly and spun around, almost causing him to run into me. I struggled to understand what he meant.

"What are you talking about?"

"At the ceremony," he rushed his words. "As a Watchman, I get to choose-"

"That's enough, Wallace," His Grace's voice cut through the night from behind us. "I'll take over from here. You may return to your post."

The dark figure of His Grace emerged from the shadows of the hill, a silent and imposing presence that made my heart race.

Wallace, with only a nod of agreement, retreated in the direction we had come from. His Grace's calm demeanor confused me, as it was a stark contrast to our recent intense disagreement.

As we made our way down the gravel path, passing by wary Watchmen, it became clear that this detour was strategic rather than random. We arrived at a small, secluded garden where potential eavesdroppers could not hear us.

His Grace's hands were clasped behind his back as he

matched my pace, "I owe you an apology," he began, his voice gentle. "I wasn't myself - too much drink, too many temptations."

I was taken aback by his sincerity and struggled to find the right words to respond.

Before I could even utter a reply, he continued. "I'm ashamed at how I acted - arrogant and impulsive. I underestimated you and your abilities."

He stopped before a patch of baby's breath and plucked one, extending it towards me. "Please accept this as a token of my remorse."

I was hesitant to take the flower, still unsure how to process this change in his behavior.

"I must confess, I refuse to see flaws in my plan," he resumed as we continued to stroll. "But now I realize I didn't properly prepare for someone like you - someone who couldn't adapt as easily as others. And for that, I apologize."

"Be careful, Liz," Despite Brant's warning ringing in my mind, I couldn't shake the feeling of his absence.

It felt like he was right behind me, his presence familiar and comforting. But I couldn't turn around and face the reality that he wasn't there. A bittersweet smile tugged at my lips as I longed for his protection, even though he was just a figment of my imagination.

His Grace chuckled, pointing towards my face. "I see I can make you smile." He softened his tone. "I want us to work together, Liz. I know you want to return home-"

"But it won't happen," I finished for him, understanding his true intentions.

His Grace nodded with a sly grin, his eyes sparkling in the moonlight.

"You're catching on fast," he murmured, his voice low and smooth like velvet.

We arrived at the garden's center, the air thick with the

scent of flowers and the soft glow of moonlight. His Grace paused, closing his eyes and taking a deep breath as if savoring the moment.

"If I were to send you home, what about the next disgruntled person?" His tone was filled with tension. His heavy steps led us through the backside of the garden, his mind consumed with worry. "And what about the person after that? It will only be thrown back in my face."

The moon cast a gentle light over us, highlighting the lines of concern on his face. "There is too much risk. Everything I have worked for would be pointless if I sent you back." His words were coated with frustration and desperation.

"I'm trying to make peace with never going home," my words caught in my throat.

His Grace's eyes narrowed, and he seemed to see my struggle for the first time. "I see how other women look at you," he mused, sympathy softening his tone. "They admire your courage as you try to adapt to this place." He paused, studying me before asking, "What can I do to help ease your transition?"

I took a deep breath, knowing that this was my chance to regain some control over my fate.

"I was told the Watchmen choose their brides, "my tone even as we walked side by side. "Could I choose not to participate in the nuptial ceremony?"

I knew my question was far-fetched. I continued, not wanting him to lose interest. "I could be a nun or something along those lines that meant I chose to be celibate."

My words struck a chord with him for a second. He took a deep breath through his nose and lifted his head in consideration.

But just as the idea appeared, the look of contemplation vanished from his face, and he shook his head. "Again, if I make an exception for you, others will follow and ask for the same."

As we walked, I couldn't shake off the thought that this is what it must have felt like for women in centuries past. It made me grateful for my time when women had more choices and opportunities. Yet, I felt unfortunate for those not afforded the same luxuries.

Coming from a family of strong, educated women who made their way in life, the idea of being forced into submission and having no control over one's destiny was unfathomable to me. It left me feeling conflicted and unsettled.

The weight of my situation was bearing a heavy burden each day that I had no control over.

"But Hunter told me the Watchmen get to choose who they want," I said, shaking off the dark conversation.

Then, I remembered Wallace's words and him asking if I would want him to fight for me. Had I missed an opportunity? "I won't marry that man," I continued, "I refuse to be trapped with a man like him. Any woman married to him will suffer."

We arrived near the tower, His Grace slowing his pace. He listened intently. I could see the wheels spinning as he took in our conversation.

"In time, you will understand what all of this means. I appreciate your honesty. Things will work out as they should, and I need you to trust me."

The word trust echoed in my mind, a constant reminder of the expectations placed on me. Everyone seemed to want to trust me, but I couldn't help feeling like I was the one being shortchanged.

His Grace nodded and bid me a good evening. I curtsied in return and excused myself, eager to retire to my chambers for the night.

The other women in the room gathered around the

warmth of the fireplace and fell silent as I entered. Their questioning and pitying gazes followed me as I crossed the room.

"Are you doing alright, Liz?" someone asked, breaking the heavy silence.

I forced my lips to stretch to a polite smile and nodded, not wanting to reveal the actual turmoil that still plagued me from my brutal attack.

With a polite farewell, I climbed the stairs to my room. As I rounded the corner, I heard laughter and chatter resume behind me.

It was clear that it would be some time before they felt comfortable enough to include me in their company again.

BRANT

As Brant's mother meticulously packed the boys' suitcases, he felt uneasy. He watched her with a heavy heart, knowing that she was trying to fill the void left by Liz's absence.

His mind was in turmoil as he remembered how Liz used to fold their clothes with such effortless carelessness.

But his mother criticized her methods under her breath, claiming they were sloppy. He wanted to defend Liz but couldn't bring himself to do it.

The thought of spending the Fourth of July without his beloved wife at his parent's summer cabin in Lake Tahoe weighed heavy on his heart. He knew his mother was right. He should let the police handle the search for Liz.

But he couldn't relinquish the hope that she would return to him and their boys. Despite his mother's pleas for him to move on and explain the situation to the boys, Brant couldn't face the reality that his wife may never return. It tore him apart, but he couldn't give up on her yet.

Their morning had been consumed by constant bickering over how to tell the boys about his absence for the summer.

Despite Brant having packed a suitcase, she couldn't help but frantically gather more of the boys' belongings.

His mother added fuel to the fire, criticizing Liz's house-keeping skills and insisting on bringing unnecessary items for the boys.

He could feel his frustration building as he watched his mother meddle in their affairs, disregarding Liz's efforts to maintain a neat household. He knew his mother never approved of Liz, but now her actions pushed him to his breaking point.

"Why are you doing that?" he snapped, marching over and ripping a tiny shirt with a dinosaur print out of her hands.

Eden rolled her eyes and huffed, "You didn't pack enough. They are two rowdy boys. They will rip and tear their clothes."

She was unprepared to handle her son's outbursts. She wasn't fond of Liz because she felt that Brant hadn't had enough time to grieve after his first wife's sudden death in a car accident.

When Brant came home with Liz not even a year later and said they were engaged, she kindly discussed taking time and didn't want them to rush into things.

She was aware her son was handsome and vulnerable, but in Liz, she only saw a woman who latched on because he was a catch with kids.

When Brant brought Liz to the family home, he clarified that he wanted no more children. It seemed a perfect arrangement for them because Liz couldn't have children. That was until that engagement ring slipped on her finger, and what seemed out of nowhere, Liz became obsessed with having a child.

She was willing to spend all their money on expensive doctors promising miracles, even if it drove them into poverty.

At first, Brant had considered borrowing money from his parents to appease Liz's desire for a child. Still, then, his parents had a long discussion with him about the ethical implications of bringing an unwanted child into the world and how he should stand his ground.

Eden always felt she could see through Liz's ulterior motives. It was obvious to her that Liz had always been after Brant's family name and fortune in northern California.

As time passed, Eden knew deep down that once Liz realized she couldn't get what she wanted, she would like out of the relationship.

It was about protecting the family name and business. Even when Liz swept her son off his feet, she remembered how the Seattle Police had suggested that Liz may have run away and started a new life. In her heart, Eden always suspected Liz could make such a dramatic exit to get what she wanted.

Brant folded Steven's shirt with care, mimicking how Liz had it. He was trying to control his emotions.

"Fine." Eden tossed down the clothes, raised her hands, and gave up. "We're leaving in ten minutes." Her sandals smacked the bottom of her feet as she walked away.

Brant's cell phone pinged with a text notification, snatching his phone out of his pocket with hope and desperation for some new information from Detective Knight.

But as usual, there were no leads or evidence to go on. Despite this, the detective always answered his calls and replied to his messages, giving him a glimmer of comfort in these dark times.

DETECTIVE KNIGHT:

I'm sorry, but I have nothing new. I have some footage turned over from the gas station across the street, but it glitches at the time frame and doesn't show anything. How are you doing?

BRANT:

Mom is taking the kids to Tahoe for the 4th. I'm thinking of coming back up and trying to help.

DETECTIVE KNIGHT:

Can you afford that? I know you mentioned the other night that money was tight.

BRANT:

Julian is helping. I'm doing what I can. I just took out a HELOC from my house.

DETECTIVE KNIGHT:

Wish I had more information to give you.

"PUT THAT DAMN PHONE DOWN!" Eden snapped at her son, breaking through his thoughts and frustrations. "I'm sick and tired of you being glued to that thing."

His jaw clenched, and in his grip, he squeezed the phone in his hand. How could she not understand? She knew he had to be available if anyone had any information about Liz.

"Why are you being like this?" he asked through gritted teeth.

Eden stood with her arms crossed, her son's defensive

stance mirroring hers. Her thick, mauve lipgloss held back the words she longed to say.

Brant reached his breaking point. Frustrated by his mother's constant manipulation, he stormed out of the room, leaving Eden alone with her thoughts.

"Brant, please," Eden pleaded, following him out of the room.

She bit down on her lip, struggling to hold back the emotions that threatened to spill out. She couldn't risk saying something hurtful and damaging their already fragile relationship. It was a tug-of-war between keeping up appearances and being honest with those she loved most.

Julian's voice rang out, and the boys' raised and excited voices rang out as they dropped their bikes in the front yard to greet their uncle.

Seeing Julian outside with the boys was a sweet relief. She was happy to see how he had been dropping everything to help her son in his desperate need, even though he was Liz's brother-in-law.

Julian was an FBI agent with the government, knew people, and had connections. She was hoping that out of everyone, Julian would be the one to set her son straight and get him to accept that Liz had left him and the boys.

Then again, she wouldn't put it past her that, because of his connections, Liz was playing cat-and-mouse and hiding out somewhere.

She was hoping to speak with them before they left for Lake Tahoe. She needed Julian to make Brant see that everything that could be done had been done. She excused herself from Brant, reminding him to finish packing and that she'd be waiting outside.

Julian's smile strained as he greeted Eden out in the yard. He couldn't help but notice her stern face and arms swaying in his direction, revealed by the slight downturn of her lips.

The botox in her face only gave her one look these days. To him, she always appeared disappointed, no matter what the occasion.

"Boys." She addressed her grandkids with a warm grandmother smile. "I need to speak to your uncle. Go in and help Pop in the motorhome."

No one ever had to tell the boys twice. They were always eager to help anyone with anything. Eden made sure she and Julian were at the motorhome's rear so she could talk with him.

Warren swung open the creaky RV door, his face lighting up as he welcomed the boys inside. "Hey there, my little campers! Come on in and pick out your bunk beds."

Eden closed the compartment's side door, ensuring it did not break her new manicured acrylic nails. "This is the last trip I will endure. Brant needs to face the truth," her voice dripping with frustration.

Julian's confusion was evident as he asked, "Eden, she's your daughter-in-law."

Eden crossed her arms and jutted out one hip in an insufferable attitude.

Julian needed to let this situation roll off his shoulders. He felt sorry for Brant and his father, who had to deal with a woman like her.

"Look, I've heard the wild stories of the doppelganger," Eden began, "the bathroom that is not permitted, Detective Knight withholding information, and blah...blah..blah..." Eden's eyes sparkled with vindication as she leaned in, her voice low and filled with venom.

"I know she's your sister-in-law, but I have friends with connections, too." She said with a cocky determination. "That woman was always after my son's money, not his love. Now that she can't get what she wants, she's throwing a tantrum like a spoiled child."

Eden's words hurt, and Julian now became suspicious. Over the years, he heard from Liz that Eden was a hard woman to please and always praised Brant's first wife.

Liz always felt like she could never compare, and she tried many times, but Eden kept her at arm's length.

The hairs pricked on his neck as she smirked and claimed she had connections. He couldn't shake off the suspicion that there was more to her than met the eye.

He made a mental note to dig into Eden's past, searching for possible links to her mysterious connections. As he opened his mouth to question her further, he caught a glimpse of his two mischievous nephews making silly faces in the rear window of the R.V.

He hesitated, knowing that any further interrogation would delay their trip to Seattle. After all, it was just a hunch, and he didn't want to risk ruining the family vacation. But he promised himself to do some research on Eden's connections once they returned home.

They could even make a pit stop in Reno and visit Eden, Warren, and the boys at their lake house.

Without missing a beat, Eden continued, "Oh, I know exactly where she is. She's hiding out. You and her sister are probably in cahoots with this whole damn plan. Liz is waiting for the perfect moment to come back and claim what she thinks is hers."

Julian couldn't take it anymore. He turned away from Eden and stormed into the house, determined to help his brother-in-law through this challenging time. He didn't want to hear any more of Eden's hateful theories about their family.

Now, all he could think about was looking into Eden's past and seeing if there was a connection to Liz's disappearance.

WISHFUL NIGHTS

As the days grew hotter, the midnight sky felt shorter, its deep blue fading into a hazy purple before giving way to the blazing orange of the sunrise.

I lay in bed, with my window facing East, anticipating when sunlight would burst through and envelope me in its warmth, signaling the start of another sweltering day.

My skin was already slick with sweat; I swiped at it with the back of my hand as I stepped out onto the cool grass, knowing that by midday, it would be scorching hot and my feet would burn if I dared to walk barefoot.

The sky was filled with sparse and wispy clouds, unable to provide much relief from the scorching sun's heat. The clouds did one of two things: glide over the sun, giving a few seconds of reprieve. Or linger above the piercing ball of heat and drift by.

It was a joke among us that when this happened, we were denied from the relentless rays. Despite summer now, I wish I had known when we arrived here. Was it now the beginning of June or mid-July? The days blended in a blur, and time had become meaningless to everyone else.

I kept track of the days on a makeshift calendar written on parchment, but even that was starting to blur together. How long had it taken us to get here? A week? Maybe almost two?

All I knew was that the sun beat down relentlessly on us, causing us to sweat and making the sour stench of body odor almost unbearable.

Living off the land meant using natural ingredients for everything, and I desperately missed antiperspirant deodorant.

Despite the scorching heat wave that enveloped the land, the castle's stonewalls stood firm and provided a calm oasis within its confines. The air was crisp and clean, a welcome relief from the oppressive heat outside.

However, this also meant we had to wear long sleeves at all times, shielding our skin from the sun's harsh rays. Angela's talented hands made our clothes light and airy, a blessing in this dry climate.

Yet even with these measures, we couldn't escape the relentless thirst that consumed us daily. We often trek to the nearby stream to fill buckets with refreshing water to quench our dry throats.

A warm glow spread across the land as the days passed and the sun descended behind the towering West mountain. I always called these evenings "Sherbert" because the sky turned a delicate shade of orange and pink, like the ice cream I used to buy for the boys as a treat after a long, hot summer day.

The vibrant colors lingered in the sky, painting the mountains with shades of gold and apricot until fading into a dreamy hue of cotton candy as night settled in.

The remaining rays of sunlight clung to the edges of the

horizon before disappearing into darkness, signaling the end of another beautiful day.

When a cool breeze swept in like a sweet escape from the day's scorching heat, my skin tingled with relief as I welcomed the refreshing sensation. Around me, my fellow weary villagers let out sighs of gratitude and flashed thankful smiles, grateful for the respite brought by the setting sun. It was as if nature understood our struggles and gave us a moment of reprieve before another day began.

Coming from a warm desert climate with constant smog and humidity, living in this mountain range was a new experience. The air was crisp and refreshing but also very dry.

Luckily, we had aloe vera plants to help soothe our skin and rose oil to add moisture. These small luxuries made all the difference in our daily lives.

I spent most of my time working in the medical building, crushing herbs and blending ingredients under Doctor Ferrarius' guidance. When he didn't need me, I would head to the sewing building, where Angela would have me cutting fabric while filling me in on the latest gossip. Despite keeping to myself, I couldn't help but feel like this place and its people were becoming a part of me.

Sitting on the bench in the garden outside the dining hall, I felt tranquility. A few Watchmen stood on guard nearby, providing a sense of safety. From this spot, facing North, I could catch a glimpse of Zak and give him a friendly wave. It had been days since I last saw him, and Hunter remained in the locker.

The night sky was clear and filled with stars, more than I had ever seen. Each time a shooting star streaked across the sky, I made a wish for Brant and the boys to be safe and happy. As I stared up at the half-moon, lost in thought, footsteps approached from behind me.

Amara plopped beside me, her long, chestnut hair tied

halfway back and cascading over her shoulders, growing like a weed as her roots showed, like all of us women who missed the salon. She held a bowl of plump, deep purple grapes in her hands.

A wave of relief washed over me as I returned her smile and my attention to the peaceful night sky above us.

"I'm sorry," I apologized, "I was lost in thought."

Amara shrugged, "I could tell. I called your name a few times." She offered me a handful of plump green grapes. "So, we'll have a new roommate." Her weary eyes flicked towards me. "Are you sure you can handle this?"

I had almost forgotten about Nellie. Rumors had been circulating that she had been with Mother for the past few days, learning to transition from being kept in the locker. As much as I dreaded caring for her, what else was I supposed to do to pass the time?

I popped one of the crisp grapes into my mouth, savoring its sweetness as my teeth broke through the tough skin. The crisp and refreshing taste was what I needed on this warm summer night.

Mother strolled down the corridor as if fate tempted with time, with Johanna by her side. Nellie followed behind, her head down and long blonde hair covering her face.

"There goes trouble," Amara commented as we watched them round the corner.

"I think she's trying," I countered.

Amara tilted her head. "No, she's just laying dormant, waiting for the right time to unleash her chaos." She plucked a dandelion from the grass and fiddled with its petals. “Enjoy the peace while you can,” she said with a hint of concern. "Rey told me that His Grace will make the announcement this Sunday," she tossed aside the wilted flower bud.

"Rey? Is that what you call him now?" I couldn't help but tease her. They must have grown closer than I realized.

Amara blushed and gave me a playful shove. "Okay, okay, I need to be careful about my name for him."

"How serious is it between you two?" I had my suspicions about their closeness, but now, nicknames?

Her smile grew wider as she talked about Reynard. She bit her lip in that shy, lovesick way only a young teenager would.

"It hasn't been long, but he just knows how to make me happy."

I knew Amara well enough to know that this was new territory for her. She deserved someone like Reynard, who made her light up with joy.

"I'm happy for you," I formed a smile. I was genuinely happy for her.

"I hope His Grace sees how we feel about each other, " Amara's hands were restless. "Reynard says the Watchmen get to choose their wives, but I can't help but worry."

"I feel everything will work out for you two," I remarked.

A shooting star streaked across the sky as we sat on the bench. Amara gasped and grabbed my hand, urging me to make a wish.

"Did you make one?" Her body perked at the sight.

"Of course," I did, but my superstitious brain made me keep it to myself. Wishing that Zak was close to finding a way for me to escape was something I couldn't share with everyone, not even Amara.

AT BREAKFAST the following day, Mother approached me with a nervous energy that set me on edge. She beckoned me to follow her to her study, her long white hair cascading over one shoulder like a waterfall of silk. Her dress, a vibrant yellow velvet adorned with cream-colored ribbons, glided as I trailed behind. The same ribbons were woven into her hair, adding an elegant touch to her appearance.

A pang of jealousy crept over me as I compared our outfits - my simple dress was no match for her extravagant attire.

She shut the door behind us as we entered the room, creating a sense of privacy and importance.

"Please, sit," she gestured towards one of the plush couches, her movements restless and fidgety.

Before sitting across from her, I couldn't help but smooth out the wrinkles in my dark skirts from my morning duties in the stables.

Something was weighing heavy on Mother's mind as she struggled to maintain a smile. The tension in the room was palpable, and it was evident that she struggled to get out the words to finish her sentence.

"The pairing is starting this Sunday," she muttered, her words heavy with significance. "I have removed Yasmin and Esther from your room, and Nellie is moving in as we speak." The gravity of her words hung between us, filling the silence with anxious anticipation.

She couldn't leave it at that; she had to keep going. "Hunter has been released," her hand resting on her chest as if trying to calm her racing heart. "I'm sorry." She softly uttered.

I was speechless, my mind reeling with questions. But for the moment, I could only sit there in shock and try to make sense of everything. I feel a sinking feeling in my stomach from her words.

My body was in turmoil, my temperature rising as I sat frozen. My heart was pounding so hard it felt like it would burst out of my chest. I wanted to escape, but I couldn't move. Mother's lips were moving, but the chaotic thoughts in my head drowned out her voice. Would I pass out? Should I stay, or should I run? The conflicting emotions inside me only added to the confusion and fear.

I managed somehow to get to my feet. Mother followed suit and was still trying to apologize. "His Grace has a plan. Something that we should--"

"I no longer trust your plans," I interrupted, my chest heavy with anger and frustration. "Why would he do this and not warn me?"

"You'll be closely watched," Mother answered, taking a step toward me. "Hunter is aware of the consequences if he approaches you."

"What about the twins?" I asked, my voice shaking. "Why would you move them?"

"Liz, I'm asking you to trust us." Her hands went on my shoulders to help calm me. Her big brown eyes looked into mine. "I know it's a lot to ask. His Grace believes he found a way around this."

I felt foolish for thinking that Hunter could stay hidden in the locker forever. I should have known that he would eventually have to come out, but I couldn't help wishing there was a way to make him disappear. The realization that I was an outsider in this situation hit me hard, and it seemed like they didn't trust me as much as I counted on them—which wasn't saying much.

A knock on the door caught our attention. Marshall opened it, revealing Hunter standing on the other side with piercing ice-blue eyes. Despite the summer heat, his gaze sent shivers down my spine, making me feel like a snow-storm was brewing within these castle walls.

His appearance was still disheveled and unwashed. He had worn the same clothes since the day he attacked me, now covered in dirt and hay.

His hair was matted and greasy, his skin paler than usual, and he had dark circles under his eyes. The stench emanating from him was almost suffocating.

"His Grace instructed me to bring him here first," Marshall also addressed me. "Liz, he wants you to see Hunter too. I'm relieved you're both present," he pushed Hunter forward, the sound of chains rattling around his wrists and ankles echoing in the room, reminding me he was still confined and couldn't attack.

Hunter looked like he had something difficult to say. His voice rasped and strained as he took two steps into the room, never breaking eye contact with me.

"I owe you an apology," his direct tone tried to convey pain and remorse. He was trying, but I had no sympathy for him.

Marshall entered the room, grabbed Hunter by the arm, and spun him around. My gasp was involuntary as I took in Hunter's back - covered in lashings and dried blood. His shirt hung from his body in tatters, clinging to his skin like a second layer. I didn't know what to say or do, but a part of me couldn't help feeling satisfied seeing him suffer from the consequences of his actions.

Hunter broke free from Marshall's grasp and turned to address Mother and me. "I understand now that what I did was wrong," he began, "and I am constantly reminded as I heal from my injuries." Though his words held weight, there was still an underlying tension between us that couldn't be ignored.

Mother's words cut through me like a knife, pulling me out of my thoughts. "You've said enough," her words cut through the tension.

I could feel his eyes burning into me as he stood next to Marshall. Hunter’s smirk directed at me as they left the room, sending me waves of anger and hatred. For once, I didn't cower in fear. Instead, I stood my ground, ready to face whatever twisted fate awaited me.

NEW ROOMMATE

Amara's intense gaze was like the look my parents gave me when I was a child when I shared bad news with them. It was a look of disapproval, asking why I hadn't thought things through before acting. She wasn't pleased with our new roommate and the sudden change, especially since the twins had already left.

She thought the best thing was to change her work schedule so she wouldn't have to see or deal with Nellie. She didn't appreciate my attempts to convince her that we could make things easier for Nellie.

"You're on your own," she scoffed at me as I stood there, dreading the thought of welcoming Nellie into our living quarters.

I stood outside my room, hesitant to press down on the latch. I already dreaded Nellie's presence because I couldn't believe what I had gotten myself into. Just as I was about to press my thumb down, a sudden reminder of Brant's presence hit me as he cleared his throat behind me.

"Are you sure about this?" His question mirrored my doubts.

As I turned to face Brant, memories of our past flooded back. Seeing him in his UCLA windbreaker and blue jeans made my heart ache. His white shirt still had a small mustard stain from the last time we ate together before we walked into the Chihuly Gardens.

I couldn't help but smile at the familiar yet painful sight. "No, but what else can I do?" I asked, trying to suppress my conflicting feelings.

Brant took a deep breath and leaned against the railing, hands in his pockets. His sympathetic gaze and soft puppy dog eyes added to my inner turmoil.

"You take on too much, you know that," he reminded me. You always need to fix someone when you should be fixing your problems." He crossed his arms.

As he spoke, I could feel my argument crumbling. He made a valid point, meaning I should follow the voice of reason in my head. But how could I fix what was broken in my life without prioritizing others' happiness over mine? It was my nature to prioritize their happiness over mine. Was that the right thing to do, or just another form of self-sabotage?

As I opened the door to my room, Mother stood in the center, watching Nellie make her bed on the bottom bunk where Esther used to sleep.

Nellie's head tilted in confusion as she struggled to remember who I was. After a moment, she exclaimed, "Oh, you must be Liz!" There was a glimmer of recognition in her voice. "The one Hunter fancies." Her tone was playful, enjoying my immediate displeasure.

As soon as the words left her lips, my heart sank. Nellie had wasted no time starting her games; it hadn't even been thirty seconds since I arrived.

Bitch!

My hands itched to clench into tight fists, but I

suppressed the urge and forced myself to remain calm. Mother scolded Nellie for her rude behavior, but she only smirked and made a snide comment about Hunter mentioning my name when they were in the locker.

As much as I wanted to lash out at her, I reminded myself of why I had taken on the task of helping her. But deep down, I couldn't shake off the feeling that Mother and His Grace had their hidden agenda for Nellie - one that I was not privy to.

Nellie's reintegration into the village was a tricky task and another obstacle for me to overcome. Before entering the room, I had to clear my mind and set aside my issues, just like I was advising myself in Brant's vice. I pushed my struggles to the side to assist her.

AS I escorted Nellie toward the bustling dining hall, all eyes turned toward her. Her expression of wide-eyed wonder reminded me of a student on a field trip to a museum. She often stopped to take in the scenery and to take a deep breath, picking wildflowers and admiring stained glass windows.

It reminded me of my past experiences leading field trips with my students, where I would allow them to explore and wonder at their own pace, never stopping.

"Nellie, are you hungry? We have a limited time for lunch," I reminded her.

"But I didn't get to explore the grounds fully," she replied, holding a handful of dandelions to her nose to inhale their scent. "It feels amazing to be free." With a contagious smile, she tossed the flowers into the air and skipped along, taking everything around her with childlike curiosity."

We made our way through the food line. Nellie piled her plate with chicken, carrots, asparagus, and bread as she had never seen such a bounty. We sat at our usual table, where the twins were already waiting for us.

"I'm Nellie," she said, extending her hand to shake theirs.

"We know," Yasmin said matter-of-factly. "You were the one who pulled my hair on our first night here."

Nellie's cheeks turned pink with embarrassment. "I wasn't feeling well that night. I hadn't taken my medication."

"Medication for what?" Esther's eyes grew big as she took a bite of her apple.

"Oh, just schizophrenia, anxiety, body dysmorphia, cancer, and depression," Nellie rattled off.

The table fell silent as everyone processed this information. Nellie continued eating her chicken dumplings, moaning with each bite and exclaiming how amazing they were. Some women blushed at the sounds, while others tried not to give her attention.

When she went to get up and thank the chef, I touched her arm to remind her that we weren't allowed in the kitchen during meal times.

She sat back down, juices from the chicken dripping down her chin. As she wiped it away with the back of her hand, I felt Amara's eyes on me from across the table.

GREENHOUSE WHISPERS

The following day, Nellie and I went to the women's showers. Amara was already at the medical building. She didn't speak to Nellie; when she did, she gave short answers, which didn't phase her.

"She'll come around." Nellie is light on her feet, like a ballerina.

As we passed other women, they would stop and introduce themselves to Nellie, but she barely took notice or seemed uninterested. She seemed to absorb our energy and adapt, almost like a chameleon. I observed her, noting her behavior. In the presence of others, she seemed to become more reserved, as if being the focus of attention made her anxious.

I showed Nellie the designated spot for her dirty laundry and then guided her to the communal showers. She seemed amused at showering with a group of strangers without hesitation. We both undressed and walked into the open room, feeling the warmth of the heated floors against our bare feet. We could see other women entering or leaving as steam filled the room. I noticed Nellie covering her breasts with one hand and the other covering her crotch. I could empathize with her discomfort; my first time showering in a group setting was also nerve-wracking.

I lathered my hair with tea tree oil. The minty smell relaxed my senses as the cascading jets from the shower head massaged the muscles on my shoulders. I pointed to dispensers that worked. I made sure not to touch her; the intolerable gaze against the warm water seemed daunting as she had to clean herself.

I was still learning about her triggers and didn't want to make her feel uncomfortable. In my child development courses, I knew about personal space and how everyone has different boundaries, so I respected hers and kept my distance during the shower. Despite feeling exhausted and dirty, I breathed relief as the warm water washed away the day's stress.

We may have come in like cattle, but we were just two women seeking comfort and cleanliness. A sense of relief washed over me as the warm water cascaded down my body. Closing my eyes, I took a deep breath and allowed myself to be in this moment. The sound of the rushing water drowned out the chaos of the outside world.

IN THE vanity room, I preferred to let my damp hair rest on my shoulders while I pressed and squeezed the towel to remove excess water.

Nellie had her long blonde locks wrapped in a turban style. As she applied rose oil to her skin, I couldn't help but notice the thin, faint scars on her arms and legs. They seemed to blend in with her skin now, but I knew they were the remnants of her past struggles.

I first learned about cutting in high school, where some kids talked about it as a way to deal with emotional pain and escape from their troubles. When Nellie caught me glancing at her scars, feeling awkward, I stood up to focus elsewhere.

"You can ask," Nellie pumped lotion into her hands. "I don't mind."

I shook my head, feeling overwhelmed. "We must find out what Mother has in store for us," I said.

I left the room, knowing I needed to change into something fresh and clean. I couldn't quite explain my reluctance to know everything; it was almost as if part of me already knew that I would be faced with a convoluted tale or a lengthy story that I didn't have the energy to process.

AS WE WALK towards the kitchen and turn the corner into the dining hall, an irresistible scent of baked bread hits our noses simultaneously.

Nellie's stomach grumbled, "I'm already hungry." She patted her stomach. "Oh, I need to thank the chef."

Taking off on her feet, I found myself calling after Nellie and jogging to keep up with her pace. Reaching the back of the kitchen, nothing blocked her determination to find Maestro Roberto and thank him.

In the back, he grabbed a tray full of hot rolls from the stone fireplace. Nellie caught a roll to toss it around as it cooled. She couldn't help but exaggerate how much she enjoyed the meal. The wrinkles around Meastro's eyes crinkled as he blushed at her compliments.

"Could you do me a favor?" he asked with a smile, handing her a parchment list. "I need some fresh herbs for tonight's dinner."

Nellie's face lit up with excitement at the chance to help. She practically skipped out of the room like a child eager to please. I followed behind, carrying a basket for our herb-collecting adventure.

As we strolled toward the greenhouse, Nellie held her hands behind her back and took in the scenery around us. Her posture was graceful and elegant, like that of a ballet dancer. The sun peeked through the clouds and illuminated her face, creating an ethereal glow around her.

She paused and closed her eyes, inhaling as if taking in all the freshness and warmth of the sun's rays. Watching her bask in this simple pleasure, I couldn't help but feel happy for her. It must have been so long since she had experienced something fundamental yet beautiful.

"I desperately need my vitamin D," she chuckled, shielding her eyes with one hand as she gazed up at the sun. She scanned the grounds. "I'm just trying to keep up appearances," she said with a forced smile.

There she was.

I could see right through her facade. She took a few steps closer, suspicion evident in her eyes.

"Do you trust them?" Her eyes narrowed on me.

Angela approached us, holding a bundle of woven silk. Nellie's demeanor changed, and she became shy once again. She played a sweet and innocent victim, ready to share how terrible it was to be in the locker and gain sympathy from anyone who would listen.

Angela showed us the soft, delicate, cream-colored bundle. Nellie's fingers trailed over it, tracing the fabric's top with delicate care. Admiration shone in her eyes, but she was distracted by talking about the feel of the bundle and how long the process of weaving the skeins took.

"I'll need more hands to help with the cleaning and stoving the cacoons," Angela remarked.

"That sounds wonderful," Nellie said, her eyes widened with delight. I'd love to know how this whole process works."

My eyes met Zak's in the distance, from behind Angela, and he gestured toward the back of the sewing house.

"I can show you where we keep the Mulberry trees and silkworms in the greenhouse," Angela said. Full of excitement, Nellie bounced up and down, asking permission to come along.

"I'll gather the herbs," I said quickly. I seemed too eager to leave their presence.

As Nellie bounded off ahead, Angela paused and scanned the surroundings with a narrowed gaze.

"You don't mind being alone in the greenhouse?" Her eyes narrowed at me.

I shrugged my shoulders. "I'll catch up," I assured her. She glanced behind me one last time before following Nellie, her wariness evident.

Carefully timing until they were safe inside, I approached the sewing house on the right side. My eyes scanned the area, searching for any sign of Zak. The next moment, I felt a light touch on my shoulder, and I instinctively spun around with my basket, ready to strike.

Zak stepped back just in time to avoid being hit. "Whoa! Liz, it's me," he said, holding his hands up in surrender.

Feeling embarrassed and foolish, I lowered the basket. "I'm sorry," I mumbled. "I didn't mean to--"

"No need to apologize." He interrupted me. "I didn't want to startle you." His expression grew serious as he took a step closer to me. His gaze swept over our surroundings. "I might have found a way out of here," he whispered.

My heart swelled with hope and curiosity as Zak leaned in close and whispered his plan. His warm breath tickled my ear, and I caught a faint hint of mint on his breath.

"How?" My eyes grew as big as the grapes.

"The Eastside of the forest, past the moat, during dinner. Can you sneak out?" he replied, glancing around to ensure no one was listening.

I nodded, eager for the chance to escape this place. But then Zak's words hit me - it would only be me leaving.

"What about you?" I couldn't help but worry for him.

He tried to appear brave, but I saw a trace of sadness in his eyes. "Someone has to stay behind and lock the gate."

Disappointment washed over me. I had envisioned us leaving together, helping each other on our journey.

"I promised to return you to your husband and children," his gaze on me, seeing the sincerity and listening to his stubborn determination, did make me feel better. "This might be our only chance before the nuptial ceremony. I can't bear to watch you possibly marry..." He couldn't finish the sentence.

"Hunter." The name tasted bitter on my tongue. "If the plan doesn't work. I want you to know that if Hunter ends up being my chosen husband, I would rather take my own life." My voice shook with determination and fear.

Zak seemed disappointed in my choice, or I already had a plan if this escape didn't work. He stepped back, giving me space to process everything. We both knew how high the stakes were - escape or certain death.

I heard Nellie calling out for me as she rounded the corner. Always thinking on his feet, Zak handed me a pair of garden clippers.

"Here you go," he said, slapping the old rustic tool into my hand. "I knew Alex had another pair." He nodded towards Nellie before walking away.

Nellie walked over to me, her footsteps light and graceful. She already had herbs in her basket. As she watched Zak leave, she bit her bottom lip and dragged her teeth along it.

"That man is going to be my husband," she licked her lips, watching him leave.

CHECKERS

Corina appeared from the east side of the sewing house, where they wash and clean garments. She didn't waste time asking questions and handed me a stack of pressed clothes.

"Someone needs to take these to His Grace's chambers," she said matter-of-factly. Her Spanish accent was apparent through every other word.

The whisps of her thick, long, dark brown hair swirled in the wind as her hazel eyes were set on me to understand the determination in her tone.

I hesitated, not wanting to take on this task, but before I could protest, Corina gave me a wink when Nellie turned away to chase a butterfly. She wiped her brow with the back of her hand, baby hairs of her sweat-soaked brown hair pressed to the sides of her narrow face. "You should probably go," she suggested. "I've been asked to show Nellie around the laundry area," She added with a smile.

I was reluctant to accept the pressed garments from Corina's clammy hands, which smelled of fresh air and cotton. I was relieved to be rid of Nellie for the time being.

As I strolled through the vast grounds, across fields, and through castle corridors, I couldn't help but notice more Watchmen through my travels. I was reminded after hearing the electronic movements as the cameras up in the rafters made it seem like they were monitoring my every step.

Mother had promised me better protection now that Hunter was out, and this was the security measure that the castle needed. The Watchmen stood tall and vigilant, their gazes fixed above me rather than on me.

Each of them exuded a warrior-like aura, resembling the famous wrestlers Brant and the boys often watched on television. Their height, weight, and ethnicity varied, showing His Grace's inclusive approach to his algorithm.

My feet shuffled along the cold stone floor, my footsteps echoing through the castle corridors. I held His Grace's garments, grateful for this moment alone to collect my thoughts.

"What do you think he'll ask of you?" Brant appeared by my side, dressed in the Watchmen uniform.

I kept walking, not wanting to slow my pace or look at him.

"I'm not sure. Maybe he wants to check on me," my shoulders shrugged.

"Bull..." Brant smirked. "Just be careful. I'll be right beside you."

I stopped in my tracks, turning to face him.

"But you're not here," I said with a hint of sadness.

Brant opened his mouth to respond but closed it again, unsure what to say.

"Liz?" Wallace called out to me. He stood guard at the bottom of the staircase leading to His Grace's chambers.

His usual bright eyes were dull and full of sadness when they met mine. He was the type of man who wore his heart on his sleeve, and I could see that now.

During our last encounter, he asked if he should fight for me, but I couldn't give him a straightforward answer because I didn't want him to get the wrong idea. Wallace's eyebrows raised in recognition as I held up the crisp garments.

"I was told His Grace needed these," I explained.

"I know," he responded with a knowing nod. "He mentioned you might be coming up."

Wallace's gentle fingers grasped my elbow as I started to climb the staircase, stopping me in my tracks.

"If you want me to fight for you, Hunter doesn't stand a chance," he whispered, his touch lingering on my arm.

Taking a step back, I didn't want to give him false hope or expectations.

"I appreciate your concern, but I don't need anyone to fight for me. Besides, I'm already married," my voice firm.

"Liz, you don't understand," Wallace insisted, closing the distance between us. "There is no way out of this. This is your new life."

I should have been flattered that a handsome man with such a muscular build and rugged features would be interested in someone like me. I felt like the plain Jane in my story, not even giving myself the credit to be the cutesy girl next door.

If I didn't know any better, It felt like we were enacting a scene from a romantic movie, where the charming hero tried convincing the distressed damsel that she needed his assistance. But I didn't want or need his help.

Little did he know Zak and I already had a plan in place. And if that plan failed...I couldn't think about that. I had to stay positive and believe I would leave this situation by tomorrow.

"I can't give you what you want," I told him. My eyes turned away from him, and I continued to climb the spiral stairs.

My knuckles tapped on the sturdy wood door. His Grace opened it, and I curtsied and greeted him, offering his clothes in my arms.

"Here are your garments, your Grace." Speaking to him in such a formal manner made me feel foolish.

"Please, enter," he said, moving aside to let me pass.

As I entered the room, I felt like stepping back in time. The high peaked ceilings were decorated in an impressive and overwhelming mid-century medieval style.

The tapestry hanging from the walls depicted a replica of the castle. One also displayed a family coat of arms—a beautiful blue and white shield with three white stars across the top and three fleurs-de-lis in blue. A knighted helmet sat atop the shield, representing their noble status.

As I walked into the opulent bedroom, I was drawn to a large painting of a replica painting like the Renaissance-era, of His Grace, his proud stance with his hands on his hips, hung above the fireplace.

One teacher I worked with, Gary, an enormous history enthusiast for the medieval era, would have been fascinated to be in a room like this.

His Grace stood before me, wearing a fitted purple dress robe with the same crest embroidered on the lapel as the Watchmen's uniforms – two bears standing upright. His presence was regal as he addressed me, speaking in a smooth and refined voice.

I followed his instructions and placed the clothes on the giant chest at the end of his bed. I went to leave when I heard the door close, and a slight shiver of fear crept up on me.

His Grace asked me to sit across from him at the chess table next to the crackling fire. I paused, still wary of his intentions, but his gentle expression reassured me. Being so tense was silly of me; he only wanted to get to know me and show me kindness. I needed him to trust and believe in me if

I wanted to succeed. So, with a forced smile, I took my place across from him, ready to play my part.

"I'm not much of a chess player," I admitted as I walked over to sit across from him.

His Grace chuckled at my comment and suggested we play checkers instead. As we played, he asked me about my new roommate and how things were going between us.

"She's quite feisty," I said, trying to hide my nerves as I moved against him on the checkers board.

But His Grace continued to chuckle in response, focused on the board. As I made my next move, I purposely played carefree and without strategy because the game was not my primary concern; I wanted to get straight to the point.

"Did you arrange for me to deliver your clothes and inquire about Nellie?" My tone was gentle yet probing.

He paused before moving, placing the piece, and leaning back in his armchair. "Our discussions have been deep lately," he admitted. "I do not wish you to suffer any longer within these walls. What can I do to ease your transition?"

Mimicking his body language, I leaned back in my chair, my hands resting on my stomach. From his relaxed posture, he seemed interested in me enough to want to help me.

"What is troubling you?" he asked with genuine curiosity.

I knew I needed to give him something. I couldn't dismiss the conversation or make it difficult; that would attract more attention and eyes. If I had behaved and made this discussion easy, I might have gained more insight into this place, which might have worked to my advantage.

"I'm curious," I started. "What is this place about?"

The question brought a slight smile to his lips. "In time, you'll understand."

Darn it!

"Alright," I caved, not wanting to come off so brash. "Can we discuss the courting and the nuptials?"

His eyebrows raised in interest, and his fingers steepled together. "I'm afraid I must decline any further discussion on that subject," he waved off my question. "Doctor Ferrarius has shared your medical chart with me and told me how he can help." His eyes gleamed, and he was intent on directing this conversation.

I know it is physically impossible to feel your organs shift, but in that moment, I could have sworn my heart plummeted into my stomach. The sudden lack of blood rushing through my veins drained the color from my face and left me feeling cold and clammy.

Terror washed over me at the thought of undergoing corrective surgery in this place, sending electric shocks of fear pulsing through every nerve in my body. I felt like a balloon about to burst at the seams, ready to explode with anxiety and panic.

"Since our last conversation about the Watchmen having the first pick," I mused out loud, trying to avoid the topic of surgery altogether. "Do women have any voice in this decision?"

"It's not up to me," his fingers teasing which move to make next. "The system chooses."

I bristled at his words. "But what about the promises you made to the Watchmen?"

His lips twisted into a condescending smirk. "What happens when a woman has two suitors?"

There was that feeling again like my organs were all falling into the pit of my stomach. I wanted to understand the point of this conversation.

"Your Grace, you asked how you could help, and I feel this conversation has no point." Sitting straight, I clenched my hands at my skirts to dry my clammy palms. "Fine, I'll play your game," my jaw tightened. "What would happen if a woman has two suitors?"

Sitting up straight, his elbows rested on the arms of his chair, his intent gaze fixed on me. "I asked you to trust me. I decided the people need to be entertained, make this nuptial ceremony worth fighting for."

I was trying to maintain my composure. "Your solution is to make the men fight? This is barbaric." I was astonished to believe it. "What about the women?" I interjected, my voice shaking with anger. "What about our choice?"

He chuckled mirthlessly, and I had to hold myself back from lunging across the table at him. How dare he treat us like objects, pitted against each other for their entertainment?

"Your choice?" he scoffed. "That's a luxury you no longer have."

A strong scent of woodsy musk permeated the air as His Grace rose from his chair and strode towards the fireplace, placing a hand on the intricately carved mantle. The embers from the burnt log still glowed, and despite their dying heat, I felt like I was standing in front of an inferno.

"You are influential, whether you realize it or not," he spoke with a hint of disappointment. "They know your story and pity you. And yet, despite my pleas for trust, you continue to plot and scheme behind my back."

How could he possibly know?

I tried not to give anything away, recalling a small trick my brother-in-law Julian had taught me while playing cards at my sister's house one night. He would tell bits of a story and then explain how someone could have gotten away with a crime if they hadn't done specific actions, like shuffling their feet or looking to the left or up while telling a lie, how just the slightest pressure could make someone spill all their secrets when Julian barely scratched the surface.

I rose from my seat, desperate to escape the room. But I took a moment to steady myself and remember that I only had one more night here. He wouldn't have been so calm since I arrived if he knew about Zak's plan.

"There is no scheme," I reminded him, trying to keep my temper in check. "I already promised Mother and you that I would cooperate. It's just going to take some time for me to adjust." Controlling my anger was becoming increasingly difficult. "You expect me to marry a stranger and undergo a procedure that may or may not fix me?"

With his back turned to me, I couldn't read his reaction. But I knew this conversation would go in circles, and I didn't have the patience. I curtsied in response before leaving the room.

"Liz," His Grace called out after me.

My feet stopped, and I turned to face him before reaching the door.

The *Klunk-tap, Klunk-tap* boots approached me, his gaze filled with purpose and sincerity. "You ended up here by mistake, and for that, I apologize deeply. But there is a reason for your presence, and I am determined to make it right for you. Just tell me what you want." His words were empathetic, a gentle twinge pulling at my heart. "I can make your dreams come true and grant you the opportunity to become a mother."

My eyes pooled with tears. My body quivered, fighting and struggling to refuse to show any more weakness. His Grace took my hand, but I stepped back, gathered my skirts, and decided to leave the room.

"My heart belongs to another man, one whom I pledged my life to years ago," I spoke without turning back, leaving His Grace speechless.

PARCHMENT

The sun warmed my skin, and Brant's hand intertwined with mine. Our backyard was surrounded by lush green grass and colorful flowers. The boys ran through the sprinklers, giggling as they got soaked. The smell of charcoal wafted through the air as Brant tended to a dozen burgers on the grill.

"Who are we feeding? The entire neighborhood?" I joked, taking a sip of Rosé wine.

"Our new friends," he replied, flipping the burgers. I watched as he moved around in his Hawaiian shirt and shorts.

"New friends?" I questioned.

Before he could reply, I heard voices coming from behind me. I spun around on my heels and saw a large picnic table on the lush green lawn, with the magnificent castle in the background.

Our simple backyard had been transformed into a picturesque scenery, and all the Faithful villagers were gathered around the table enjoying the food. The spread included delicious sides such as baked beans, coleslaw, salad, and other dishes stretching down the long picnic table.

A fog of shock and disbelief consumed me. I stood frozen, watching the villagers devour the food, gratitude etched on their faces as they thanked me.

I jolted at the sound of a sharp sound piercing my ears like a blade slicing through flesh. I spun around to see an empty backyard - no Brant, no boys playing, no sprinklers, and the grill sizzled with food.

Zak's voice called out from the picnic table, and my heart sank. His eyes were heavy with sadness and longing as he approached me. His fingers gently grazed my cheeks as he reached out to touch my face.

"I've missed you," his raspy voice pulled at my heart. "I didn't want you to leave me, but I made a promise."

His touch was warm and comforting, making me yearn for his embrace. My eyes fluttered, and I pressed my face in his hand.

"I didn't want to leave," I admitted with a tear rolling down my cheek.

"Babe?" Brant's confused voice interrupted behind me.

Alert to my behavior, Brant's face became focused, his brows furrowed, and his lips twisted in anger. His strong fingers squeezed the empty beer can, and it crumpled like paper in his hand.

"What about our family? How could you be so selfish?" His voice boomed, causing me to flinch. But as I tried to explain who Zak was, Brant disappeared along with the castle grounds, picnic table, and people. In the blink of an eye, I was back in my ordinary backyard, with its familiar grass and swing set. My two young boys ran past me, their playful laughter ringing in my ears.

Brant's booming voice snapped me back. His hands gripped my shoulders, his fingers digging into my muscles.

"We are your family, Liz!" he exclaimed, his tone filled with anger and pain. "But he took you away from us! Can't you see that?"

But I refused to let him guilt-trip me. "You don't understand. Zak needs me."

Brant stood frozen for a moment, then took a step back. "No, he doesn't. We need you. All he did was help set you free."

I shook my head in disbelief. "He's my friend."

With each word, Brant's face saddened. "It'll cost you everything."

I WOKE up startled, my eyes snapping open. I blinked and tried to regain my composure and sense of reality. The dream felt incredibly vivid, with Brant's anger toward me and Zak's affection challenging me. It was a strange feeling to shake off. I rubbed my face as my brain slowly attempted to wake from its slumber.

The room's faint was lit by a small lantern on the nightstand. Amara climbed down from her bunk and asked if I was okay. She mentioned that she had been awakened by my heavy breathing and was concerned.

My face rested in my hands, and I struggled to shake off the remnants of the intense dream. I saw Nellie's untouched bunk and her tucked sheets.

"Where's Nellie?" My brows furrowed at the sight, still trying to grasp reality.

Amara raised an eyebrow in concern. "Everything ok? Remember, Mother asked her to stay near her chambers at dinner."

I rubbed my eyes and tried to shake off the uneasy feeling from the dream. Brant's words echoed in my mind, making it hard to distinguish what was real. After leaving

His Grace's chambers, I couldn't remember much of the night.

"That was a bizarre dream," I mumbled as I sat up and placed my feet on the cold stone floor. The sensation helped anchor me and bring me back to reality.

Amara settled on the end of my bed and rested her chin on her knuckles, intrigued. "Do tell. Your dreams are always fascinating."

I took a deep breath and recounted the details of my dream to Amara, including how Brant had appeared angry with me and how confused I felt about it.

"That does sound concerning," her almond-shaped eyes drooped. "Speaking of your journey, I have something for you." Amara reached under my bed for a large medical sack and placed it between us on the bed. "Supplies for your travels."

Words escaped me as I opened the top of the small medical kit Amara had prepared for me. Inside were wrapped strips of cloth and a sack of food containing pieces of fresh bread, apples, oranges, and pears. A warm blanket was folded on top. I rummaged through the kit and found ointments for cuts, scrapes, and other survival essentials. This kit was unlike any I had ever seen.

"How...how did you do this?" I asked her in disbelief.

Amara smiled and shrugged. "You're not the only one Zak talks to. He was worried you wouldn't know what to pack, so I said I would take care of you."

Amara handed me a folded parchment. I saw a few drawings and written instructions inside as I unfolded it.

"So you don't get lost trying to locate him," she explained.

"You knew about his plan? About me leaving?"

She pressed her lips together, tears threatening to spill from her eyes. "I'm really going to miss you," she cleared her throat.

Without hesitation, I pulled her into a tight hug. "I can't believe you would do this for me," I whispered, trying not to cry. "You have no idea how much this means to me."

"What kind of friend would I be if I didn't help give you a fighting chance?" Amara's voice cracked with emotion. "And I'm going to miss your stories."

At that moment, I realized how lucky I was to have such a caring and selfless friend like Amara.

THROUGHOUT THE day, I kept Zak's parchment tucked in my pocket, stealing glances at it whenever possible. By noon, I had memorized every detail of his message. He wanted to meet me just before dinner while everyone was distracted and gathered in one area.

I rehearsed the steps, ensuring I had them all down in the order they had been written. When the time came, I would be on the castle's north side, with fewer guards and less chance of being caught. If a Watchman questioned me, I had a cover story ready—I was going to the kitchen to help Meastro Roberto.

But until then, there wasn't much for me to do in the medical building. So, to keep myself occupied, I made my rounds in the stables and helped feed the animals. Their eager faces and happy snorts were a welcome distraction from my nerves.

As I dumped the remaining scraps into the pig trough, I couldn't help but grin at the sight of the pigs devouring their meal. Behind me, the goats and sheep bleated in anticipation, patiently waiting their turn. Caring for these magnificent animals reminded me of a simpler life outside the bustling city, with more space and wild creatures.

My life may have been full of hard work, but it brought such fulfillment at the end of each day. I never complained about the challenges or tasks. This lifestyle was rugged but vastly different from my urban upbringing.

I now understand why people leave the city for a slower, more peaceful life. That's what I would take away from this place—a reminder to slow down, appreciate the small moments, and admire Mother Nature's breathtaking scenery.

I returned to the women's tower and noticed Angela's blonde locks shining in the sunlight. She waved for my attention and met me halfway, her arms wrapped around a beautiful cream-colored satin and silk dress.

"I need a model for this dress. Can you help me out?" she pleaded, her eyes big and blue.

The sun wasn't ready to settle over the West mountain, meaning I had plenty of time before my next task.

"Sure," I replied.

We entered the women's chambers, and Angela helped me slip into the dress. The soft fabric clung to my skin, highlighting my toned curves. My breasts perked up over the material, and I couldn't help but admire myself in the floor-length vanity mirror.

The mirror showed off every inch of the dress, from its hand-stitched floral vines to its delicate green spirals and intricate patterns of roses, tulips, magnolias, and other flowers.

I was amazed at my newfound slimness and overall health. The diets and trends I had experimented with in Los Angeles seemed pointless now that I lived in this secluded location. The daily tasks that kept me active and moving were something I hadn't appreciated until now. Despite my physical changes, I still struggled to accept how this place molded me into a different person.

But as I stood in front of the mirror, wearing this stunning dress that fit me like a glove, all those insecurities seemed to fade away. For the moment, I felt confident and beautiful.

I slipped my arms into the flowing chiffon fabric, feeling the intricate vines hand-stitched and intertwined at the neck. Angela's talent in medieval gowns was undeniable.

"Wow, this is stunning on you!" she exclaimed as she stepped back to admire her work on me.

But I didn't share her enthusiasm. I didn't want to look or feel beautiful as Angela began to pin the hem. She spoke about facing stiff competition from thousands of other talented designers, but here, she was one-of-a-kind and reveled in it.

"Seriously, Liz...this looks amazing on you," she said through pins clenched between her teeth.

My lips turned upward as she talked about her fashion days in New York. My thoughts went back to Zak's instructions for tonight's escape plan. I recounted in my memory where to go, what times to be there, and how many paces I needed to take before reaching our meeting point. Tonight was my only chance to escape this place.

CHANGE IN PLANS

I sucked up a deep and held my breath as I gazed at my reflection in the full-length mirrors adorning one wall of the room. Despite the unconventional setting, I couldn't deny how beautiful and vibrant the silk gown made me feel.

As I slid out of the dress, the smooth material gliding against my skin, a twinge of sadness washed over me. The coarse cotton of my regular clothes didn't have the same elegant touch as the luxurious silk. However, I reminded myself I was not in a situation where luxury mattered.

I needed to focus on practical matters. Time seemed to move slower than usual, making this day feel like the longest of my life. Just as I was leaving, I heard someone call out my name. Looking up, I saw Aldrich. His bright and cheerful attitude was contagious as he waved at me.

"It's good to see you," he said with a wide smile.

"I haven't seen you this week," I realized.

He shrugged off my comment with a sheepish grin. "Someone has to keep an eye on this place. How is my sister?"

His question caught me off guard, "don't you talk to her?"

Aldrich put his hands in his pockets, a clear sign he was uncomfortable, but he tried to make small talk. “I want to hear from her roommates too," he said, "to get a more honest perspective."

"She's trying," I kept it short and sweet, wanting to find a place to study the parchment again. "Good seeing you," I managed to say before excusing myself.

Aldrich followed me, "can we talk?" He jumped ahead of me, blocking my view.

He gestured towards the lush gardens where His Grace and I had leisurely wandered just a few nights ago. Despite my initial reluctance, I yielded to his request and walked by his side, interested in what he had to say.

The air was thick with the sweet scent of magnolias, their vibrant blooms towering above us like colorful guardians of the garden. As we made our way through the winding paths, I couldn't help but notice other members of the Faithful strolling and conversing, casting curious glances in our direction. Aldrich led us to a secluded corner of the garden, where a small stone seating area was nestled among the foliage.

He joined me, crossing his legs and putting on a fake smile for anyone passing by. "I want to make this easy for you, so I thought, why not share some information that gave you insight?”

I relaxed, crossing my legs, intrigued at this kind gesture. "By all means..."

“To obtain his Watchmen soldiers, his Grace had to make promises," Aldrich explained earnestly. "He promised them they could choose their brides. But when Hunter harassed you, His Grace changed his mind." He leaned in closer, continuing in a hushed tone. "His Grace shared everything with me and mentioned your game of chess and your distress over more than one suitor."

Frustrated, I just wanted someone to cut to the chase in this place. "What's your point?"

"The information I'm about to share could potentially put others in harm's way, but you have people who care about you," he said in a sincere tone.

He glanced around and noticed others walking by, getting closer to eavesdrop on our conversation. "Can you do me a favor?" He asked. "Let out a little laugh." He spoke through a wide grin, barely moving his lips.

I nodded, understanding his motive, and let out a small giggle while covering my mouth with my hand. This made the nosey uninterested in our conversation. They assumed we might have been talking nonsense, and they wandered away.

"Satisfied?" The sarcasm in my tone made him stretch his lips across his face.

Aldrich's face softened as he prepared to divulge more details, "Reynard proposed a unique approach to courting. And Zak was the one who suggested having another suitor."

My voice dropped to a whisper, "Zak?"

He nodded, "he's still doing what he can to help. He's working on a contingency plan."

"When? How?" I asked, disturbed by this information.

"Reynard and Zak asked for a meeting a few nights ago. Zak pitched the idea that most women should have another suitor matched to them, which throws Hunter off. Reynard pitched the idea that the men would need to ask if a woman wanted to be fought for or something like that."

I understood and realized Wallace's true intentions: He wanted to fight for me, to save me from Hunter. But doing so would also mean that I would become his wife. The thought of this becoming a twisted game made my stomach churn.

Aldrich's words snapped me back to reality. "This isn't a fight to the death," he clarified. "There are three non-lethal weapons to choose from. If another man challenges the one you've been matched with for your honor, they can settle it on the field."

My stomach churned with disgust as I heard this grotesque idea. My mind raced, trying to understand why His Grace, Wallace, and Aldrich were all pushing me to see something I wasn't ready to face.

Then it hit me like a sledgehammer - Hunter would choose me, and after everything he put me through, His Grace would allow it. The realization made my throat go dry and my hands tremble. I tried to maintain my composure, but inside I was crumbling.

Aldrich's gaze dropped to the ground, unable to meet my eyes. "A few nights ago, the men were asked to put their names in a box for who they wanted to be paired with." He hesitated before speaking softly, “Your name was on his request."

My hands rubbed together, the weight of this revelation sinking in. If tonight didn't go as planned, I would face the harsh reality that Hunter was one of my suitors. A thought that sent shivers down my spine and left me feeling conflicted and unsure of what was to come.

"Was I on anyone else’s list?" The question nagged at me. Part of me wanted to know, but another didn't want to find out. My mind was racing with fear and confusion.

Aldrich's eyes drooped as he shook his head. "I'm sorry."

Feeling desperate, I shook my head as well. "No, there has to be another way. How is it possible that a man who attacked me could also end up being chosen as my suitor?"

Aldrich let out a heavy sigh. "His Grace approved this plan a few days ago. The men are aware of it, but they don't know who they will be paired with or if there are any other suitors they may have to fight against."

My hands covered my mouth to keep myself from getting

sick. I had rejected Wallace's idea to fight for me, feeling like a fool, thinking he meant more. He might have, but he was trying to protect me. But as Zak remained quiet and didn't try to vouch for me, it dawned on me that he must have his sights set on someone else. And for some reason, that thought hurt.

"Why are you telling me this?" I asked while my emotions were in turmoil.

He rested his elbows on his knees. "I feel guilty for not protecting you that night. And you're also trying to help my sister." His eyes welled up as he struggled. "It pains me to know I can't physically defend you against Hunter. And after all this time working towards this life, I don't think I can accept being trapped in a loveless marriage."

Worry consumed my thoughts and heart, leaving no room for words. If tonight did not go according to Zak's plan, I could be forced to marry Hunter. Zak and Reynard's attempts to have other suitors for me had failed; no one else had shown interest. As I reflected on the situation, regrets flooded my mind, and I realized I should have considered other options. However, my focus had been solely on surviving in this place, leaving no room for rational thoughts.

I struggled to control my emotions as I asked, "Will His Grace allow this marriage?"

"I will not allow it," Aldrich declared, standing up from the bench. "I cannot reveal all the details yet, but trust me when I say I have a plan."

Once again, everyone seems to have their hidden agendas. I am caught in the middle and still clueless about everything happening since the beginning.

THE NIGHT OF

Marshall's footsteps crunched on the gravel as he hurried towards Aldrich and me in the garden. His brow was furrowed, and his breaths were quick. "His Grace requires your presence," he said, urgency lacing his words.

"Of course," Aldrich's shoulders relaxed, but I could see a hint of concern in his eyes as he turned to look at me.

"Don't worry about me, I'll be fine," I assured them, even though my voice lacked conviction.

After they left, I wandered aimlessly through the sprawling gardens. The scent of magnolias filled the air, and a gentle breeze brushed against my skin.

The sunlight filtered through the leaves, creating a beautiful dappled effect. The sun was West, just above the mountain's peak, as the fluffy white clouds gathered in pillows above the top, teasing for the weather to come.

My mind was consumed by thoughts of Zak and his mysterious list. I couldn't help but wonder whose name he added. As much as I tried to convince myself that I didn't care, I couldn't help but feel disappointed at the thought of not being chosen. But then again, why did I even want to be a part of this twisted game?

No one else beat themselves up for wanting to escape this idyllic place. Each day brought me closer to understanding why so many people felt rejuvenated. There was less stress and noise from the outside world. No one had to pretend to be someone they weren't. There was less financial pressure from our usual society's social standings. I could understand why so many found contentment in their new lives.

It made me question whether I was the only one seeing through the facade or if there were others like me silently rebelling.

It made me think of that cult in Southern California that made everyone drink the 'purple juice,' they all perished for one person. No one had mentioned this about being a cult, but the word never wavered from my mind. I just chose to be careful.

Yet, despite my doubts, there was no sign of revolt or resistance from anyone, which baffled me.

I came across a tranquil creek near the front of the castle. I couldn't resist dipping my hands into the cool water and splashing it on my overheated face and neck.

As I knelt by the water's edge, gazing at the darkening sky, I closed my eyes and prayed that everything would work out tonight.

Distant and familiar voices came from the opposite direction. I recognized Amara's laugh and felt sad, knowing I would miss her and the twins. My stomach growled as the scent of beef stew wafted towards me from the dining hall where everyone else was gathering.

I stayed close to the shadows as I went North of the castle walls. I dipped to pick up my sack, which had been hidden in bushes from earlier in the morning and slung it over my back. When Amara and the twins passed by, unaware of my presence, they laughed and giggled at their conversation. I would miss their faces, their kind spirits.

"Should we wait for Liz?" Yasmin asked, looking back at the women's tower.

"No, earlier she said to eat without her. She had more work in the stables." Amara answered without a second thought. It was an answer she had cooked up all day and couldn't wait to use.

Despite everything, I couldn't help but envy Amara and the twins' ability to accept this lifestyle. Knowing their tragic pasts outside these walls made their contentment here more bittersweet.

I crouched low behind the bushes, watching as the crowd dispersed. The men headed towards the cottages while the women headed to the dining hall, where a delicious-smelling stew awaited them.

I counted to six and took a deep breath, preparing myself for what would come. With my head down, I scanned the ground for any movement.

Crossing the narrow creek, I held my breath to avoid making any noise that could give me away. My heart raced as I reached the other side and exhaled through pursed lips.

I crouched down, estimating the distance to the forest's edge - it looked to be about forty yards to my left, then another forty yards towards the northeast. Using my hands as a guide, I navigated through the tree branches, trying to stay on track as best as possible.

The night sky stretched above me, and within the depths of the forest, there was nothing but darkness. Just when I thought I had made significant progress, a figure with a lantern appeared ahead of me. My body froze, unsure if it was Zak or one of the Watchmen.

"Liz?" Zak's voice whispered out into the darkness.

Relief flooded me, and I picked up my pace, rushing towards him.

"I'm here," I said in a soft voice.

We met in the middle as his lantern was lifted at my eye level, blinding me.

"You ready?" He asked.

I shifted the bag on my shoulder, feeling its heaviness dig into my flesh. As we strolled, Zak rummaged through his pack and retrieved a canteen. My mouth salivated at the idea of drinking clean water; I was minutes away from lapping up from the creek I had seen nearby. When I was nervous, my mouth always went dry.

"Thanks," I moaned with satisfaction, taking a long sip.

Zak grinned. "Always one step ahead," he grabbed a folded sack tied to a thick stick and handed it to me. "And some extra food, just in case."

Impressed by his outdoorsman skills, I couldn't help but tease him. "Were you a Boy Scout or something?"

He chuckled, confirming that he had been an Eagle Scout when he was younger. I fondly remember him telling me about when we sat in the darkness on the cargo train when there was nothing else to do but share our stories.

As we continued walking, Zak halted and turned to face the East. He motioned for me to do the same. "Listen for the electric current," he instructed.

I strained my ears and could make out the hum of electricity in the distance. Zak explained that a latch nearby had been turned off for maintenance, causing the cameras in the area to glitch every thirty seconds.

"Follow me," he led us toward our destination while avoiding camera detection.

With only the faint glow of Zak's LED lantern leading the way, we trekked through the dense forest. The darkness enveloped us, making it impossible to see more than a few steps ahead. I stumbled over tree roots and rocks, trying to follow his steps.

When we were near, Zak placed the lantern on the ground. He warned me that he must carefully unlock a concealed part of the gate, and any sudden movements could trigger an alarm. My heart raced with anticipation as I realized this was my opportunity to break free.

"You should have warned me to work on my cardio," I joked, nervous because I had only a few more steps to accomplish.

Zak entertained my joke for a split second. As the hum grew louder, he returned to our mission. He handed me a pouch in my palm, warning me it was cayenne pepper, explaining that it would deter any animals that got too close.

As we approached the towering fence, our necks craned upwards in awe. Its imposing height of thirty to forty feet seemed almost insurmountable in the darkness.

Zak took caution, navigating through the thick underbrush, pushing away leaves and branches that obstructed our path to the gate. He mentioned the gate was down for maintenance, but it was difficult to make out any details in the dim light. He pressed on, determined to find the latch to begin the process of my escape.

“I need to place my thumb between the lock and the latch and slowly open the door.” His tone is as slow as his movements.

A mix of fear and excitement flooded through me as he prepared to take action. This was it, my chance to escape.

He turned to me, his face severe and full of concern. "Are you ready?" he asked.

My heart raced as I contemplated my options. Should I run past him, or should I walk in?

"Wait," I managed to say, trying to compose myself. "I

want to say goodbye." The knot in my throat grew with the adrenaline surging through my body. "Why won't you come with me?"

He hesitated before pressing down on the latch with his thumb. It was almost as if saying goodbye was painful for him, or perhaps he didn't want to deal with how awkward it was.

"Someone needs to stay and fix the fence," he said, motioning towards the gate. "We only have so much time."

Instinctively, my hand touched his shoulder, pulling him closer as if trying to hold onto him. I wrapped my arms around him, trying to savor every moment of his embrace before leaving.

The moon cast a soft, ethereal glow on his features as he stood before me, and the LED lantern behind us added gentle illumination. In the dim light, I could see the longing in his deep blue eyes as they gazed down at me.

His hands rested on my arms, sending warmth throughout my body. My heart skipped a beat when he took a small step closer, closing the distance between us.

I was taken aback when he leaned in towards me, but I felt excitement and anticipation instead of my usual panic. I tilted my head to meet him as his lips drew closer to mine. But just as our lips were about to touch, his body stiffened, and he pulled away and positioned himself in front of me protectively, ready to shield me from any potential danger.

Zak's voice boomed like thunder as he shouted to someone in the distance. My heart raced as I peeked around his towering figure, only to see Hunter standing there with a maniacal grin, holding a lantern that cast an eerie glow on his face.

"What are you doing here?" Hunter taunted, his eyes flickering with malicious intent.

"I could ask the same," Zak retorted, his voice laced with

confidence and a hint of danger. He squared his stance and balled his hands into fists, ready for whatever confrontation may come.

Hunter's hand gripped around the electric stick as he brandished it threateningly. "She is not allowed out here!"

Zak stepped forward, his body tense and ready to defend us. I could feel his intense energy radiating from him, his chest rising and falling with each quick breath.

But I couldn't just stand by and watch this unfold. With shaky courage, I stepped out from behind Zak, terrified we might be outmatched.

"I asked Zak to meet me out here," I announced, trying to sound bold and unafraid.

Hunter's narrowed eyes scanned the scene, honing in on Zak's work pouch discarded on the ground. His grip on the electric stick tightened, crackling with dangerous energy.

"You are aiding her escape," he accused, his voice laced with anger. "Stand down or face the consequences." His gaze then turned to me, cold and calculated. "Elizabeth, come with me."

Fear clutched at my heart as I realized there was no way out of this without a fight. My feet were frozen in terror as Hunter's steps came toward us. The crunching of leaves and twigs under his feet made the fear creep up my body. Seeing the steely determination in his eyes, he was ready to apprehend anyone who dared defy his rules.

Zak refused to back down, his body coiled like a spring ready to unleash its full force. "She will not go with you," he declared with disdain. "We were simply enjoying each other's company before you decided to interrupt."

Hunter scoffed, his sneer dripping with contempt. "You expect me to believe that?" He took menacing steps toward us. "She's been planning this escape since day one, and you fell for it like a naive fool." His electric stick maneuvered like a professional swordsman in his grasp as he came closer. "There are still miles of dangerous terrain and obstacles separating her from true freedom."

A wave of detectable tension swept through the air as Hunter's steely gaze fixated on Zak. My heart raced with fear and guilt, knowing Zak had only helped me out of loyalty.

"Don't hurt him," I begged Hunter, my voice trembling with desperation and defeat. I offered myself up as a sacrifice for his safety.

My legs turned to jelly as the fear in my throat was so thick it was suffocating me. Zak begged me to stay with him, but before he could move, Hunter was upon us. He grabbed my arm with a vice-like grip, wrenching me around to face Zak. And there it was, the electric stick inches from Zak's face.

"Don't even think about taking another step," Hunter growled, a sinister smirk creeping across his lips. In one swift motion, he turned the stick towards me, the glowing tip inches from my cheek. "Or I'll make sure her pretty face is scarred for life."

Zak's body trembled with pent-up rage as his eyes bore into Hunter, a tangible aura of hatred radiating from him. I hated watching how I made him look like this while he watched Hunter's grip around my torso tighten as he played around, his putrid breath on my neck.

"Stay there," Hunter sneered with a sadistic grin, "if you hear her scream, it'll be because she's enjoying me."

But Zak's confident gaze shifted as if he knew I had the strength and determination to fight back. In that split second, I channeled all my fury and power into one swift blow—driving my elbow with brutal force into Hunter's gut, silencing his taunts, and igniting a fierce battle for survival.

Hunter recoils in shock, dropping his electric stick as my fist connects with his jaw. I dodge his flailing arms, feeling the electric stick's warmth splicing the skin on my cheek.

I retreated as Zak delivered powerful blows to Hunter's face with the fistful of cayenne pepper, sending him staggering backward. The remnants of cayenne pepper stuck to his skin ignite into a fiery inferno, searing his eyes shut and leaving him writhing in agony.

The electric stick fell to the ground with a resounding thud, sparks igniting the dirt beneath it. I reached for it, trembling as I wrapped my fingers around its still-crackling surface. I watched the device sputter and die out in my grasp.

Hunter's howl of pain pierced the air, his face contorting with rage as he clutched at his blistering skin. "What the hell! I'll kill you for this!" he roared, staggering to his feet with a determined fury. His features twisted and mangled from the heat of the pepper.

Hunter tripped over a branch, stumbling back, trying to clear his vision as the snot ran down his nose. "I'll give you courage," he spat through gritted teeth. Striking a Watchmen twice is punishable by death." The look in his eyes was wild and crazed. Now, she will indeed be mine."

"Drop the damn weapon!" The command from Reynard cut through the forest like a sharp blade, shattering the peaceful sounds of nature. The booming voice seemed to reverberate and echo among the trees, causing a nearby flock of crows to take flight in fright. Their loud caws filled the air as they frantically searched for a new roost to settle in for the night.

I stumbled backward, throwing the electric stick to the ground in surrender. Reynard, Wallace, and Marshall charged toward us, accompanied by a battalion of Watchmen.

They swarmed Zak, who offered no resistance as they apprehended him with swift and brutal force to the ground, along with Hunter, who blamed Zak for attacking him as his face contorted with fear and defeat as they were taken into custody.

SAME STORY

Mother paced back and forth in the study, her hands resting on her lower back as she listened to my story. I left out the valid reason for Zak and me being in the forest, but I gave a detailed account of Hunter's actions and words.

To cover up the truth, I fabricated a tale about why we wandered into the forest. I claimed I needed some alone time and that Zak had been a good listener.

"You don't understand," I pleaded. "Everyone looks at me differently. They judge me with their eyes." I pulled the blanket tighter around my shoulders.

"So you just happened to wander into an area that needed repair, and security was down?" Mother's tone was skeptical, but I couldn't let her see my doubts.

I pulled the quilt up to my shoulders, relishing its cozy warmth. Even though I wasn't thirsty, my hands held a cup of lemon tea. The mug's heat was comforting, and I couldn't help but gaze back and forth between Mother and the door as we waited for His Grace to arrive and decide my fate.

A lemon slice bobbed in my cup, and the steam rose,

filling my senses with a refreshing aroma. As I took a deep breath, memories of our walk back from the woods flooded my mind. We walked in silence, Reynard and I trailing behind the rest of the group. He stayed by my side, speaking only in hushed tones as we returned to the castle ground in the darkness.

"You two got lost in the woods and ended up here. Do you understand?"

I nodded, following his lead as he glanced at me. Our plan had gone awry, but we stuck to our story to avoid suspicion.

Mother's words snapped me back to reality as she questioned my honesty. "I'm sorry, Liz...either I must have missed something, or you're not being entirely truthful," she said in disbelief.

"You should explain that lingering look between you and Zak." Brant's voice sounded irritated from behind me.

I couldn't bring myself to look over at him. Instead, I kept my composure and shrugged.

"I didn't ask."

Despite my efforts, Mother's face still remained doubtful. And when Brant snorted from his spot in the room, I felt even more guilty for not knowing which look he was referring to.

I reminded myself that it wasn't just about Zak and me exchanging a glance; it was about what could have happened if we hadn't been interrupted—a potential kiss.

The pressure to explain my feelings intensified as I felt the weight of Mother's gaze and Brant's unspoken judgment. My mind was already racing with the events that had transpired in the forest, and having both a natural person and my subconscious scrutinizing me made it even harder to find the right words.

"I want to embrace this new place, but Zak is the only one

I trust here," I admitted, unsure if that was true or just a coping mechanism.

Mother kept her eyes on me and crossed her arms, wanting more details. Her eyebrows lifted in curiosity, and her lips pouted as she waited for me to continue.

Reluctantly, I felt compelled to explain. "We just needed some time alone together. He's my friend, and I feel like I can confide in him more than my husband," I confessed, feeling a pang of guilt.

"Ouch," Brant responded.

The memory of Zak and I in the woods, feeling his embrace and then the touch of his hands run down my arms, vividly remembering that lingering intent gaze and the smell of him, fresh pine and mint on his breath, enveloped my senses. I remembered a sweet musk of his skin when he stepped closer, enclosing the space between us.

His scent created a heady aroma that filled my lungs with comfort and kindness. At that moment, I couldn't help but feel a quickening in the pit of my stomach as I anticipated the warmth of his breath on my lips.

My cheeks tingled with heat at the thought of giving him a goodbye kiss. But most of all, it was how he looked at me with longing and sadness, knowing that this would be our last time together. I cleared my throat to push away these memories. Mother was tired on her feet. She sat in the armchair beside me, her index finger rubbing her temple in deep thought.

"That's all you have to say?" she asked, breaking the silence.

The study door creaked open before I could respond, and Reynard entered. His face was unreadable as always.

"His Grace has requested Liz to return to her room," his voice was assertive. "I will escort her."

Mother was in shock. "Is she in trouble?"

"That is not for me to say," Reynard answered. "Liz, are you ready?"

I set my cup down and shrugged off the fleece blanket. I stood up, feeling nervous butterflies fluttering in my stomach.

"What about Zak?" I couldn't help but ask.

Reynard's jaw clenched before he replied briskly. "Are you ready?" He ignored my question and gestured towards the door with a curt nod.

I HELD off until we were outside, away from potential eavesdroppers lurking in the halls. Our walk was leisurely, with no need to rush. Based on his rigid stance and reserved demeanor toward me, I could sense that Reynard was displeased with the situation.

"What's going to happen to him?" I voiced my concern.

Reynard remained tight-lipped, his eyes fixed straight ahead. "His Grace is still deliberating. He finds it coincidental that you and Zak walked in the same area where the cameras were down."

"Mother is struggling with my story as well," I replied. "Do you know anything? I care about what happens to him."

The creases on Reynard's face relaxed, but his body remained as still and tense as a statue. "Unfortunately, I am not aware of what consequences he will face," he admitted, his tone lacking reassurance.

"Why did you choose to help?" I inquired empathetically. Don't I go against everything you strive to protect behind these walls?" My mind was trying to wrap around how someone like Reynard would want to help a rebel like me.

"Zak is my friend and only wants to see you happy. Amara is fond of you as well," he said, his voice soft and gentle. His eyes held unwavering loyalty as he spoke, his words tinged with a hint of sadness.

Taking a deep breath, Reynard's chest rose and fell like waves in the ocean. "You don't belong here. Our ways are foreign to you, and you will never truly understand them." He paused, his gaze searching mine for understanding. "There is no point keeping you here if you refuse the faithful way."

His sincerity was tangible, and I couldn't help but be touched by his words: "I wish His Grace saw things the way you do."

Reynard's face was somber as he replied, "Unfortunately, His Grace has much more at stake." His words hung heavy in the air, a reminder of the weight of responsibility on His Grace's shoulders.

"Just be grateful that your lies matched up," he said, his voice strained with worry. "I don't know what will happen to Zak now." Reynard's biceps bulged as he pulled the door to the women's tower and gestured for me to go inside.

As I entered the room, the heavy door shut behind me with a sharp click, its rusty lock latching into place. The only light source was the dying fire in the hearth, casting eerie shadows that danced across the walls and floor.

The sparse candles around the room emitted enough light to pierce through the darkness. With a heavy heart, I sank to the cold, hard ground and enveloped my arms around my legs. My breaths came out in short gasps as I fought back tears, trying to convince myself everything would be alright. But in this lonely room, surrounded by bleakness and silence, I couldn't help but feel utterly alone and helpless.

What have I done?

THE SHARP PAIN

As the sun crept over the horizon, I felt my eyelids flutter open, adjusting to the soft glow of morning light.

In the corner of the room, I could make out Amara's graceful figure as she tip-toed towards our bunkbed, her silhouette outlined by the faint rays of sunlight peeking through our window. She carried a delicate bowl filled with plump apples, juicy grapes, and ripe pears - imagining their sweet aroma on my tongue, my stomach growled in anticipation.

She perched on the edge of my bed and placed the bowl in my lap, her expression mixed with worry and tenderness.

"You need to eat," she said, her voice laced with concern.

As I lifted myself into a sitting position, my eyes traced the names etched into the bunk above me—Brant and the boys. The weight of guilt settled in my chest as I thought about how I had let them down, how my hesitation and inability to say goodbye had caused this mess.

My fingers plucked the ripe, plump grapes from their stems. The juicy tang of the green fruit exploded in my mouth, a burst of heavenly flavor that made me realize how long it had been since I had something to eat. Amara's curious gaze followed my movements. Setting the bowl of fruit aside, I mustered the courage to bring up the topic.

"I guess no one was watching Hunter." My mind was still reeling with confusion and fear over what had transpired.

"The Watchmen wear trackers." She shared, "In the security room, Rey said he gave one to Zak, and then he saw Hunter walking in the same direction as you two." Her sorrowful gaze fell upon me. "He couldn't share everything. What happened?"

I poured out every detail of my ill-fated adventure, recounting when Zak and I stumbled upon each other in the depths of the woods and how quickly it all ended.

As I relived the memory, a wave of regret washed over me, knowing that if I hadn't hesitated, Zak might have been able to lead me past the gate and toward freedom. But instead, here I was, still trapped in this place.

I should have awoken in the forest this morning with a clear plan to escape and reunite with my husband and family. But my lingering feelings about saying goodbye to Zak clouded my judgment, causing me to hesitate.

Amara gently squeezed my hand as if trying to absorb my pain and guilt through her fingertips.

"I'm so sorry," she whispered with sadness as I looked into her beautiful almond-shaped eyes. It was as though she could feel my pain as deeply as I did.

A loud knock on the door startled us, and we jumped to our feet in alarm. Amara hurried to the door, pulling it open to reveal His Grace standing outside, with Reynard following behind.

With grace and poise, Amara greeted His Grace with a deep curtsy before inviting him into our cramped room. I mimicked her actions, attempting to smooth out the wrinkles in my disheveled clothes from a restless sleep.

Despite my efforts, I couldn't help but feel self-conscious under his piercing gaze, studying me as he entered the room.

"Amara, could you please wait downstairs for us? I want to speak to Liz alone," His Grace requested, turning towards her with a slight nod. Amara's expression displayed concern as she left the room, leaving me alone with His Grace.

My heart pounded like a drum in my chest, sending adrenaline rush through my body. I nervously fidgeted with my fingers, trying to hide the tremors they gave off.

His Grace, adorned in regal black and emerald attire, took a few slow, deliberate steps towards me. His intense stare fixed on me, making me feel small and insignificant.

I longed to shrink away from his piercing gaze, but I stood rooted in place, unable to move or speak. Every fiber of my being screamed to run, but I remained still, trapped under his powerful presence.

"Last night--"

"It won't happen again," I blurted out before he could finish his sentence.

His raised eyebrows expressed his surprise at my interruption, and I lowered my head in shame.

"I'm sorry," I murmured.

"As I was saying," His Grace continued, regaining control of the conversation.

He stood tall, fists clenched on his hips as if asserting his authority and displaying his strength. His chest rose and fell rapidly, his breaths coming in quick succession. His flushed face and narrowed eyes betrayed his attempt to control his anger toward me.

"My patience wears thin," he growled, voice edged with frustration. "You broke my most stringent rules and dragged others into your reckless plan."

I bit my lip to keep my composure, but my chin quivered. "Zak and I--"

"Don't!" His sharp tone cut me off, his frustration evident. Taking a deep breath, he raised his hand to stop me from speaking.

"Your stories may match, but I know your true intentions." He pointed a finger at me. "Isn't it ironic Zak put in an order last week to work in an area where the cameras are malfunctioning, and the gate needs to be repaired? Then, why don't we discuss where Hunter had heavy traces of cayenne pepper on his face from being struck by Zak." He stepped closer to me; I could smell the sweet meat and eggs on his breath. "Cayenne is a spice to help deter animals."

I kept my mouth closed, refusing to mention the sack of food and supplies Amara had given to me. My fingers itched with the memory of Reynard taking the sack from my shoulder and tossing it into the woods as we trailed behind.

A knot formed in my stomach as I thought about Wallace's expression when he caught sight of Reynard's callous action - a mixture of hurt and sadness glazed over his eyes. The sack's contents were meant to sustain me on my journey, but now they lay abandoned in the forest, symbolizing my shattered trust and fractured bond.

The sound of *klunk-tap, klunk-tap, klunk-tap* of His Grace's polished leather boots on the cold, stone floor made my mouth dry in anticipation as he approached the door. Every step seemed to reverberate in the room, causing my heart to pound.

I watched with bated breath as he reached for the doorknob and pressed down. The metal latch creaked open to reveal a figure wearing a black feathered flat cap.

As His Grace stepped aside, I could see that it was none other than Doctor Ferrarius, his face adorned with an amused smile.

The dim light from the window cast intriguing shadows on his features, making him seem almost mysterious. My eyes couldn't help but drift to his hand, discreetly hidden behind his back, sparking curiosity.

The hairs on my neck stood up as he approached me. His lips twitched, trying to lift into a smile. I could only imagine what he held in his hidden hand—something he didn't want me to see.

Anticipation and fear mingled within me as he closed the door behind him, positioning himself to block the only exit in the room. I stepped back, my hands rising in defense against whatever may come next.

"What's going on?" My voice trembled with panic.

"Liz...I knew you would be trouble." His Grace's words were laced with frustration. "I have provided for you, given you food and shelter, even offered to fix you."

My eyes locked on Doctor Ferrarius as fear and dread filled my chest. He revealed a large syringe filled with clear liquid and removed the cap with his teeth.

In a panic, I sprang toward the small table and threw a chair to block his path. They both were amused as Doctor Ferrarius approached me, kicking the chair from his path. I pushed the table at him, striking him in the upper thighs.

He toppled over as my last move and in a desperate attempt to escape. But there was no way out - I was trapped in this hellish room with these heartless men who saw me as nothing more than a lab rat. The realization fueled an uncontrollable rage within me.

His Grace grabbed me, and with all my strength, I kicked him in the shin and scrambled to get away, my dress catching my footing at the same time, and I fell onto Nellie's bed. Doctor Ferrarius grabbed my ankle and pulled me down hard onto the floor.

Gasping for air, I thrashed around, screaming for help

that I knew would never come. His Grace's cold eyes gleamed with sick amusement as he ordered the doctor to inject me with something.

Doctor Ferrarius hesitated, torn between following orders and intervening in my pleas not to do this to me. In the end, he knelt and pinned my struggling arms above my head.

As I fought against their hold, I felt a sharp prick in my arm, and a searing heat exploded throughout my body, rendering me powerless. In the last moments, before everything went black, I could hear the distorted voices of those two monsters discussing their plan to get me out of the room.

And then all sounds faded away as I slipped into unconsciousness, trapped in this nightmare once again.

BRANT

Brant was perched on a weathered barstool, his rigid muscles coiled with tension as he nursed an IPA. His eyes darted to his watch every few minutes, the furrow between his brows deepening with each passing moment.

Where the hell is he?" he muttered under his breath.

The glass in his large, calloused hands trembled as he took another swig, the bitter hops mingling with his mounting irritation. The jingle of the entrance of *Red Door* stirred a flicker of hope in him, but it dissipated when he saw it wasn't his brother-in-law walking through the door.

Detective Knight strolled in a few seconds later, her piercing blue eyes scanning the room before locking onto Brant's form at the counter. She gave him a slight smirk as she slid into the seat beside him. Startled by her sudden appearance, Brant was about to spill his drink as she slid a manilla envelope towards him.

Without a word, she gestured for the bartender to bring her an IPA before returning to Brant. He opened the envelope to reveal documents about his wife's case and photos he gave her to help find Liz.

Detective Knight sipped her beer with practiced ease. As an ambitious and determined Seattle Police Officer, Detective Knight set her sights on impressing Brant's brother-in-law, Jullian, and Brant himself. She couldn't help but feel a touch disappointed when she noticed Brant was the only one at the bar.

However, she pushed it aside as the tall, tattooed bartender with his long hair in a bun approached them with two fresh pints. She subtly slipped her credit card to him before Brant could refuse it.

She couldn't help but think about Brant's financial struggles, knowing he had traveled from his home in Los Angeles to travel back up North a month later. She wanted to help ease any pain or burden he may be feeling.

Frustration gnawed at her as she thought about the case they were working on. Despite countless hours of investigation, there was no evidence of anything other than Liz vanishing into thin air.

The bartender smiled kindly at her and leaned across the counter. "Your money's no good here tonight," he said, gesturing towards the card she had tucked into her wallet.

"You're too kind, Mikey," Detective Knight replied with a grateful smile as she sipped her pint.

Brant flipped through the organized paperwork, his sharp eyes scanning each written statement from the Chihuly Gardens employees. The grumpy woman who gave them directions had scribbled down a brief note about being late for lunch, but nothing else seemed out of the ordinary to her.

He moved on to another statement from the young punk who had given them the tour, Patrick. His handwriting was sloppy, and his memory was vague, mentioning only a blurry recollection of seeing Brant and Liz among the sea of tourists. Brant snorted in annoyance, remembering how the cocky young man had thought himself funny with his dry humor.

Then, his identical twin brother was in the lobby of the Edgewater Hotel, where they had stayed for one night. A twinge of anger flickered in Brant's mind as he considered paying them another visit to jog their memory, but he pushed that idea aside.

These statements did not provide any helpful information. No one in the gardens knew anything about the incident.

Tired of sitting at the bar with limited space, Brant moved to a small booth on the opposite side, with more light and large window panes looking out to the street. He didn't expect to find much here, but Detective Knight had pulled some strings to allow him access to this paperwork, and he wanted to make the most of it.

She followed behind him, attracting the attention of several single men in the bar whose eyes couldn't seem to resist wandering down to her service weapon on her right hip.

The Red Door was a haven for her, a famous cop hangout. The smell of delicious greasy meat and fish food filled the air, making her stomach growl in anticipation.

The building was an old corner structure with tall ceilings and rustic wooden beams running along its length. Every inch of the pine wood seemed to shine with cleanliness and care.

Despite being a Tuesday evening, the place was relatively empty, and she relished the quiet and calm atmosphere it provided.

As Brant shuffled through more papers, he glanced at his watch impatiently before gazing towards the front door.

Detective Knight noticed his distraction and sat across from him, following his gaze. She couldn't resist teasing him, trying to lighten their tense atmosphere.

"You waiting for another detective? Should I be insulted?" She touched her heart, but Brant's expression remained severe and unamused. He was focused on finding answers and not in the mood for jokes.

She sipped her beer, observing the clear signs of stress on Brant's face - the dark circles and bags under his eyes. She could tell he hadn't been sleeping and couldn't blame him. He looked much thinner than the last time she saw him, perhaps having lost around fifteen to twenty pounds.

His eyes were red and puffy, most likely from crying or lack of sleep; she noted that both were probable. This man was broken over his missing wife, and she couldn't help but feel a hint of jealousy.

In her last case, it was the husband who plotted to murder his wife, and the way he talked about her disappearance with such disdain only fueled her anger towards how someone could do that to their spouse.

This memory reminded her of how guilty she felt when Brant was the prime suspect for over a month. She had been determined to prove his involvement in Liz's disappearance, but there was no evidence to support it. Their endless phone calls, discussions, and theories made her doubt herself and feel remorseful for jumping to conclusions based on her previous case. After all, a husband like Brant wouldn't be working so tirelessly to find his wife if he had something to do with her vanishing.

She observed Brant watching the door and knew who he was waiting for.

"So, when was Julian supposed to arrive?" She took a swig of her beer, gulping the bitter hops, which soured her expression. Her nose wrinkled in disgust as she pushed the pint away. "Can I get a real beer, please?" she raised her voice to the bartender.

Mikey laughed and grabbed a glass to pull the spout to her liking. “On it, detective." He walked over and set down the rich darkness of the Guinness.

Brant paid no attention, reading the statements. Detective Knight took a sip and savored the smooth, rich malt taste, smacking her lips in satisfaction.

"That's beer," she declared with a grin.

Brant's eyes caught the dark draft and looked up. He saw her eyes light up as she took a large gulp. He chuckled at her comment, grateful for the moment of lightheartedness.

He then returned to being serious as he reviewed the long list of missing women. He scribbled down notes on her notepad as he read off names from various states: Oregon, California, Idaho, and Nevada. The amount of information was overwhelming, considering that these leads all related to sex trafficking cases she was working on.

Liz didn't seem to fit the typical victim profile - a woman in her early thirties, taken from a public place like the Chihuly Gardens. It was known that sex traffickers target younger women who are vulnerable and have a reputation for being prostitutes. Still, Brant knew better than to underestimate someone's preferences in these cases.

Detective Knight reached into her front pocket, pulled out a small USB stick, and placed it on top of the stack of paperwork in front of him.

"This is the video surveillance from Chihuly Gardens," she explained. "It covers the 24 hours before and after your arrival."

Brant held up the USB card, his hopes rising with anticipation. "Did you see anything?"

Detective Knight took another sip of her Guinness before responding.

"I've watched the footage three times now, and...nothing." Seeing the disappointment on his face made her feel like a failure. She wrapped both hands around the bottom of her glass. "I can't put my finger on it, but something just feels off about this case. That's why I'm lending you all of this evidence. I need you and Julian to take a fresh look at it."

"I keep circling back to the doppelganger. What are the odds that when Liz and I are in the gardens, so is this woman? Liz is taken that day, and then two days later, the doppelganger is in the morgue." Brant's eyebrows raised as the memory of seeing the body in the morgue made him suppress a wave of nausea.

"That's what keeps me up most nights." Detective Knight took another swig, haunted by the vision.

DECEITFUL

As I stirred from my deep and peaceful slumber, the steady beep of a heart monitor welcomed me back to consciousness. The past few days had been filled with strange and unsettling dreams, but now all seemed quiet in my mind.

The room softly glowed through the white curtains, dancing gently in the breeze. As I struggled to focus my vision, I noticed the dull ache in my body intensify. It wasn't until I tried to move and felt a sharp pain in my abdomen that I realized something was different.

Faint memories started to resurface - Amara's support, Reynard and I walking in the forest, something about Zak, but what were we talking about?

My confusion turned into discomfort as I reached up to adjust the oxygen tubes in my nose and found myself too weak to move. The heaviness in my arms reminded me that I was still recovering from whatever had put me in this hospital bed.

"What?" My voice came out hoarse and audible.

Anxiety began creeping into my body as the fog of sleep

lifted. Yasmin pulled back the curtain and rushed over to check my vitals.

"Liz!" She exclaimed, surprised to see me awake. She told me to relax and explained that I had been sedated for a procedure. "I didn't know until afterward. I'm so sorry." She whispered.

"What...happened?" I managed to croak out, still struggling to make sense of everything.

My throat felt parched, and I desperately needed a drink of water. Yasmin checked a machine beside me and jotted notes on her tablet.

Her eyes avoided mine as she asked, "How do you feel?" But I could see the concern in her deep brown eyes.

A wave of nausea hit me, and I warned Yasmin that I was about to vomit. She grabbed a small bucket and held back my hair as bile and sour liquid erupted from my mouth. I coughed and gagged, feeling weak and helpless.

"It's probably just the anesthesia," Yasmin reassured me as she helped me sit up and handed me a glass of water. I drank it greedily, hoping to wash away the awful sour taste in my mouth.

But then, memories flooded back to me. I recalled His Grace, Doctor Ferrarius, pinning me down and then a sharp pain in my arm.

"What did he do to me?" I demanded, anger rising in my chest.

Yasmin was afraid to answer. Her eyes were scared, yet sad, to be the one to tell me. A tear rolled down her cheek, "He...he...Doctor Ferrarius performed the Strassman's abdominal metroplasty." Her voice croaked.

My heart plummeted into the pit of my stomach and drained me of all feeling as though it had bled out onto the bed. The surgery I had researched back home, the one I pleaded with Brant to have done to me despite its exorbitant cost, was now revealed to be a cruel and non-consensual procedure.

My body convulsed with violent retches, my insides churning as if they were trying to escape my throat. Each inhale only fueled the rage in my chest, igniting a wildfire that made me howl in fury at this wretched place.

"Tell me everything," I growled through gritted teeth, my voice dripping with malice and determination.

Yasmin grabbed the bucket and set it on the floor, removing the robust and sour stench.

The curtain slid open, and Doctor Ferrarius strutted in with a smug expression, almost as if he had just performed the most extraordinary surgery of his career.

My blood boiled at the sight of him, and I longed to jump out of my hospital bed and do something unspeakable to him. I muttered curses under my breath, unable to stand the sight of this man who had caused me so much pain.

He cleared his throat, snapping me out of my thoughts. "Yasmin, other patients need your attention," he said before dismissing her with a wave and then turning to face me.

He closed the curtains around us with two quick steps, trapping me with him.

My grip on the bedsheets tightened as I tried to understand what was happening. The realization that this man had violated my rights and my body hit me like a ton of bricks. How could someone who took an oath to protect and heal do something so heinous? I thought Hunter was evil, but now I couldn't be sure.

"What did you do to me?" tumbled out of my mouth.

Deep down, I wanted to hear him confess, to validate my anger and hatred towards him. But at the same time, the thought of him being responsible for fixing my broken uterus filled me with conflicting emotions.

Did vanity and pride drive him, or was there a part of him

that wanted to help me? My heart and mind were at war as I struggled to process his response. My hand rested on my lower abdomen, where I felt soreness and tightness that shouldn't be there.

My body shook as I forced out the words, "You took away my choice and violated me." Tears streamed down my face, a mix of anger and helplessness.

"I did as His Grace asked of me," he replied, matter-of-factly, trying to justify his actions. "I examined you thoroughly, taking X-rays and scans. I am very confident in your future ability to have children. The procedure wasn't that complicated."

His words repulsed me. He saw me as nothing more than an experiment, thinking he was doing me a favor by "fixing" me. The rage inside intensified as I glared at him with pure disgust. But my silence only seemed to make him feel uneasy.

"You're healing exactly as predicted," his unwavering tone and arrogant expression continued. "In six weeks, you'll be good as new."

I fought with all my might to hold back the hot tears that threatened to pour out of my eyes like a dam breaking. My chest heaved with the pressure building inside as if a balloon was about to burst.

"I will never forgive you," I seethed, my voice shaking with conflicting emotions.

As if my words had sudden clarity to his pride, his gaze changed to a mix of regret. His thick, dark brown eyebrows dropped. "I had no choice, Liz," he pleaded, his words only adding to the turmoil inside me.

Feeling desperate to fix the situation, he took out a syringe from his pocket and injected it into the I.V. bag next to my bed.

My eyelids became heavy within ten seconds, and my consciousness slipped away as sleep overtook me again.

He laid me back down on the bed, and I was too weak to resist him. His words were slurred and hard to understand, but I thought I heard him apologize. But it didn't matter; I could never forgive him for what he had done to me in the name of "saving" me.

IN MY dream, I found myself in the center of a vast meadow. The bright sun cast warm rays over the fluffy white clouds floating above. The tall grass surrounding me rustled softly in the gentle breeze as I sat cross-legged, posed meditatively.

My senses were alive and attuned to the sounds of nature around me. The sweet melodies of birdsong filled my ears, with one particular bird making a playful call that sounded like *"cheeseburger."* The sound made my stomach growl with hunger.

I reveled in the tranquility and solitude of this place. It was the most peaceful moment I had experienced in a long time. As I sat there, basking in the warmth of the sun and the beauty of my surroundings, I heard approaching footsteps.

But instead of feeling fear or anxiety, I welcomed them with open arms. With my gaze fixed ahead, I awaited the arrival of this mysterious figure.

As they drew closer, their shadowy form slowly taking shape, I could feel an electric jolt of energy in my chest. Though their face was initially obscured, I sensed a comforting warmth emanating from their spirit.

"You found me." I couldn't contain my excitement when Zak, a few feet away, walked towards me.

My smile was wide and wild as he reached out his hand for me to take. Just as I was about to grab it, another voice broke the moment.

"What are you doing?" Brant's annoyed voice came from behind me.

I turned to see his puzzled expression. I was caught off guard and didn't know how to respond.

"Brant, you're here?" I blurted out as I got up from where I was sitting.

"I've been here," he replied with suspicion in his tone. "I've been with you this whole time, yet you hesitated to say goodbye. What are you doing?"

I looked back at Zak, still smiling with care and understanding. He waited for me to make a decision.

"Take your time," he offered kindly.

I BECAME aware of the rhythmic beeping from my heart monitor as I opened my eyes. It was a harsh reminder of my current reality, and the pain in my abdomen served as a constant reminder of the events that had led me here.

I heard a slight snore and gargled breath, causing me to startle and look over to see Aldrich sitting in a chair beside my bed. He must have fallen asleep, sitting upright in his chair.

He woke up with a start at his snore, rubbing his face in embarrassment. When he saw I was awake, he leaned back in his chair and tried to relax. I could see the conflicting emotions on his face - wanting to smile but feeling sad about my current state.

"He played God with me," I croaked, struggling to gather my strength. "He took away my choice." The way Aldrich hung his head only confirmed my suspicions. "Did you know this was going to happen?"

Resting his elbows on the chair's arms and clasping his hands together, he remained silent and looked at me with questioning eyes. His mind was working overtime, trying to figure out how much he should tell me.

"You used to want this," he said as if trying to convince me of something. "Children, only the financial burden held you back."

I strained my ears to hear his soft voice, wondering if I had heard him correctly. In my current state of mind, I couldn't grasp the true intention behind his words.

"Aldrich... what do you mean?" My mind was muddled from exhaustion, stress, and mental fatigue caused by this place. I needed someone to help me make sense of everything.

When he didn't respond and allowed the weight of his words to sink in, I realized he was just as guilty as His Grace and Doctor Ferrarius.

"You think you know everything about me?" I spat at him.

"Your government ID, social security, certificates, and credentials tell me who you are," the confidence in his tone changed his demeanor.

"But your online presence reveals what is truly in your heart." He stood up from his chair, ready to leave the room. "Someday, you'll thank us," he moved the curtain with one hand, leaving me alone with my thoughts.

REALIZATION

Brant's strong hand gripped mine as I lay on a hospital bed with my legs in metal stirrups. The room was filled with the sound of my grunts and straining breaths echoing off the sterile walls. Sweat glistened on my forehead, dampening my hair, and I could feel the pressure building with each contraction.

Doctor Ferrarius, with his distinguished, thick Sicilian accent and piercing gaze, stood at the foot of the bed, guiding me through each push with unwavering determination. Amara hovered over me, monitoring my vitals and offering words of encouragement.

Brant's presence alone strengthened me as I pushed with all my might. My muscles screamed in protest, but I refused to give up—not without Brant's steady hand supporting me. Then, a strange tugging sensation followed by sweet relief as our baby was born.

Exhausted and trembling, I collapsed back onto the bed, feeling every muscle in my body ache from the intense effort. But all of that faded away when we heard the cry of our newborn baby.

Doctor Ferrarius and Amara rushed to clean the baby while Brant stayed by my side. He tenderly kissed my forehead and told me how proud he was of me.

As they offered Brant the chance to cut the umbilical cord, I drifted in and out of consciousness. In one brief moment of clarity, I saw him standing there with tears in his eyes as he snipped the cord connecting our child to me - a symbol of our new little family member joining us in this world. And with that final snip came an overwhelming rush of love and joy for this precious new life we had created together.

Amara's face was lit with the broadest, proudest grin as she cleaned the tiny bundle on the changing table. My eyelids felt heavy, but I fought to keep them open and focus on her words.

"She is so precious!" Amara was tender and took careful measures on the newborn.

As I struggled to get comfortable, a sharp wave of pain washed over me, causing my stomach to twist and constrict. Then, panic surged as I realized an eerie silence fell in the room. Everyone else seemed paused in time.

"Where is my baby?" I croaked out with long-stretched echoes as if trapped in a cave.

I turned toward where Brant had stood moments before. But instead of his familiar face, Hunter stood there now, his features twisted into a cold, menacing mask as he cradled my newborn child.

Terror seized me as he took slow, deliberate steps towards me, a cruel smirk playing on his lips. But he was just out of reach, taunting me with brutal words as he held my perfect baby in his arms.

"You've done your job," he sneered. "Now it's time for me to take over."

My screams echoed off the walls as I fought against the invisible restraints that held me down like a strong magnet.

My heart shattered as he walked away with my child, leaving me alone and helpless. The people in the room remained motionless as though they were statues. My emotions were a tangled mess of fear, anger, and heartache, unsure of what to do next in this living nightmare.

A SHARP gasp escapes my lips as I jolt awake, my body trembling with adrenaline. My hands are clenched around the bed sheets, and I hear a rip. I can feel my heart pounding against my chest like I had run a marathon.

I scanned the room, my eyes wide with fear. In the corner, I see Zak sitting in a wooden chair, his arms resting on the armrests. But something is off - he's wearing a shirt I don't recognize, except it's not a shirt. His torso is wrapped in blood-stained bandages. The sight of him sends waves of panic through me.

My gaze locks onto his sleeping figure, his head bobbing up and down in exhaustion. But then he startles awake, his eyes immediately drawn to the erratic beeping of my heart monitor. He rushes over to me, his voice hoarse with concern as he tries to calm me down.

He stood by my bed, gripping the frame as if it were the only thing keeping him upright.

"Liz," he said with a concerned expression, "I've been so worried about you."

I noticed bruises and cuts on his knuckles from when he struck Hunter in the forest. The yellow and deep purple bruising looked sensitive to the touch. My gaze traveled up to his bandaged torso, and I couldn't resist asking what had happened.

"It's nothing," he dismissed my concern. When he met my

eyes, there was that look again, the longing to share something with me.

"You can't dismiss this," tears threatening my eyes. "What happened to you?"

Zak's hand hung in the air, hesitant and unsure. He murmured as he reached for my hand. "It doesn't matter right now," he murmured, his eyes filled with concern. "How are you doing?"

My heart twisted in my chest. He was hiding something from me. I could tell by that look he was in pain, and it was all because of me.

My hand trembling, I reached out to touch the bandage on his chest, desperate to apologize for what had happened. But my words caught in my throat, a knot forming that threatened to suffocate me.

"I'm fine. It's nothing." Zak's gentle hand squeezed mine as he spoke, "Liz, they said you needed surgery. What happened?" His voice strained with worry.

He didn't know.

They had sent him to sit by my side. So, I would say the words aloud and face the reality of what had been done to me.

Tears stung at my eyes, but I turned my head away to hide them. "It's not fair," I choked out, the sensation crushing me.

"Liz, don't blame yourself. You've done nothing wrong," his words are a bittersweet comfort that only deepens my guilt.

But I know the truth; my stubbornness has caused his pain and suffering, and now we are paying the ultimate price.

Exhausted and broken, I confess to Zak, "I can't keep fighting. Every decision I make seems to bring more harm than good. I want it all to end." My voice falters as I realize what that means, and the weight of defeat crushes down on me. "But to find any semblance of peace, I know I must surrender to their will," my voice feels heavy with sorrow and regret.

My body shook with uncontrollable sobs as I lay in the hospital bed. Zak sat by my side and, with his thumb, wiped away my tears without a word. His presence reminded me I wasn't alone in this dark and uncertain time.

As my cries turned into sniffles, Zak used a corner of the bedsheet to clean the tears and mucus from my face. He had been a pillar of support for me throughout this ordeal, always there when I needed him.

But as I mustered the courage to ask about Amara, her missing presence seemed unlike her, and Zak's demeanor shifted. His eyes dropped, the realization that I wasn't aware of something.

"There's something you need to know," he said gravely.

The blood on my face drained as I frantically began to think of all the possible outcomes of what could have happened. Is she injured? Did Nellie hurt her? Did Hunter get to her?

"On the day of your surgery," Zak began, "they took Amara to the locker...and she hasn't been seen since," he revealed.

My breath caught in my throat as his words sank in. The pain in my chest intensified as I realized that while I lay here recovering, Amara was in the locker.

Panic set in as I wondered what could have happened to her and why no one had told me until now.

THANK YOU

I can't thank you enough for finishing Forever Deceitful. It's been a long journey coming, and there is more to Liz and Zak's story.

If you wouldn't mind taking the time to leave a review, it would mean the world to me.

Select the book with flowers for digital readers, and it will take you to the review page. Or scan the QR Code if you are holding a copy in your hands:

Danielle Kathleen

Book Review

ABOUT THE AUTHOR

Danielle Kathleen is no stranger to storytelling. Residing in Reno, Nevada, she loves a good series where characters unfold.

Her current works are in young adult fiction, but this tempting psychological thriller wouldn't leave her alone during the pandemic. She wrote it back in 2020 and then sat on the idea, waiting for it to emerge.

The release of Forever Faithful, the first book in the series, has been the highlight of Danielle's 2023 year. She is excited to continue the series with this second book…maybe another is in the works?

Join her newsletter to receive monthly insights/book signing events and much more.

www.DanielleKathleen.com

If you are on the social media links below, follow and say hi. She loves the interactions and reading your reviews.

- facebook.com/DKathleen20
- instagram.com/dkathleen_author
- amazon.com/stores/author/B072L6Y8NN
- tiktok.com/@authordaniellekathleen

ALSO BY DANIELLE KATHLEEN

Psychological Thriller: Forever Faithful Series

Forever Faithful

Forever Deceitful

YA Murder Mystery: Summersville

Summersville

A Never Ending Nightmare

Untold Stories

Made in the USA
Monee, IL
13 June 2024

59362639R00144